THE ROAD TO YOU

A SPICY VACATION ROMANCE

ERIKA VANZIN

Edited by
STACI FRENES

*To my editor, Staci,
the fearless human who painstakingly restored every em
dash I "accidentally" deleted while pretending I knew
better.*

1

LENA

The morning light filters through my bedroom window, painting the room in soft hues. I blink against the gentle glow, turning over just enough to catch a glimpse of the impossibly blue sky welcoming me.

I'll never tire of this view, with the lush green of the trees peeking out from the property below mine, and the Los Angeles sky stretching bright. A stark contrast with the Minnesota weather of my childhood. Even on those rare, foggy mornings when June gloom sweeps the coastal neighborhoods, the Los Feliz Hills always seem to be spared those cloudy skies.

I stretch, toss the covers aside, and pad barefoot across the cool hardwood floors. Swinging open the French doors to my garden, I breathe in the warm, jasmine-scented air and smile. It's the perfect weather for morning meditation.Finding this house had been a year-long journey of open houses, bidding wars, and not-so-veiled disappointments. But the moment I stepped inside with my realtor, I just knew. The light, the energy, the way the walls seemed to call my name, I knew it was The One.

A lot of A-list actors and fellow colleagues don't even bother with the house-hunting. They send assistants to weed out the ones that don't meet their requirements, stepping in only at the last minute to sign papers and take selfies in front of their new swimming pool.

Not me. I want to feel the vibes of a place and let its welcoming energy wrap around me like my favorite blanket. Preston, my boyfriend, loves to tease me about it. He calls me a spoiled Hollywood star with an under-tone of insecurity. But I think he's just jealous. While I'm sipping tea on my sun-drenched patio, he's shuffling boxes between rentals, grumbling about bad layouts and street noise.

But hey, if a busy, famous director doesn't have time for "mundane things" like finding a home, that's on him. Let him talk while I enjoy every bit of my sanctuary.

After a blissful hour of meditation, I wander into the kitchen, greeted by the quiet humming of a sweet song by Rose, my housekeeper, who stands at the counter with a bowl of colorful, freshly cut fruit before her.

"Good morning, Miss Sinclair," she says when she notices me.

I've asked her a thousand times to call me Lena, but she insists on keeping things professional. I stopped fighting it years ago.

"Morning, Rose. How's your day going so far?"

"Very well, thank you." She sets the fruit bowl and a steaming cup of coffee on the counter in front of where I'm sitting. "If you don't mind, I'll take your dress to the dry cleaner's this morning. I couldn't quite manage to get rid of that stain."

Ah, yes. A splash of red wine now mars the gorgeous, ivory dress, courtesy of Preston's waving hands as he animatedly talked about his latest movie at a party. I'd been hoping to save it from the trash, but hope is fading now. It's a shame. I loved that dress and hoped to wear it again this summer.

"If you want, I can drop it off on my way back from the gym," I offer. "I'll be heading that way anyway."

The suggestion horrifies her. Her eyes widen, and she clutches her chest like I stabbed her.

"Oh, no, Miss Sinclair. Please enjoy your morning. Don't worry about the dress. I just wanted you to know in case you wondered where it went."

I smile, not surprised. Rose never lets me lift a finger when she's around. Sometimes, it feels strange, this change from my childhood, where chores were done by the whole family. My sister and I grew up washing dishes, folding laundry, and cooking alongside my parents. I come from a middle-class family where both our parents worked long hours to make ends meet, and everyone in the house helped out. Now, the only thing I fold is a yoga mat.

"Thank you, Rose. But you know if you ever need a hand, I'm here."

Her smile softens. "I know, Miss Sinclair." With practiced grace, she wipes down the countertop and disappears down the hall, moving so quietly I half wonder if this house has secret passages.

I finish my breakfast, rinse my bowl, and tuck it into the dishwasher before grabbing my gym bag. As I drive my SUV through the gate, the world shifts from calm to chaos.

A wave of paparazzi invades my driveway with their cameras flashing and their bodies pressing too close to my car. I'm almost afraid I'll hit some of them on my way to the gym.

"What the heck?" I mutter, gripping the wheel as I inch forward, careful not to drive over anyone's foot.

I'm no stranger to the attention. Being a famous actress comes with its fair share of lack of privacy. But this is madness. They're never this aggressive, especially when I'm not filming and just living my life.

I finally break free of the horde, and the roar of

voices fades behind me. My blood pulses in my ears as I glance into the rearview mirror.

What on earth had set them off this morning?

When I finally make it to the gym, the uneasiness from the paparazzi still twists in my stomach. I'm grateful to have a space where I can burn off the lingering worry with a good, sweaty workout. Already dressed in my gym attire, I give Sam at the front desk a quick wave and head straight for the treadmills.

Choosing this gym had been a strategic move. Concealed in a gated commercial complex, it offers a level of privacy that is hard to find in Los Angeles. Only gym members and those working in the offices above have access, which means no lurking paparazzi and no strangers sneaking photos over the lifting bench. The steep membership fee and strict vetting process explain why the place accommodates celebrities and high-profile clients. Here, nobody cares that I'm Lena Sinclair, the Hollywood star.

The main workout room is bright and airy, and rows of treadmills are lined up to face floor-to-ceiling windows. Outside, the murals covering the gray wall are a pleasant, colorful distraction to look at. But my eyes are drawn to the three big TVs hanging above the windows, all tuned to the same talk show. The hosts lean in close, their expressions practically vibrating with gossip.

I drape my towel over a treadmill and wander to the water dispenser, filling my bottle while trying to shake off the morning's weirdness. That's when I catch the two women by the free weights sneaking glances at me with their heads tilted together, deep in a hushed conversation.

They're not new here. We've exchanged small talk before, and opinions about the yoga classes we attend together. But today their smiles are tight, like I caught them doing something wrong. My skin prickles.

It could be nothing. After run-ins with the paparazzi, I always feel like everyone is staring. I look down to make sure I'm appropriately dressed—leggings, a sports bra, a loose tank top. *Not naked. Not a bad dream. I'm fine*. I reassure myself.

I return to the treadmill, pulling my phone and earbuds from my bag, only to find my phone dead. That explains why I haven't heard from anyone this morning. Normally, I don't check my phone until after my work-out. I like keeping my mornings stress-free, easing into the day without the noise of emails or social media. My entourage knows better than to bother me unless it's urgent.

I step onto the treadmill, set it to a light jog, and let my eyes drift back to the talk show. There's no audio, just the hosts' exaggerated expressions and a montage of clips behind them.

I squint.

The screen flashes to an old interview of Preston and me, side by side, promoting our latest movie. My pulse quickens.

Did I miss a media alert? I need to call Greta, my publicist. She never forgets to keep me in the loop, but maybe something slipped through her busy schedule. Before I can piece it together, the screen shifts, a magazine cover fills the frame, and my heart stutters.

In the upper corner is my headshot—the same smiling photo from my IMDb page. But it's the image beneath it that squeezes the air out of my lungs.

It's a blurry shot, probably taken from a great distance, but unmistakable.

Preston, my boyfriend of four years, is passionately kissing Ronan Kavinsky, the lead actor in his new movie. Preston's hand is shoved down the front of Ronan's pants, their bodies pressed against the side of a trailer.

Everything around me falls away, and my ears buzz with the rush of blood pumping into my body.

The treadmill keeps moving, but I don't. My foot catches, and I lurch forward, gripping the handrails just in time to avoid hitting my face on the hard equipment. My knees buckle, and I hit the emergency stop button, stopping the machine before making a fool of myself.

Breathe, Lena. Hold it together.

The room feels suffocating. The thud of weights, the steady hum of treadmills, and the distant rhythm of pop music blend into a confused noise. My vision blurs with tears, and I force myself to blink. I focus on the polished floor beneath my sneakers. Years of smiling on red carpets and dodging uncomfortable questions teach you one thing: how to hold back tears until you're safely behind closed doors.

I grab my towel and gym bag, slipping off the treadmill as smoothly as I can manage. My limbs feel wooden, and my expression is locked in a polite mask. The women by the weights watch me. Their eyes are a little too wide, and even their whispers cease as they witness my walk of shame.

I nod at Sam as I pass the front desk, my lips stretching into a tight, unnatural smile.

Outside, the sun shines too brightly, and the air is too sharp. I fumble with my keys, slide into my SUV, and slam the door shut. The silence hits me like a wave, and I suck in slow breaths until I'm sure I won't shatter.

But the image is still there, with Preston and Ronan passionately kissing, seared into my mind. I feel my perfect morning, my perfect life, shaking so hard I'm sure it will soon shatter.

I let Tabia in and close the door behind her. The paparazzi who had swarmed my gate this morning are now more insistent than ever, and I can't shake the fear that one of them might try to jump over the perimeter wall. My hands are shaking as I turn the lock.

Tabia smiles gently before wrapping me in a tight hug. Her soothing hand moves in slow circles on my back, and it's a miracle I don't shatter right there on her shoulder. I pull away and guide her into the living room, collapsing beside her on the couch. A bottle of wine sits on the coffee table with two glasses already waiting.

"Have you heard from your publicist yet?" she asks, picking up where our phone call ended less than two hours ago.

I nod, grabbing the bottle and filling both glasses. I hand one to her.

"Greta called. She said they're already working on damage control." My voice is hoarse, every word scratching its way up my throat.

Tabia's dark eyes study me over the rim of her glass. Concern is taking up every inch of her face. She's searching for a hint of how I'm holding up, but the truth is, I'm numb. I didn't even cry when I got home. I just plugged in my dead phone and sifted through the flood of messages from Greta, switching from shock to management mode without ever truly processing what happened.

Preston cheated on me. And he didn't just cheat, he humiliated me publicly. I can't tell what hurts more: the betrayal or the fact that the downfall of my personal life is plastered on gossip sites for everyone to see.

"That's it? Just 'damage control'?" Tabia's voice tightens, and I can practically see the wheels turning in her mind, ready to call Greta herself and demand more action.

I take a long sip of wine, letting the warm feeling it ignites settle me before answering. "She talked me through all the steps they've already put in motion, and what comes next depends on Preston's response. But basically, I'm supposed to lay low and wait for the storm to pass."

Tabia sighs, and frustration veils her expression. "Did you hear from him?"

Her voice is soft and careful, like she knows the precarious balance I'm clinging to. She should. We've known each other for ten years, ever since I moved to Los Angeles at twenty with a dream of becoming a famous actress. She was my roommate back then, my first supporter through every audition and rejection. She's seen me fight tooth and nail for everything I have, and she knows that when I break, I break hard.

I shake my head, and a fresh wave of bitterness crashes into my chest. "I know he's seen my texts, but every time I call, it goes straight to voicemail. He won't even give me the courtesy of a conversation."

"What an asshole," she mutters into her glass, her tone low and deadly.

The silence stretches between us. I swirl the wine in my glass and stare at the red liquid catching the light. This morning, I woke up feeling like the luckiest woman in the world. Now, it feels like fate sucker-punched me for even thinking such a thing.

"It doesn't feel real," I admit. "I mean, I saw the pictures, I know it is. But not hearing it from him feels like I'm living someone else's nightmare, not my own."

"Do you want me to call him? I can be scary when I want," she offers, and I know she means it. With her six-foot-tall frame and statuesque beauty, she can be intimidating, especially when she puts on her "model mask," as she calls it. That blank, impassive expression she wears on the runway that can make even the most confident men squirm.

I huff a sad laugh. "He knows your number. If he doesn't want to face me, he won't face you either. That's just him. If he doesn't say it out loud, then it's not real. Nothing is happening."

It's a trait I've never liked about him. That ability to slip into denial and hide from anything unpleasant. I was foolish enough to think he'd change. What a joke.

Tabia scoffs, and her disdain is sharp enough to cut. "Did you know he was into men?"

Coming from anyone else, that question would have stung, but not from her.

"Not a clue." I shake my head. I've replayed that thought in my mind a hundred times since I saw those pictures, but no clues ever stood out. I feel like a fool for that, but I don't even know if there are telltale signs that someone is into both genders. That's not even the point. He cheated, that's the thing I hate, not with whom.

"You know what's worse?" I don't wait for her to respond. The words tumble out before I can hold them back. "Now I'm stuck in this house for the entire summer because every time I step outside, they'll be on me like vultures. I don't even know how to face our friends. What are they thinking? What are they saying behind my back?"

Tabia places a warm hand on my knee, setting her glass down on the coffee table. "Don't worry about what other people think. It's clear as day that he's the one in the wrong. And if your friends can't see that, they're not worth keeping around."

Her reasoning is rock solid, but the ache in my chest doesn't ease.

"And as for the summer," she continues, "why don't you fly to my apartment in Milan? It's empty, and you could use the break. Get away from the paparazzi, recharge without feeling like a prisoner in your own home."

I let the idea sink into my mind. I can almost taste the freedom. The thought of wandering Milan's streets without paparazzi following me feels too good to be true. I could finally breathe without cameras flashing in my face, without gossip following me everywhere I go.

"I might take you up on that." For the first time all day, I feel something like relief. This could be a way out of this nightmare, and a spark of hope ignites in my chest.

2

———

LENA

I wake up half an hour before the plane lands, just in time to pull my hair into a messy ponytail and put on a bit of makeup, just in case someone recognizes me. I've done everything possible to avoid attention, from ducking under the back seat of Tabia's SUV driving out of my house to boarding the plane in the plainest sweatpants and baggy T-shirt I could find. Greta will spend the next couple of weeks tipping off the paparazzi with fake sightings of me around Los Angeles, buying me time to settle into my Milan apartment and lay low.

I take a deep breath, trying to rein in the nervousness wreaking havoc in my stomach. It's been six days since the news broke, and the worst part is that I haven't heard a single word from Preston. Not a text, not even a message through his lawyer or publicist. Nothing. He has tightened security around his set and hasn't even bothered to release a statement to explain the situation.

Every gossip magazine is wildly speculating about the timeline of our relationship. Some say I must have known all along; others suggest our relationship was nothing but a cover for him until he was ready to come out. That accusation stings more than anything else.

Our relationship was real, or at least, it was for me. But now I'm questioning everything. I've spent hours replaying every moment, scrutinizing every touch, every small confession, every kiss that seemed to be too rushed. Maybe he really didn't like me, or maybe he's bisexual and just fell for a man, but I need to hear it from him. I need him to tell me that there was something real between us. After four years, I deserve at least that much.

A flight attendant cautiously approaches me, her sweet smile curving her lips. She's been attentive throughout the flight, helping to calm my raw nerves just enough to fall asleep.

"I don't want to overstep, but I can make sure you get off the plane first," she whispers. Her voice is so gentle that my heart squeezes in my chest. "I'll buy you some time to get through immigration before the rest of the passengers."

My chest lightens a bit with relief. Bless her.

Whether it's solidarity or sheer pity, I'm grateful. I want to hug her, maybe even kiss her for this small mercy.

"Thank you. I really appreciate it. I hope this won't get you in trouble."

She shakes her head slightly, the soft smile never leaving her lips. "I already spoke to the captain. He's on board with it. He makes the rules." She winks before moving on to help another passenger.

I'm not sure what story she spun for him—perhaps that a broken-hearted woman needs a few minutes of respite to disappear before the world swallows her whole —but I don't care. I take this kindness and make the most of it.

When the plane touches down, I move quickly, slipping through the airport with my head down, my sunglasses and ball cap firmly in place, and my heart pounding. I'm lucky enough to snag a taxi without much of a wait. The driver doesn't give me a second glance as I tell him Tabia's address, and I sink into the back seat, grateful for the anonymity.

The soft hum of the radio fills the car with a comfortable blur of Italian words I don't quite understand. It's soothing, this bubble of not knowing, not needing to process anything for a few more minutes.

I watch as the city unfolds outside my window. The landscape shifts from the industrial sprawl around the airport to the mix of tall buildings and single-family homes on Milan's outskirts. As we draw closer to the city center, the streets grow narrower, the architecture older, belonging to another era.

When we finally pull into the *Brera* neighborhood, I can't help but marvel at its beauty. It's vibrant and a bit bohemian, just as Tabia described. Not the polished, high-fashion glitz of the *"Quadrilatero della Moda,"* another Milan neighborhood, where she spends her time when she is here for Milan's Fashion Week, but a place with character. The streets are cobblestone, and the buildings are exquisitely restored. Their facades are a blend of soft pastels and weathered stone. Tiny balconies overflow with flowers—bursts of red, pink, and yellow, thriving in the early June sun.

As I step out of the taxi, heat and humidity wrap around me, making my sweatpants feel even more suffocating. I feel underdressed and out of place among the elegant locals. A couple of women sit outside a corner café, their cocktail dresses effortlessly chic as they sip tiny espressos. To my relief, they don't even glance in my direction.

I pay the driver, drag my luggage to the side of the street, and slip through the massive wooden door that leads to Tabia's apartment building. As it swings shut behind me, it feels like closing the door on the last six days of chaos, betrayal, and endless questions.

For the first time since my world imploded, I have a

chance to breathe. An opportunity to find myself again, far away from the flashing cameras and the ever-persistent rumors.

THE APARTMENT IS SMALL BUT IMMACULATE, A PERFECT mix of modern charm and old elegance. The entryway is paved with a stunning black-and-white mosaic, creating a welcoming first impression. Just beyond it, the flooring transitions to light hardwood, bathing the living room in a warm, inviting glow.

A plush white sectional couch and mid-century wood coffee table sit in the corner, but my attention is immediately drawn to the window—the most unique one I've ever seen. It stretches along the far wall, continuing around the corner and seamlessly connecting the living room to the sleek, modern kitchen. The massive glass panes are divided by delicate white frames, offering a view of the communal courtyard below.

The courtyard is a postcard brought to life. Wrought iron balconies hold draped terracotta pots brimming with vibrant flowers, and neighbors' curtains flutter lazily in the breeze. It's quintessentially Italian with a mix of contemporary design and historical character.

This place is breathtaking.

I drag my suitcase into the vibrant bedroom, which

has bold, flowery wallpaper and rich blue linens, and pull out a few essentials. I settle on a light, floral summer dress and a pair of low sandals, something comfortable for exploring.

The bathroom is a tiny sanctuary. The white marble tiles and brass fixtures make this space so luminous, you almost don't notice there are no windows in sight. The glass-enclosed shower beckons to me like an oasis. One look at it, and I don't even have to think: I strip off my travel-worn clothes and step under the warm spray.

I let the water wash over me, rinsing away the stale airplane smell, the smudged makeup, and the exhaustion clinging to my bones. I take my time, lathering away the remnants of the last few days—the betrayal, the heartbreak, the ache of unanswered questions. Even my legs seem to breathe a sigh of relief as I scrub away the stickiness of those suffocating sweatpants.

Forty minutes later, I emerge from the bathroom with a fresh burst of energy bubbling beneath my skin. Despite the jet lag, I feel more awake and grounded. My stomach growls in a loud reminder that I haven't eaten since…well, I can't even remember. The flight is a blur of short naps and a lot of sparkling wine.

A quick search on my phone reveals a small grocery store nearby. I don't bother drying my hair or applying makeup. I just twist my damp hair into a messy bun, slip into the dress, grab the keys, and step out into the warm Milan air.

As I wander through the cobblestone streets, I'm captivated by everything around me. The city hums with life. The architecture is a layered history of stone, tiny balconies, and pastel colors. Pale yellow and pink are predominant, but patches of white or stone give this place a relaxing vibe. Each turn offers a new view: a unique café, a woman tending to her flowers, soft music coming from one of the open windows.

I've been to Italy countless times, but never like this. Before, it was always a whirlwind of photo ops, interviews, and tight schedules. This feels different. This feels like I'm seeing it for the first time through the eyes of someone who finally has the luxury of *visiting* a foreign country.

When I reach the grocery store, it's like stepping into another world. Back home in Los Angeles, grocery shopping is a clinical experience with fluorescent lights, endless aisles, and everything pre-packaged for convenience. Here, the store is small and intimate, with wooden crates full of fresh produce, the scent of herbs and ripe tomatoes filling the air.

I find myself smiling at the simple act of bagging my own salad, selecting ripe peaches, and asking the clerk for a few slices of prosciutto. The clerk smiles, and she takes her time to select the best piece of meat, as if time moves differently here. The kind of tranquility I've only experienced in movies.

But then, as I approach the register, reality slams into me. A rack of gossip magazines lines the counter, and my face is everywhere. My heart drums a heavy, uneven beat. Preston's betrayal is plastered across every glossy cover, our lives dissected by bold, unmistakable headlines. I don't need to read Italian to know what they say.

I knew we were so famous the gossip would spread, but I naively hoped I could escape it here for a little while.

My hands tremble as I place my groceries on the conveyor belt. I focus on the beeping of items being scanned. The girl behind the counter doesn't even glance at me. She moves with practiced efficiency, entirely unaware of who I am or the chaos I left behind.

Relief rushes through me, and I exhale a slow breath.

For now, at least, I am just another face in the crowd, a girl in a floral dress, buying bread and fruit in a quiet corner of Milan.

I unpack the groceries, humming a song I heard on the radio in the grocery store, filling the small fridge with fresh produce, and neatly stacking the pantry with bread and a box of pasta. The kitchen feels even cozier now that I have my supplies for my stay here.

I prepare a simple salad, a meal that requires little thought but can settle my growling stomach. I rinse the crisp lettuce under cool water, chop the tomatoes, and layer thin slices of prosciutto over a piece of crusty bread. The aroma of fresh bread and salty cured meat fills my nostrils, and my stomach responds with another low, demanding growl.

I drizzle olive oil into the salad bowl, add a pinch of salt and a dusting of pepper, and carry my dishes to the kitchen table. The seat faces that incredible window, and I settle in, letting the view soothe me.

Outside, on the other side of the courtyard, curtains billow softly in the breeze. Their slow dance has a hypnotic rhythm that pulls me back to a memory I wasn't ready to face.

I'm suddenly in the middle of the African desert, the sun long gone but the air still warm, carrying the almost absolute silence of this isolated place. Preston and I had taken that trip after the chaos of the film premiere. It was a rare escape where no one knew us, and we basked in almost total solitude.

We had slept in a canvas tent, its fabric flapping gently in the wind. I remember the candlelight casting shadows on his face, the way he looked at me with something I thought was love. We had tangled together that night, wrapped up in a passion that made us spent, sweaty, and breathless.

The memory crashes over me like a sudden, icy, unavoidable avalanche. My heart breaks open in my chest, and before I know it, hot tears spill over my cheeks. It's the first time I've cried since the news broke, and the floodgates open with a force I can't control.

I cry for every moment of happiness we shared, every kiss that now feels tainted, every promise that now is broken. I cry for the woman I have been with him, the one who believed in us.

Time goes by in a blur of tears and sobs. My salad turns dark and soggy, and my eyes burn with the sting of too many tears. When the sobs finally subside, I'm left hollow, emptied out, as if every tear carried away a bit of sadness, leaving me with nothing inside.

But beneath the ache, something else tugs at my mind like an insistent voice I can't ignore. An unsettling truth rises to the surface, and I can no longer push it away: in four years together, Preston and I never once talked about our future.

Not about a home together, not about marriage, not even a shared pet or a silly what-if about growing old side by side. The realization settles over me like a cold shadow. I've been mourning the past, not the future. Because, in truth, there was never a future to mourn.

A slow, simmering anger replaces the grief. My

fingers curl around the edge of the table, and my breath steadies, each inhale feeding the flame inside me. How dare he? How dare he not only break my heart but vanish without a word, leaving me to drown in speculation and scandal while he hides behind his security and silence?

The rage grounds me. I wipe my cheeks; my skin is raw, but my resolve is taking root in my chest.

No more tears for Preston. *Not one more.*

If he can't acknowledge the shitstorm he created, if he can't even muster a single text or offer an explanation, then he isn't worth my tears. He never was.

I push the soggy salad aside, the last remnant of my breakdown, and stand up. I am not a victim. I refuse to be.

This is my fresh start, my chance to rebuild without the weight of him holding me down. And I'm going to take it.

3

MICHELE

Pain shoots up my leg and slams into my back as Dr. Marini bends my knee. He's the best orthopedic specialist at Italy's top private clinic, but right now, I'd trade him for anyone who could give me a massive dose of painkillers. My teeth grind together, and my knuckles turn white as I grip the exam table's paper-thin sheet. I've been here for half an hour, stripped down to my boxer briefs and a T-shirt, but it feels like days.

He's been poking and prodding me for what the clock over the door says is thirty minutes, but it feels like that damn thing is dragging the second hand through mud. Its slow tick is taunting me, reminding me I'm still stuck in this hell of a place.

"Aren't you supposed to ask if I'm in pain?" I

manage through clenched teeth, trying to inject some humor into this horrible situation.

He doesn't miss a beat. "I don't need to ask," he says, still avoiding my gaze. "Your muscles are stiff, your forehead's shining with sweat, and your grunts are… well, not exactly subtle." He smirks, but his eyes remain fixed on my leg.

Nobody looks me in the eye these days. They're either hyper-focused on fixing me or too scared to deal with my less-than-charming attitude. I get it. It's easier to look at my leg than at the mess I've become. They all think the same thing, they just don't say it out loud: six months and you're still not back? Hell, I'm not even at fifty percent of my previous shape. But hey, at least I can walk, right?

"You can sit up. We're done." He pats my knee like I'm a kid at the dentist, then strides back to his desk.

"How long before he can play again?" Marco's sharp and cold voice cuts through the silence. My agent has never been known for his patience, but today, he's barely holding it together.

I stare at the wall as I pull on my pants, my fingers clumsily fiddling with the sweatpants' string. I don't look at Marco or at the gruesome sight of scars on my leg. There's nothing left to focus on except the stark, white wall.

"We can't say for sure." The doctor's voice is professional but with a practiced edge of sympathy. "The bone has healed, but the muscle is taking longer to recover."

"It's been six fucking months," Marco snaps, and I wince.

Dr. Marini doesn't even flinch. His attention shifts to me, ignoring Marco completely. I'm the patient, not my agent. "The accident did a number on your leg," he says with a steady tone. "The bone snapped in two places, tore through muscle and tissues, and nearly broke through entirely. It shredded tendons, muscles, and vessels. The surgeons did their best, but the priority was saving your leg…and your life."

I've heard this speech before, but every time it feels like a fresh punch to the gut. They did what they could, but finesse wasn't on the table. It was survival.

"Are you saying they botched the surgery?" Marco's voice is a low growl.

"No." The doctor's jaw tightens. "I'm saying that if they hadn't realized you were *the* Michele Moretti, they'd have amputated. They took risks to preserve your career. Regular patients don't get that luxury."

An icy wave washes over me. I can still hear the crash, the metal-on-metal screech, the sharp, searing pain in my leg that faded to a chilling numbness. Flashes of light, sirens, and voices that went in and out of focus. I was drifting between reality and unconsciousness.

"What can I do to fix this?" My voice comes out hard with an edge of annoyance to cover the fear.

Dr. Marini sighs, and his expression shifts into a mix of patience and pity. "Stick to physical therapy. I'll talk to your trainer and adjust your workload, but beyond that, it's time and effort. You have to push through and wait."

"That's it?" Desperation creeps in, cracking my voice. "I just sit around and wait?"

I'm thirty years old. I should have another ten years on the field, another decade of being the best. But hope is slipping between my fingers. The future I've envisioned for myself is coming to a screeching halt right before my eyes.

"There's an option for surgery," he offers, though he sounds doubtful. "We could address the adhesions causing pain, but it's a gamble. No guarantees the recovery would be quicker, or complete."

He speaks to me like I'm a wild animal ready to snap. "Look, considering the extent of your injuries, you've come a long way. A week after surgery, we didn't even know if you'd walk again, let alone play. This wasn't a clean sports injury. You're lucky even to be talking about going back to the team. Don't take that for granted. Some people don't have that chance."

The reprimand is sharp and necessary to drag me out of my self-pity. It's a reminder that I'm not some entitled asshole who thinks the world owes him. But lately, this battle feels impossible. I'm drowning, and the surface keeps slipping further away, no matter how hard I fight to resurface.

Out of the corner of my eye, I see Marco shift uncomfortably, his chest deflating. He's not wrong to be pissed—his job is to keep my career alive, and right now, I'm dragging us both down.

"I'm sorry," I mumble, rubbing my hand over my face. The exhaustion is crushing me.

The doctor nods. "I know it's tough. Take the summer to heal, not just physically. Your mental state matters. The right mindset will help your body recover."

Marco sighs, and I know what he's thinking. He's never believed in all this "mind over matter" bullshit, but I'm desperate enough to try anything. What the hell do I have to lose?

We leave the office in silence, our footsteps sounding loud in the empty corridor. Marco moves with a sharp, angry pace, and I trail behind, feeling the weight of the injury in every step.

"Marco, wait!" I grab his arm, spinning him to face me.

He jerks away. "Shut up, Michele. You've fucked this up, and I need to walk away before I say something I'll regret."

"Are you serious?" My frustration flares hot in my

chest. "What, you're never going to talk to me again? Grow up."

His eyes flash with anger. "Your contract expired two weeks ago. They aren't even pretending to negotiate. They're stalling, waiting for another team to take a chance on you. They won the championship without you. You were out for half of the fucking season. Why would they pay for a player who might never be the same again?"

His words hit like a punch to the gut. For months, he's been my lifeline, the voice of optimism when all I saw was darkness. Was it all a lie?

"I've been with them since I was twenty. A decade, Marco. That has to count for something."

He shakes his head. "This is business. And right now, you're a liability."

I open my mouth, but the truth is a cold, hard weight in my chest. The management's calls dried up months ago. When they did call, it wasn't about me, it was about my timeline, my usefulness. Only my teammates still check in regularly. Real friends who saw me as more than a jersey and a paycheck.

Marco's face hardens. He spins on his heel and walks away without another word.

This time, I let him go.

I WALK OUT OF THE CLINIC, BUT INSTEAD OF HEADING straight to my car and driving home, I take a detour. My feet carry me around the block to the little bar that's become my refuge over the last six months. Franco and his crew have seen it all. Cup after cup of coffee, they watched me as I went from a wheelchair to crutches, and finally, to standing on my own two feet.

They never ask too many questions. Never pry for the gory details of my injury or push for a story to sell to the tabloids. When the paparazzi got too aggressive, Franco himself would push them out the door, armed with nothing but a broom and a dirty dish towel. He treated me like a guy who needed coffee, not a celebrity trying to hold his life together.

I'm not naive. I know I'm a big deal. I'm one of the top football players of my generation, and I have been with the best team in the league for a decade. I'm practically a rockstar in this country. Privacy isn't part of the deal. I can't expect to be left alone, but here, at least, I get a little bit of quiet.

"Hey, Michele! How are you doing?" Franco's cheerful voice pulls me out of my thoughts as I approach the tables outside the bar.

I force a grin. "I can't complain." I'm still walking, right? I'm lucky. "What about you?"

"Counting the days until I can finally retire." He

chuckles, clearing a tiny espresso cup from a nearby table.

"What will I do when you're not here to make my fabulous espresso?" I tease.

He's been here forever. Took over this bar in the nineties and hasn't stopped since. Six in the morning until close, seven days a week, except for the two weeks in August when he and his wife head to Rimini. Same hotel, same beach umbrella, same first two weeks of the month. It's practically tradition.

"Not my problem." He nods toward the younger guy behind the counter, already crafting cappuccinos with the precision of a surgeon. "You'll be just fine."

I chuckle and step inside and breathe in the scent of freshly ground coffee. A genuine smile spreads across my face. But as I approach the counter, a blonde whirl-wind with a messy bun spins around, and before I can react, hot cappuccino cascades down my T-shirt.

"Shit!" The burn is immediate and almost painful. My first instinct is to yank my shirt off, but instead, I grab the fabric between my fingers, holding it away from my skin. The cup clatters to the floor, leaving a trail of milk and foam splattered everywhere.

I'm two seconds away from cursing this clumsy idiot when a soft, breathy voice whispers, "I'm so sorry." The words drip with an English accent, so sweet it catches me off guard. Wait, they are actually spoken in English.

I look up and find myself staring into the bluest irises I've ever seen. For a heartbeat, I'm lost. Those eyes lead to a button nose and lips so full and soft they could make a grown man forget his own name. I'm talking from experience here.

"I'm so sorry," she says again, her cheeks flushing. She snatches a pile of napkins from the counter and starts patting my chest, the motion so awkward and clumsy it melts my irritation on the spot.

The stain is beyond saving, a beige disaster spreading from my chest to my sweatpants. But who cares?

"Don't worry." I chuckle, trying to put her at ease. "Let me buy you a cappuccino, unless you'd rather try to squeeze this one out of my shirt."

She looks up at me, wide-eyed, and suddenly, nothing else matters. Not my leg, not the clinic, not Marco's pissed-off expression still seared into my mind. Right now, my world has shrunk to the hope that she'll say yes.

4

LENA

Yes or no? A simple answer to a simple question.

This gorgeous man just offered to buy me a cappuccino after I thoroughly ruined his shirt. Logic says I should be the one offering to pay for dry cleaning, not accepting free coffee from him. And more than that, I shouldn't even stay here. I should turn around and disappear. Lay low, Lena. You have one job this summer: *lay low*.

But how am I supposed to say no when he looks like *that*?

Warm brown eyes, a sharp jawline dusted with the perfect amount of dark scruff, and full lips that appear to be far too easy to fantasize about. I always thought that the whole *Italian men are next-level attractive* thing was an exaggerated stereotype. But if he's the standard, then yeah, I get it now. This man could convince me to rob a bank, right here, right now, and I'd probably ask which getaway car he prefers.

"Yes," I breathe out, and the smile that spreads across his face is *blinding*.

He says something in Italian to the barista—something deep and smooth that I don't understand but *definitely* wouldn't mind hearing again—then places a firm hand on my back, guiding me toward a small table outside. His touch is light, but it leaves a trail of heat against my skin. The bar is quiet at this time of day. Most people are tucked away in air-conditioned offices, while we sit beneath a large umbrella shielding us from the hot Italian sun.

A gentleman, he pulls my chair out for me like he's done it a thousand times before. It looks effortless, second nature for him. When he takes the seat across from me, he extends his hand with a confident, easygoing smile.

"I'm Michele Moretti. Nice to meet you."

Oh, that voice. It's rich and deep, laced with something that makes my stomach dip in a way that is *very* dangerous.

I clasp his hand way too clumsily, and my fingers are sweaty against his warm palm. "Lena. Lena Sinclair."

The second the words leave my lips, I regret them.

Idiot. I should have just said *Lena.* But it's too late. His eyes flicker with recognition, and my stomach clenches in a grip.

"*That* Lena Sinclair?"

My heart sinks. It was too good to last. I made it fifteen whole days without being recognized, and now my anonymity is over.

Heat creeps up my neck, but I force myself to nod, staring down at my hands. The urge to bolt is strong, but if I run now, I'll make a worse scene.

Instead of an over-the-top reaction, he simply leans back in his chair, studying me like he's debating whether to say something or let it go.

"I'm sorry," he finally says, his voice still smooth but now careful. "I didn't mean to embarrass you. I just prefer to be straightforward. Pretending not to recognize you would feel dishonest, and I'm not that kind of man."

My head snaps up, and my eyes lock onto his. I was bracing for *something else*, the usual fake nonchalance, then the casual request for a selfie, maybe even a veiled attempt at getting more details about my situation. But he just says it like it is. No big deal.

And for some reason, that makes my shoulders relax.

"I'm just not used to people recognizing me *and* keeping it cool," I admit. "Most of my encounters end with a 'quick photo' that's on social media before I even walk away."

His brows pull together slightly, but his lips stay tilted in that barely-there smile. "Would it make you more comfortable if I asked for one?" His voice is teasing. "I could sell it to the gossip magazines. Make a fortune."

I scrunch my nose at him, but my lips betray me with a small smile. "Oh, absolutely. I hear they pay big money for blurry pictures of me covered in cappuccino stains."

He lets out a low, warm chuckle that makes my stomach quiver.

"Trust me, I'm not selling *anything* to those vultures," he says in a firm voice. And for some unexplainable reason, I believe him.

Something about the way he sits—completely at ease, legs sprawled out like he has all the time in the world—makes me settle into my chair a little deeper.

The barista places our drinks in front of us and Michele thanks him before turning his attention back to me. "So, Lena. What brings you to Brera?"

I pause, unsure. Does he really not know, or is he being polite?

"I'm staying at a friend's place for the summer," I say carefully. "She has an apartment nearby and isn't using it, so she offered it to me." I lift my cappuccino to my lips, hoping that's enough to end the subject.

He nods, sipping his espresso in one go like a true Italian. "Unusual choice for a summer getaway."

I tilt my head. "Why's that?"

He shrugs. "Most people go to the coast or the lakes. Milan in the summer is, let's say, *hot*. Most locals escape the city, especially around August. It's only June, but still, not a typical choice for a tourist."

That actually makes sense, considering the streets have been emptier than I expected. But before I can ask more, I see the shift in his expression, the playful curiosity replacing casual conversation.

"So why are *you* here in the middle of a workday?" I raise an eyebrow at him, mirroring his earlier question. "I've noticed people take their jobs *very* seriously in this city."

That earns me a full, head-tilted-back laugh, and I swear I stop breathing for a second.

"Fair enough." He grins, his dark eyes gleaming with amusement. "I had an appointment nearby, then decided to grab a coffee. And, well..." He gestures at his shirt, smirking. "I got a cappuccino too."

He winks. And my stomach does a *whole backflip*.

I press my lips together to stop a smile from spreading too wide. "I really *am* sorry about that. I'll pay for the dry cleaning."

He waves a dismissive hand. "Don't worry about it. A washing machine will fix it."

I hesitate for a second, my gaze flicking to his left hand. No ring. Not that it necessarily means *anything*, but still. It makes me wonder if there is someone who will wash his shirt while I'm here, having a coffee with him.

Then I remind myself, rings don't mean much, not in my world. And look how *that* turned out.

Four hours.

That's how long we've been sitting here, lost in conversation, oblivious to the world around us. We only realize the time when the barista, now looking a little sheepish, approaches our table with a hesitant smile.

"We don't make dinner, but I have some sandwiches if you want," he offers.

The bar is empty now, the nearby tables wiped down, chairs stacked. It's obvious he's closing up, but he's also clearly a friend of Michele's and doesn't want to rush him out.

"I'm sorry, we didn't realize it was so late," I murmur, feeling a little guilty.

The man's smile is warm, reassuring. "Don't worry, I'm used to him staying late. He can talk for days if you let him."

Michele lets out a low chuckle. "We appreciate the offer, but I think we should let you go home to your wife." He pulls out a bill and places it on the table without waiting for change.

After two weeks here, I've learned that Italian coffee is absurdly affordable. What he left probably covers at least four overpriced Starbucks lattes back home. I instinctively reach for my purse to contribute, but before I can even touch my wallet, Michele's hand lands lightly on mine. The contact is brief, but it still sends a jolt up my arm.

"I offered you a cappuccino, and I meant it," he says, shaking his head.

I pause, then murmur, "Thanks."

A silence settles between us as the barista disappears inside. It's not an uncomfortable silence, but it's different, like both of us are waiting for the other to do something first. Like both of us understand the need to leave, but don't want to.

"So…" he finally says.

"So…" I echo.

Something has shifted. The easy rhythm we had all afternoon has been interrupted, as if we stepped outside the little bubble we unknowingly created. There's still so much to say, so much we could ask each other, and yet the words won't come. We've talked about everything and nothing, and it feels like there is a whole world to talk about. Does he feel it too? That unfinished feeling, like neither of us is ready to walk away just yet?

Michele clears his throat, and his tone is almost hesitant when he speaks again. "Okay, this might sound strange, but would you like to have dinner with me?"

I blink, surprised not just by the offer but by the hopeful edge to his voice. A sentiment that mirrors mine.

"Now?" I ask, just to be sure we're on the same page.

He nods. "Unless you have plans."

There's something endearing about the way he says it, like the thought of me having evening plans hadn't even crossed his mind until now.

I chuckle. "I'm here alone. My only plan was watching TV with a cup of gelato."

His lips curve into a slow, confident smile. "I promise you won't regret missing the gelato." He extends his arm slightly in an invitation, not too intimate, just enough to suggest we walk together.

I hesitate only a second before slipping my hand through the crook of his elbow.

As we start strolling toward a quieter street, I glance at the stain still marring his shirt. "Are you sure you don't want to go home and change?"

He shrugs, completely unbothered. "Where we are going, they don't mind if I walk in wearing only my boxer briefs."

I let out a laugh. "Is this a common occurrence? You showing up to dinner half-naked?"

Michele smirks, shaking his head. "No, but they're

used to worse. Believe me. And this?" He gestures to his stained shirt. "This is nothing. Accidents happen."

His casual attitude about it is almost charming. In my world, if I as much as step outside with a coffee stain, the headlines would have a field day.

We reach a tucked-away *trattoria* nestled between a residential building and a covered walkway leading to a small square. Above the door, a wooden sign reads Trattoria Mamma Rosa, and from the terrace above, a cascade of pink, white, and purple flowers spills over, partially veiling the windows. It's intimate and charming, the kind of place only locals seem to know about.

As soon as we step inside, a woman behind the counter looks up and her face lights up when she sees Michele.

"*Ragazzo mio!*" She sets down the bottle of wine she is opening, hurrying around the counter.

I watch as she wraps her short arms around his torso, pressing her cheek against his chest with motherly affection. Michele chuckles, resting a hand lightly on her back, murmuring something in Italian.

The brief exchange is warm and affectionate. Around us, a few tables have turned their attention our way. For a split second, my stomach clenches with nerves. Have they recognized me? But no. They're not looking at me. They're looking at *him*. Maybe because of the stained shirt? I don't linger looking for an answer, but I'm glad I'm not the one drawing attention.

After a few more words I don't understand, the woman leads us to a corner table. The trattoria is cozy, with butter-yellow walls and old-fashioned tools hanging as decor. It feels worlds away from the upscale, modern restaurants I'm used to. I sigh in relief when I realize I can relax a bit and not think about being perfect in here like I usually do when I go out in Los Angeles.

Michele settles into his chair and glances at me. "Sorry, she doesn't speak much English. She was just asking how I've been."

I smile. "No problem."

Honestly, I've noticed it's rare to find someone here who speaks English fluently, especially the older generations. Most know enough to get by, but deeper conversations are another story.

Michele picks up a menu but doesn't even glance at it before looking at me again. "Do you trust me to order for you? I'd like you to taste a bit of Milan."

There's something almost boyishly eager in his expression, and it's contagious.

"I'd love that," I say. "I've mostly been playing it safe with food since I got here. I'm sure I'm missing out."

His grin is almost triumphant as he orders an *antipasto*: cheese, cured meats, marinated vegetables, and thin, crispy breadsticks he calls *grissini*. Everything is paired with a bottle of wine.

As he pours us each a glass, his gaze flickers back to me, more curious now. "So…do you always have this much time between films, or did you take time off just to visit Italy?"

I hesitate, taking a slow sip of wine. Do I tell him the truth? He knows who I am. He will notice my face on the magazines for sure, if he hasn't already. I exhale and decide that if he's going to hear about it, I'd rather it be from me than from a gossip column.

"Usually, no. My schedule is packed. But…my ex-boyfriend was caught by paparazzi cheating on me with his male co-star. My publicist suggested I lay low for the summer to avoid fueling more headlines. Hence, my impromptu trip to Milan."

Michele's expression darkens, not with pity, but something closer to disgust. "That sucks. I hope you found out before it hit the magazines."

I let out a humorless laugh. "Nope. I heard it from the tabloids first."

His jaw tightens, and he mutters something in Italian under his breath.

I arch an eyebrow. "What does that mean?" It didn't sound nice at all, especially paired with the disgust on his face.

His lips quirk. "*Che pezzo di merda.*" He pauses before translating. "What a piece of shit."

I burst out laughing, feeling the burden lift, as if I've been holding it forever. The knot in my throat, the weight in my stomach every time I talk with someone about what happened, is not as heavy anymore. And for the first time since landing in Italy, I feel a flicker of something I hadn't dared to think of.

Hope.

5

MICHELE

"That *risotto alla Milanese with ossobuco* was something I will remember for eternity." Lena beams at me with a wide smile, and her cheeks flushed from the wine. The way she pronounces the Italian words, with that charming accent, makes my lungs forget how to work.

I knew it this afternoon, but dinner confirmed it. She makes me forget.

For the first time in months, I don't feel like a man whose career is slipping through his fingers. I don't think about the team that cut me loose, the injury that haunts my nights, or the uncertainty clawing at me like a shadow I can't outrun. With her, I forget the pain gripping my leg most of the time.

Maybe it's because she doesn't know who I am. She

doesn't see the baggage I carry, the weight of expectations, or the headlines dissecting my downfall. With Lena, I'm just Michele. No past, no pressure.

"I know! I was stunned the first time I had it after moving to Milan." I chuckle, reaching out instinctively when she stumbles on the uneven cobblestone. She catches my elbow, her fingers gripping tightly as she steadies herself.

It could be the wine, or the late hour, or the sheer absurdity of how easy it feels between us, but I don't want tonight to end. I don't want to go back to my empty apartment, to lie awake staring at the ceiling, drowning in spiraling thoughts that make my nightmares become almost tangible.

"You're not from here?" she asks curiously, looking at me with those big blue eyes that mesmerize me.

It's refreshing that she doesn't know. She has no idea how long it's been since I had a night like this, feeling light and letting my mind rest. It's been years since the last time I allowed myself to be something different than the soccer player, just Michele, and nothing more.

I shake my head, smiling. "No. I'm from a small town in Puglia, in the south."

Her expression softens. "Really? I've heard the south is amazing in the summer. I'd love to visit someday." There's a wistfulness in her voice, like she doesn't believe it's possible.

I wonder why she feels like she can't do something this simple, visiting a place she wants to see. She is already here, and from what she told me, she's staying for a while. Nothing should stop her from doing what she wants.

"It really is," I say. "The colors, the scent of fruit warm from the sun, the way people smile and live slowly like they've got nowhere else to be, it's something else. Even the taste of food is different."

Silence settles between us, but it's not uncomfortable. We walk aimlessly, just enjoying this moment. And I realize I don't want to say goodnight yet.

"Come with me," I say, the words slipping out before I can second-guess them.

She turns to me, brow furrowing slightly. "I..." There's hesitation in her voice, and I rush to reassure her.

"It's a public place. Plenty of people. Nothing to worry about." I wink, trying to put her at ease.

She exhales a soft laugh. "Sorry. I guess I'm just used to men expecting something in return after dinner. And I'm not interested in...that."

My stomach twists. It's infuriating that she even has to say it. It's disgusting how some men treat a meal like it's a transaction.

"They're not men," I mutter. "They're pathetic losers who can't get a woman any other way."

She's quiet for a beat and gazes at the paved street

under her feet. Then she says, so softly I almost miss it, "My ex was like that. He always expected something in return."

I glance at her, but she keeps her head down, shoulders slightly hunched, like she's ashamed. And that pisses me off more than anything. What an asshole

"Look how that turned out," I say, not bothering to filter my irritation. "He didn't even have the balls to tell you he had his dick buried in someone else's ass."

A sharp laugh bursts out of her, and she shakes her head. "You're not wrong."

There's something about the way she looks at me, like she's seeing me differently. She seems surprised that I don't act like the men she is used to, and the idea makes me sad for her. How can someone live always expecting the worst from the people around her? Maybe it's just her recent breakup making her distrusting, but still, it's sad.

"But seriously," she says, shifting the conversation, "where are you taking me?"

I grin. "We're here." I gesture toward a glowing neon sign up ahead.

Her face lights up, and it damn near knocks the breath from my lungs.

"Gelato?" She lets out a delighted laugh. "Are you serious? I don't know if I have room for it after that dinner, but I'll run ten laps around the block if it means I get to eat some." She giggles, and the sound tugs at something deep inside me.

When we get closer to the outdoor space, she studies the display case like a kid in a candy store, eyes wide as she scans the endless rows of flavors. "Okay, I recognize pistachio, but the others? I have no clue. I need your help."

I go through them one by one, answering every question as she listens, completely enraptured. The woman behind the counter watches us with amusement, probably used to the locals not making a fuss about it, but with Lena, it's all marvel and awe.

She settles on pistachio and hazelnut, her voice stubbornly wrapping around the Italian words. "*Nocciola*," she repeats until she gets it right and orders by herself. Her accent makes the word sound ten times sexier than it should.

We sit outside with our cups, and every time she takes a bite, she lets out a soft, appreciative moan that sends a low hum of amusement through me.

"So," I say after a comfortable silence, "are you actually going to travel around Italy this summer? Or are you planning to hide out until it's safe to go home?"

She exhales, stirring her gelato absentmindedly. "I'd love to. But the paparazzi are everywhere, even here. Trying to visit tourist spots turns into a nightmare fast."

I know it too well. After my accident, they were

relentless, circling like vultures, reminding me every damn day how much I fucked up.

"There are places that aren't swarming with tourists," I say. "And ways to avoid being seen."

She laughs. "Easy for you to say. You live here. You speak the language. I can't even read half the street signs."

"I could go with you," I blurt out. I don't think. I just say it.

As soon as the words leave my mouth, I realize how insane it sounds. I barely know her. She barely knows me.

She turns, watching me with open skepticism. "Is that a serious offer? Because I'm waiting for the punchline."

I rub a hand over my neck, ruffling my hair. "I know it sounds crazy. But if you want, I'd be happy to show you around."

And the thing is, the more I think about it, the more I actually want to. Because I don't have anything to lose. I'm stuck, floating in limbo, with no real direction. And for the first time in months, today felt like a breath of fresh air. It's almost exhilarating thinking about forgetting all my problems and living in the moment.

She tilts her head. "You expect me to travel with a stranger I just met?"

Fair point.

I reach for my wallet, pull out my ID, and hand it to her. "Take a picture. Send it to whoever you trust. If anything happens to you, they'll know exactly who to blame."

She snorts. "Not exactly reassuring. I'd still be dead in a ditch."

I sigh. "You're right. But this is the best guarantee I can offer. You've been with me all day. If I gave you bad vibes, run. Trust your gut. But if you do say yes, know that at any point, if you feel uncomfortable, you can ditch me. No hard feelings."

She studies my ID, then snaps a picture. "I'll send it to my lawyer. If you turn out to be a serial killer, he'll make sure you rot in prison."

I grin. "Fair enough."

And just like that, I find myself agreeing to something completely insane. A spontaneous trip with the most beautiful woman I've ever met.

For the first time in a long time, without a plan or even a vague direction, I don't feel lost.

6

LENA

Michele pulls up in front of my apartment the next morning, and my jaw nearly drops. A vintage Alfa Romeo, painted deep, glossy blue with chrome accents, stands near the curb like something straight out of an old Italian movie. It's compact, elegant, and effortlessly cool, just like the man behind the wheel.

I step closer, running my eyes over the sleek lines of the car. "Are you sure you'll even fit in that thing?" I ask, arching a skeptical brow as he climbs out. The door creaks slightly.

He smirks, rounding the car to take my bags. "Hey, don't underestimate my Giulia. She's taken me on more adventures than you can imagine." His voice is laced with pride as he runs a hand lovingly over the hood, like he's petting a beloved pet rather than a sixty-year-old vehicle.

I cross my arms, barely containing my grin. "You named your car?"

He opens the passenger door, motioning for me to get in. "Sort of. It's an *Alfa Romeo Giulia Super*. The name was kind of a given." He winks before shutting the door behind me, and I feel my stomach flip. That damn wink will be the end of me, I already know it.

Inside, the tan seats are buttery soft, worn just enough to be inviting but still immaculate. The scent of aged vinyl mingles with the faintest trace of gasoline, and I run my fingers along the polished dashboard. This car hasn't just survived time. It defied it.

Michele folds himself into the driver's seat, and I bite my lip to keep from laughing. He dwarfs the space, his broad shoulders nearly brushing mine, his long legs maneuvering awkwardly to fit. Our elbows touch lightly, and I glance at him, with amusement bubbling up my throat.

"What?" He shoots me a curious look.

I shake my head, fighting back a chuckle. "Nothing. I'm just fascinated to see how you plan on driving across Italy without cramping up like a pretzel."

He rolls his eyes, shifting the gearstick with practiced ease. "You Americans and your giant cars. Just wait. You'll be grateful for my Giulia when we have to squeeze between parked cars and oncoming traffic in the old Roman streets."

I huff a small laugh, conceding his point. The first time I visited Italy, I was baffled by the roads. They are narrow, winding, and seemingly designed for vehicles half the size of what I was used to. Compared to the vast highways back home, these streets feel like something out of an old movie, made for horse-drawn carriages rather than modern traffic.

"Fair point," I admit, trailing my fingertips over the pristine dashboard. "This car is in incredible shape."

Michele beams, his chest visibly puffing with pride. "It took me years to restore her. She's a *restomod*."

I glance at him, intrigued. "What does that mean?"

"It means she still looks like a classic beauty on the outside, but under the hood, she's got modern upgrades: engine, suspension, brakes, and electronics. Makes her safer and more reliable."

I nod, absorbing that. There's something undeniably appealing about the combination. Vintage charm with a strong, capable heart beneath. And, if I'm being honest, the way he talks about it, with such effortless confidence, like he doesn't need to prove anything, only makes him more attractive. What I noticed immediately about him is that he doesn't need to show off to be seen. It's a feat very few men I've met can pull off.

"We don't have air conditioning, though," he adds,

glancing at me sideways. "So I'll stick to side roads, avoid the highways. We can keep the windows down and let the breeze do the work. Sound good?"

I smile. "Fine by me. I've got all the time in the world."

We settle into a comfortable silence as he weaves through Milan's chaotic traffic. Horns blare, modern Vespas zip by narrowly avoiding us, and yet, Michele seems unbothered, driving the car with an ease that speaks of years spent navigating streets like these.

The moment we leave the city behind, the landscape shifts. The mountains in front of us replace towering buildings, and the road leads us through small towns. I lose count of how many towns we pass. In the U.S., I could drive for hours between cities without seeing a single house, just miles and miles of open land. Here, everything is connected. The small cities are stitched together like a tapestry. There's no getting lost in Italy; there's always something just around the corner.

"Where are we going?" I ask after a while, realizing I'd jumped into this car with zero clue about our destination. Probably not my smartest move, but somehow, I trust him. Hopefully, that trust won't end with my body hidden in a vineyard somewhere.

Michele flicks his gaze toward me, grinning like he's got a secret he can't wait to reveal. "I figured Como might be a bit of a paparazzi trap, considering all the celebrities who vacation there. So, instead, I'm taking you to Varenna. It's a small town on Lake Como. Less flashy but more charm."

I blink, surprised by his thoughtfulness. "Aren't there still a lot of tourists?"

"Oh, tons," he admits with a chuckle. "But tourists aren't paparazzi. No one's sitting around with a zoom lens waiting for us to show up."

He reaches into the back seat and pulls out something, dropping it onto my lap. Two navy-blue baseball caps, each embroidered with the *Alfa Romeo* emblem.

I pick one up, holding it between my fingers. "Do you own anything that isn't car-related?"

His grin is unapologetic. "I love my sweet baby, okay?" He gives the dashboard an affectionate pat, and I can't help but laugh.

Shaking my head, I slide the cap on and then lean toward him to check my reflection in the rearview mirror. He says nothing, but when our eyes meet, he winks. That. Damn. Wink.

Suddenly, I'm staring at him for far too long, taking in the dark hair peeking from beneath his cap, the way his scruff sharpens the angles of his jaw, the unbuttoned collar of his polo shirt teasing a glimpse of his chest dusted with dark hair. Usually, I go for clean-cut, polished men, the type who keep their beards perfectly trimmed and their suits pressed.

Michele is none of that. He's rougher, a little unpolished, like he belongs more to the road than in a boardroom. And damn if that doesn't make him look like he gives women the time of their life.

WE ARRIVE IN VARENNA, AND I CAN'T DECIDE WHERE TO look first. On one side, the mountains rise like a sturdy wall, their peaks covered in thick vegetation. On the other side, the lake stretches out, calm and glassy, mirroring the pastel-colored houses that cling to the mountainside. The entire town looks like it was plucked from a postcard, with red, yellow, and pink facades standing in perfect contrast against the lush greenery.

Michele parks the car near a cobblestone square lined with iron benches and a handful of trees that offer sparse shade. Across the street, a church stands tall, flanked by its ever-present bell tower. I've seen places like this in pictures, but experiencing it in person is something else entirely. This is the Italy I always imagined, the one that doesn't need filters or staged angles to feel breathtaking.

There aren't many people around, just a few elderly locals going about their morning routines and the occasional tourist snapping pictures. It's nothing like the usual chaos that follows me in Los Angeles.

"I get what you meant about this place," I say as

Michele leads me through an arched stone passageway between aged walls rich with history. "It's not exactly empty, but there aren't a lot of people who'd sell a story to the gossip magazines."

He nods, his hand brushing the rough stone wall as we descend a set of narrow stairs. "Don't let the quiet fool you. Teenagers on vacation with their parents might recognize you, but at least you won't have a mob of paparazzi waiting at every corner."

I smirk. "I'll take that over getting ambushed outside my home any day."

The winding streets of Varenna are a maze of tucked-away hotels, flower-draped balconies, and staircases that seem to lead nowhere until, suddenly, we emerge onto a terrace overlooking the lake. My breath catches in my throat.

From here, I can see the coastline stretching in the distance, tiny villages dotting the green slopes like constellations against an emerald sky. The mountains roll down to meet the water, and the lake's colors soften their peaks. The whole scene feels untouched by time, like something out of another era.

"This is incredible," I whisper.

Michele steps closer, his chest just barely grazing my back and his presence warming my skin. The touch is so light, but it sends a ripple down my spine. He lifts an arm, pointing toward the left side of the lake.

"That's the Lecco branch," he explains, his voice lower, almost intimate. "Varenna is right in the middle, facing both the Como and Lecco sides."

I frown, turning slightly toward him. "Isn't it the same lake?"

He chuckles. "Technically, yes. But there are two branches, one under the Como province, one under Lecco. They have a bit of a friendly rivalry."

I arch an eyebrow. "So, what, you guys split the lake like divorced parents?"

Michele laughs, his voice rich and warm reverberating through my chest. "Something like that. Each side swears theirs is better."

I smirk. "I guess I'll have to see both and decide for myself."

He leans in slightly, his face brushing against mine, close enough that I catch the faint scent of his cologne, something woody and clean, like cedar with a hint of citrusy soap. "I already planned on that," he murmurs, his breath teasing my skin before he straightens, giving me space. The fresh air left by his body's absence is almost bothering me.

I swallow, willing my pulse to slow down. The way he commands a moment without overpowering it is almost too much. And yet, I find myself leaning into him, reaching for that warmth he left behind.

"Come on," he says, suddenly grabbing my hand in

his firm grip. "We *need* to have breakfast on the lakefront. You can't miss that."

I let out a breathless laugh, trying to focus on his words and not the way my hand tingles where he's holding it, the way it perfectly fits in his. "You know my trainer is going to hate me after this trip, right? I swear, all I've done in Italy is eat."

Michele glances at me over his shoulder, and a smirk plays at his lips. "You'll walk enough to burn it off." He winks, and damn it, he's right.

By the time we reach the café, I feel like we've climbed half the town, ducking under low arches, navigating winding alleyways, dodging overgrown branches spilling from hidden gardens. But the effort is worth it when we finally sit at a table right by the water. The lake laps lazily at the stones a few feet away, and the late-morning sun kisses my skin with just the right amount of warmth.

I close my eyes, inhaling deeply. "This place is unreal."

Michele leans back in his chair, tilting his face toward the sun. "Yeah. I love it."

"It's so quiet," I admit. "I'm not used to this."

He watches me for a long moment before speaking. "I imagine it's a big change from LA."

I huff a laugh. "That's an understatement. I don't know how to be a tourist. Even when I'm on vacation, I bring work with me. A script to read, a book that's being adapted into a movie I might audition for. This whole 'doing nothing' thing makes me feel…lazy."

Michele smiles, but there's something knowing in his gaze. "Then I'll teach you how to live like an Italian."

The way he says it—like it's a fact, not a suggestion—makes me bite back a grin. "Deal."

Silence stretches between us, but it's comfortable, like the warmth of the sun or the steady sound of the water until curiosity gets the better of me.

"Can I ask you something personal?"

Michele's eyes flick to mine, guarded yet amused. "Go ahead."

I hesitate, but only for a second. "Aren't you supposed to be working instead of playing tour guide? You don't exactly look retired, but you're too old to be in college and have the summer off."

His chuckle is light, but for the briefest moment, something flickers in his expression, something unreadable, almost like pain.

"I'm in between jobs," he says vaguely, his fingers absently tracing the rim of the table. "Taking some time for myself."

It's an answer, but not really. There's more to it, something unspoken, something he's not ready to share. And for some reason, that makes me want to know him even more. There is an intelligence, an emotional maturity that transpires between the jokes and the laughs. And something deeper that I can't pinpoint. His eyes tell me that he's been through a lot, and that makes me assume there are way more layers to peel back before you can say you really know him. And it's a challenge I want to take on.

Michele is a puzzle wrapped in easy smiles and quiet confidence. And as I sit there, watching him with the lake shimmering behind him, I realize something. I have no idea what I'm getting myself into, but for the first time in a long time, I don't mind.

7

LENA

We arrive in Bellagio just as the sun begins its slow descent behind the mountains, painting the sky in streaks of orange and pink. The town, nestled at the meeting point of the lake's two branches, is a postcard come to life: elegant, timeless, and bathed in the golden glow of dusk. But what truly captures my attention isn't the beauty of the place, it's the way we got here.

Michele didn't drive us around the winding roads that hug the lake. Instead, he rented a private limousine boat, slicing through the water with an ease that makes me wonder just who the hell this man is.

He claims he's between jobs, yet he throws money around like it's pocket change—private boats, secluded restaurants, the kind of indulgences that don't come cheap. And judging by how effortlessly he arranged everything, this isn't a spur-of-the-moment splurge to impress me. He knows the boat guy, has his number saved in his phone, and they talk like old friends. This is his world. I just happen to be stepping into it.

A part of me itches to ask questions, to peel back the layers of mystery surrounding him. But we aren't that close, and prying into his business feels like crossing a line. I can only hope I'm not enjoying the generosity of a criminal mastermind. I mean, who has that kind of money without needing a job?

The hotel we walk into screams luxury, with its polished chandeliers and marble floors. The moment we approach the front desk, the concierge's face lights up with a broad smile.

"Signor Moretti, che piacere."

Even without speaking Italian, I can tell it's more than just politeness. It's familiarity, the kind that suggests Michele isn't just any guest; he's *known* here. I don't think this is his first time staying in this place.

"The pleasure is mine," Michele responds in English, his hand settling lightly on my back as he guides me forward.

It's a small gesture, but I appreciate it. He's making sure I'm included, that I don't feel like an outsider. The concierge's gaze flickers to me, and the recognition dawns in slow motion. His surprise is there, just for a second, before he schools his expression into professional warmth.

"It's a pleasure to have you here, miss," he says with a polite nod.

"Nice to meet you," I reply with a smile.

Michele leans casually against the counter, flashing an easy grin that feels almost too charming. "Any chance you have a couple of rooms for tonight?" His voice is smooth, but there's a hint of uncertainty beneath it. "I know it's last minute, and I wouldn't normally ask during peak season, but I want her to experience a proper Italian getaway before she goes back to the chaos of Los Angeles."

The concierge doesn't even hesitate. He smiles like he already knows the answer. "There is always room for you, Mr. Moretti."

I feel the tension in Michele's body ease slightly beside me. I hadn't even realized he was nervous. The fact that he *was* surprises me. He's gone out of his way to make sure I have a perfect time, and for what? I'm practically a stranger to him.

I've always heard about Italian hospitality, but this feels different. More than just cultural warmth, it's *personal,* and I don't know how to place it in a relationship between two strangers, because this is, ultimately, what we are.

We're given two lake-view suites, and I'm relieved

when Michele doesn't insist on paying for mine. He has a habit of picking up the bill before I can even reach for my wallet, and sometimes, it makes me feel like I'm taking advantage of him.

Tonight, at least, I get to contribute. But as I take the key from the concierge, my curiosity only deepens. Who *is* Michele Moretti? And why do I get the feeling that beneath all his easy charm, there's something he's not telling me?

THE HOTEL'S TERRACE OVERLOOKS THE LAKE, ITS GLASSY surface reflecting the twinkling lights of the town across the water. A soft breeze carries the scent of blooming flowers, mixing with the distant lapping of waves against the docks below. The candle between us flickers, casting golden light over the crisp white tablecloth, adding an air of intimacy to the night.

It's the kind of setting I'd picture for a honeymoon, a romantic getaway, the kind of night people dream about. Yet, with Michele's easygoing smile and the relaxed way he leans back in his chair, it doesn't feel awkward or forced. He isn't trying to manufacture some grand romantic moment.

And if there's one thing I've learned about him over the past couple of days, it's that he doesn't have a hidden agenda. He's not putting on a show to impress me, not orchestrating all of this as some elaborate ploy to get me into bed. He's just being him. I haven't for a single moment felt pressured by him to go further. It could be him playing the long game, but for the little I know him, it feels out of character, far from the persona he's shown me up to now.

"So," he says, lifting his wine glass to his lips, "are you enjoying your Italian life so far?" His eyes glint with amusement as he watches me, waiting for my verdict.

I take a sip of my own wine, savoring the taste before answering. "I'm loving it. The sights, the food, the company…" I flash him a teasing smile.

He chuckles, swirling the deep red liquid in his glass. "I'm glad to hear that. It's strange, but I've realized I actually enjoy playing tour guide, showing you places that aren't in the travel brochures, the kind of spots only locals know about."

"You're an amazing tour guide," I say. "Ever considered doing it professionally? I know plenty of people back home who'd pay a lot of money for someone like you, especially if you can keep them away from the paparazzi."

That earns me a real laugh, one of those deep, unrestrained ones that makes him throw his head back, his face lighting up in a way that seems to be happening more and more on this trip. I watch him for a moment, curiosity stirring inside me. There's something about the way he carries himself, the weight I sense pressing on his shoulders, that makes me wonder.

"I don't think I can change the course of my life *that* much," he muses, his laughter fading into something more thoughtful.

I tilt my head, studying him. "And what *is* the course of your life?"

For the briefest second, his smile falters. It's quick, barely noticeable, but I catch it before he schools his expression back into his usual charming facade.

"It's something I worked hard for since I was a kid," he says carefully. His voice is steady but lacking its usual playfulness. "I wished for it, fought for it. And now that I have it, walking away would feel like throwing away a once-in-a-lifetime opportunity."

It's an answer without actually answering, a way of telling me something while still keeping me at arm's length. I could press. I could push for more. But I don't because beneath the effortless charm, beneath the smooth words, I see the sadness lingering in his eyes, the hesitation just before he speaks. And I don't want him to tell me because I force him to. If he ever decides to open up, I want it to be *his* choice.

"So I guess we both saw our dreams come true," I say instead, shifting the conversation. "I always dreamed of becoming an actress. And I love my life, even if it means never doing anything crazy, like taking a spontaneous trip around Italy."

Michele's brow furrows, like I've just told him something completely incomprehensible. "Nothing crazy?" He leans forward, his expression incredulous. "Not even a *little*?"

I shake my head, feeling strangely self-conscious under his scrutiny. "Not exactly. My life is…planned. Every day, every hour, down to the minute. There's no room for detours." I force a small smile. "Sounds boring, right?"

He doesn't smile back. Instead, he studies me, his gaze soft but intent.

"No," he says finally. "It sounds…sad."

And for some reason, that hits harder than I expected.

MICHELE IS ON A MISSION. HE DOESN'T BELIEVE THAT I've never done anything spontaneous in my life, and by the look on his face, he won't stop until he proves me wrong.

"Getting drunk with your friends in high school?" he suggests as we walk along the manicured garden of the hotel, with the lake stretching out beside us in the darkness.

I let out a laugh, shaking my head. "God, no. I was

already auditioning full-time in high school. I was home-schooled."

He stops mid-step and turns to look at me. His eyebrows are raised in surprise. "You were home-schooled? You didn't have friends?"

I shrug. "I had some. Mostly other actresses I worked with, but those friendships never lasted beyond the movies we were filming together. It's strange… This job surrounds you with people all the time, but when I think about who I'd consider real friends, the list is pretty short."

Michele falls silent, thinking that over. Then he asks, "Not even the person who let you stay in the apartment in Milan?"

I smile. "She's one of the few real ones. We were roommates when I moved to Los Angeles after high school. I couldn't stay with my parents if I wanted to audition seriously, it just wasn't feasible anymore. I managed when I was a minor, but it took a ridiculous level of commitment."

He hums thoughtfully and stops in front of the stone parapet lining the lake. Leaning against it, he stares at the water and at the distant town lights reflecting across the surface.

"I know what you mean," he says after a beat. "I didn't have a lot of time to be young either. But I sure as hell did something crazy." He chuckles, and I glance at him with curiosity.

"Like what?" I lean against the parapet beside him, the cool stone pressing against my forearms.

He smirks. "Like stealing my dad's car when I was fifteen, three years short of the legal driving age in Italy, piling my friends in, and taking a joyride to the beach in the middle of the night. I drove straight onto the sand and got stuck. We had no clue how to get the car out, so I had to call my brother for help. He tried, but in the end, he had to call our dad."

I gasp, my jaw dropping. "Oh my God."

Michele grins. "Yeah. My dad showed up with a tow truck. Once he got the car out, he looked me dead in the eye and said, 'You're walking home.' Ten kilometers. I had to walk the whole way back."

I stare at him wide-eyed. "Are you serious? That's insane! You could've crashed, gotten hurt, or worse!"

He turns toward me, still smiling, but there's something deeper in his expression. "I was reckless, yeah, but I think I needed it. The pressure on me was intense. If I didn't let loose in some way, I would've cracked and screwed up royally." His voice dips into something almost wistful, like he's remembering more than just that one night.

I lower my gaze, tracing the pattern of the stone

railing with my fingers. I've known for a long time that I missed out on a lot of the typical teenage experiences. But I've never really regretted my choices. At least, I don't think I have.

"I haven't even done a tenth of what you did that night," I admit softly. "I was always the mature one. Always did the right thing."

Michele suddenly straightens, carrying a mischievous glint in his eye. "Then it's time for you to catch up."

Before I can react, he grabs my hand and tugs me toward the stone stairs leading directly into the lake.

"What are you doing?" I squeak with my heart leaping into my throat as he lets go of me and starts stripping off his shirt.

"Something crazy," he says, shooting me a grin as he unbuttons his jeans. "Are you in?"

My brain short-circuits for a second because holy hell. I figured he was fit, but seeing him like this, his chiseled torso bathed in moonlight, is something else entirely. His body is pure, sculpted strength, all taut muscles and toned legs. And then I see it. A long, mangled scar runs down his left thigh.

He turns slightly, catching my gaze on it, and I immediately snap my eyes back to his face. For a second, relief flickers in his expression. He was expecting me to ask but I don't. Not yet.

"You want to swim? At night?" I ask, trying to focus on anything but the fact that he's standing in front of me half-naked, looking like every forbidden fantasy I've ever had. Jesus, he is hot. Cover-magazine-hot. My lower belly clenches, trying to rein in the hormones going wild.

He winks. "Why not? Got something better to do?"

I hesitate. "Is it even safe?"

"Jumping into a lake in the dark at eleven at night? Probably not." He steps into the water, wading in until it reaches his thighs. "But I've survived worse."

I glance between him and the inky water. The responsible part of me—the part that has dictated every moment of my life up until now—says to stay put, to let him have his fun while I play the role of the mother hen, watching him and assuring he is safe.

But another part of me, the part that feels electrified by this night, by this man, by the way the universe keeps throwing surprises in my path, that part whispers, *What if you just let go?*

Michele takes another step, then dives forward, disappearing beneath the surface. I hold my breath until he resurfaces a bit farther, shaking his head. He drives his fingers through his wet hair, his biceps bulging with the movement and making me want to see more of him like this, while his dark eyes lock onto mine.

"Are you coming or not?"

I swallow hard, and my heart hammers in my chest like it wants to escape. I've never done anything like this. Even though it will never compare to the kind of nights Michele had when he was young, it feels huge to me.

Then, before I can think too hard about it, I whisper, "Fuck it."

Kicking off my sandals, I yank my dress over my head and toss it onto the stone steps. The night air kisses my skin, and I take a deep breath before running down the steps and diving in.

The water shocks me. It's cold, and my nipples strain against the lacy bra, sending a rush of adrenaline through my veins.

"It's freezing!" I gasp, surfacing.

"You'll get used to it," Michele says, swimming closer.

Only now do I realize how little separates us. My lace bra and underwear cling to my skin, and there's nothing but moonlight and water between his bare body and mine.

For a moment, neither of us speaks. The moment seems surreal and magical at the same time. It's like we are alone in the world, and the idea doesn't scare me like it should. I'm swimming half-naked in a lake in a foreign country, doing something probably illegal, with a man I barely know, equally half-naked. I should at least feel a bit on edge for it, but instead, I feel excited. I don't know if it's more for the situation or the fact that a gorgeous man is staring at me like he wants to devour me in the best way, but the internal turmoil is wreaking havoc in my stomach and lower, so much lower.

"Is it so bad?" he finally asks in almost a whisper.

I think about it. About how wild and reckless this feels, and about how, for the first time in a long time, I feel free.

"Actually," I murmur, "it's pretty damn good."

Michele smiles, reaching out to take my hand. He doesn't pull me closer, doesn't cross any lines. He just holds onto me as we float beneath the stars.

Then, a chill runs down my spine.

"Oh my God!" I shriek, kicking my legs wildly. "Something touched my foot!"

Michele bursts out laughing, his chest shaking as he reaches for my waist, guiding me toward the stairs. I wrap my arms around his neck, clinging to him, my legs lifted high to avoid whatever lurks below.

"This is exactly why I don't swim in lakes at night," I mutter while my pulse is still racing.

"But you did it," he teases, his voice warm against my ear. "And you loved it."

I loved way too many things about this night, but the way he is carrying me out of the water, his skin against mine, his strong arms around my waist, is reaching the top of my personal favorites.

I exhale, still pressed against him. He's right. I have no idea what's coming next in my life, but for the first time, I kind of like it that way.

8

MICHELE

I let Marco's call go to voicemail again for the tenth time today. The screen lights up with his name, the buzzing fills the small car, but I don't even glance at it anymore. Since we left Milan ten days ago, I've vanished from the world. No press, no sponsors, no rehab updates, nothing. Just me, Lena, and the open road.

I know I should at least send Marco a text, something to keep him from having a heart attack, but every time I even think about answering, a weight settles in my ribcage. I can already hear him in my head, pushing me to be smarter, faster, tougher. To do another interview, another sponsor meeting, another reminder to the world that I'm still here, relevant, capable of coming back.

But the truth is that I don't know if I am.

My leg feels stiffer every day without proper therapy,

and cramming myself into this car for hours isn't helping. Walking through the towns, climbing ancient stairs, and exploring castles balances out the damage, but it doesn't fix it. And I don't know if I even want to fix it anymore. I'm tired and hopeless, something I've never felt before, and it terrifies me.

"You know," Lena's voice pulls me from my thoughts. She's hesitant, which isn't like her. "Shouldn't you take that call?"

I glance at her, catching the way she bites her lip as she watches me from behind oversized sunglasses. The wind tangles her hair, with the strands catching in the sunlight, and for a second, she looks like she belongs in an old Italian film, with her timeless and effortlessly captivating beauty.

I smile, keeping my voice easy. "It's work-related. I've been clear that I'm taking time off." It's a lie, but I don't feel like explaining everything to her right now. I don't even know how to explain what I'm feeling to myself, let alone another person.

She studies me in silence, long enough that I feel it in my chest. "I feel guilty for accepting your offer for this trip," she finally says. "Like I'm keeping you from something important." I can hear the guilt in her tone, and that sparks a sense of uneasiness in my chest.

If there's one thing I've learned about Lena in this short time we traveled together, it's that she never hesitates to speak her mind. She doesn't play games and doesn't dance around the truth. She's direct in a way that should annoy me, but somehow, I love it.

I shake my head. "Don't be. I needed this trip as much as you did. Probably more." And this, at least, is the truth. I didn't know how much I needed this break from reality until I took it.

She watches me carefully, like she's trying to decide whether or not to believe me. "Promise me that if you need to go back, you'll tell me. You won't just ignore it until it's too late."

I exhale slowly, gripping the steering wheel. She doesn't know that I already crossed that line weeks ago. I'm not sure there is a way back anymore. But I don't want her to carry that weight.

"You're not a problem, Lena. You will never be." I glance at her, offering the best reassurance I can. "And I promise if I have to go back, I'll tell you. We'll figure it out."

She studies me for another second, then nods, easing the tension in her shoulders.

"So," she says, shifting the mood, "where are you taking me next?"

I smirk. "To drink good wine and eat good food."

She groans, but the laugh that follows is warm. "I don't even know why I ask. You've been stuffing me like a Thanksgiving turkey since we left Milan."

"Don't be so dramatic." I chuckle. "We've been exploring. You need fuel to keep up."

She sighs, but there's no real frustration behind it. "You're right. I don't think I ever would have seen those towns on my own. They looked like something out of a fairy tale. The hills, the towers, those castles on the cliffs…" She shakes her head in awe. "I don't even know how it's possible to build something like that. They've been standing for centuries, strong and beautiful. Before I met you, I didn't even know Emilia Romagna existed. How unfair is it?"

I glance at her, and something warm settles in my chest. She says it like she's talking about more than just the buildings. I saw how she enjoys the slow life in those places, the long lunch breaks, and the simplicity of small moments. I don't think she can get that in Los Angeles.

She lets out a small huff. "I still have no idea how you Italians drive on these tiny roads, though. It has to be some kind of magic trick. There's no other explanation."

I bark out a laugh, remembering how she yelped every time I squeezed the car between stone walls and oncoming traffic. "I promise you, it's not that difficult."

She mutters something under her breath, but then the road curves, opening up to rows of lush green vines stretching out forever. The vineyard sits at the top of the hill, bathed in golden light, the kind that makes everything look unreal, almost dreamlike. Lena falls silent, and her lips part slightly as she takes it all in. For the first time in weeks, peace eases through my chest.

Maybe I'm not ready to go back, but I have a feeling this trip will help me figure it out.

WE SIT BENEATH THE PERGOLA, THE ONLY TWO PEOPLE here aside from the crickets singing their hearts out in the warm July sun. The heat lingers, but the shade from the vines and the occasional breeze make it comfortable. The scent of earth, grapes, and something faintly floral drifts around us, mixing with the rich aroma of food. It's the kind of afternoon that settles deep into your bones, making you forget about time.

The vineyard owner's wife approaches, setting down our plates with a warm smile.

"This is *tortelli di erbette*. Fresh pasta stuffed with ricotta cheese and chard, sprinkled with parmesan," she explains to Lena.

Lena's eyes widen in surprise. "I thought the *gnocco fritto* with *prosciutto* and…" She hesitates with her brow furrowing. "*Squac… squac…*"

"*Squacquerone*," I supply, grinning.

She points at me. "Yes! That cheese. I thought that was our meal."

The woman chuckles, and I can't help but do the same.

"Oh, no, sweetheart, that was just the *antipasto*. This is the first course. Then comes the second course, then dessert. Coffee and *digestivo* after that."

Lena's mouth falls open. "Jesus. I'm going to roll down the vineyard by the end of this meal. The wine doesn't help either."

She shakes her head, but there's a teasing glint in her eyes. Her cheeks are flushed, not just from the heat but from the bottle of *Lambrusco* we've already drunk. And she doesn't even know about the *Malvasia* we're about to have with the *tortelli*, or the *Sangiovese* that will come with the beef.

When the woman walks away, Lena leans back in her chair, stretching her legs out. She tilts her head toward me, with her lips curling slightly. "Be honest. Do you want me to get drunk? Because we're almost there."

I chuckle, swirling my wine. "Not on purpose. But we're in a fantastic winery, eating an authentic meal, and drinking their best bottles. When's the next time we'll get to do this?"

She raises an eyebrow. "Fair point. But it's almost three in the afternoon, and we're not even halfway through. We won't have time to visit anything else today."

I lean back, watching her over the rim of my glass. "Are you in a hurry?"

She shrugs. "Not exactly, but…"

"So relax." I smile, setting my glass down. "This is an Italian meal. It's meant to be slow and savored. We're not supposed to rush through it just to check the next thing off our list."

She exhales, shaking her head, but I see the way she lets go, just a little.

"You're right," she admits. "I'm just not used to it." She shakes her head, and I feel a bit sad for her. How is it even possible to live always in a rush? My career is not a slow one, but at least I take my time whenever I can to relax and enjoy my life.

We take our time eating, drinking, and talking. The conversation flows effortlessly, and laughter slips between us like it always belonged there. She tells me stories about her childhood, moments that make her wrinkle her nose in embarrassment or cause her to throw her head back in laughter. And I find myself watching her more than I probably should, catching the way she gestures when she talks, how she plays with the stem of her glass, how her eyes light up when she teases me.

Maybe it's the wine, or maybe it's just her beauty, but I'm paying too much attention. I know I am, but it seems like I can't tear my eyes from her mesmerizing face.

By the time we finally push back from the table, it's nearly five. The vineyard around us is lazy with afternoon warmth, and we're both drunker than we should be.

I take her hand without thinking as we wander into the vineyard. Her fingers are soft, her grip easy, and for a moment, I let myself enjoy the way it feels. She doesn't pull away. If anything, she holds on tighter when she stumbles slightly on uneven ground, laughing breathlessly.

"We might've overdone it," she murmurs, pressing against my side for balance.

"I have a feeling we did. It's probably best if I don't drive and we stay at their bed-and-breakfast for the night instead," I suggest.

She nods absentmindedly. "I think that's the right call."

She steps forward, misjudging her footing, and suddenly, she's tumbling. I catch her around the waist before she can hit the dirt, pulling her against me. She turns in my arms, her hands landing on my chest, and then she's just there. Close. Too close. Her perfect body molds to mine like they were made to complement each other.

She tilts her face up, flushed from the wine, and her lips are slightly parted. A few freckles dust her nose, ones I hadn't noticed before, and I wonder how I missed them. Maybe I didn't. Maybe I just hadn't let myself focus on them because they are too tempting, too distracting. It would be so easy to just shut off my reasonable self and brush them with my fingers. Or my lips. So, so easy.

I should let go. I know it's the right call, but I don't.

Her breath hitches, just barely. It's subtle, but I notice the breath caught in her throat. Just like I've noticed the way she leans toward me sometimes, the way she lets her gaze linger, the way she laughs a little softer when it's just the two of us. Being together day after day has created the sort of intimacy between us that normally only happens after months of dating. And the fact that this thought crosses my mind should be enough to let her go, but I linger a moment longer, savoring her breath on my skin, coming closer and closer.

Is it real, or am I just drunk and imagining what I want to see? Her eyes flick to my mouth, just for a second. But I see that too. I didn't imagine it.

"Thank you," she whispers.

I don't know what I'm supposed to say. My grip tightens on her waist before I force myself to loosen it. We're drunk. That's all this is. I can't trust my judgment when I can't even walk straight.

"We should head back before we hit our heads out here." I keep my voice light, forcing a grin as I turn her toward the path.

She doesn't argue. Just slides her arm around my back as I drape mine over her shoulders. It's practical; we need to keep each other steady. At least that's what I tell myself, but even drunk I know it's bullshit.

But the way she fits against me feels far too good to ignore.

WE STUMBLE INTO THE WINERY, LENA STILL GIGGLING beside me. She's been laughing at a butterfly for the last five minutes, watching it zip back and forth like it's drunk too. And now she's got me chuckling along with her. Our steps are unsteady, our bodies warm from too much wine and summer air.

The woman who served us earlier greets us with a knowing smile.

"I don't think I'll be able to drive tonight. Do you have a couple of rooms left in the bed- and-breakfast?" I ask.

Lena covers her mouth, trying—and failing—not to laugh, and the woman's lips twitch like she's holding back her own amusement.

"I only have one room left," she says, almost apologetic.

I glance at Lena, still clinging to my side. She shrugs.

"It's not like we can drive anyway. It's this or sleep in the car."

The mere idea of sleeping all cramped up makes my back ache in protest. "We'll take the room," I say, and the woman nods.

We barely make it to the door before Lena almost trips over her bag.

"Jesus, I'm drunk, drunk, drunk," she giggles.

I steady her, my hand instinctively settling at the small of her back. She's warm beneath my touch, and I have to remind myself to let go.

Inside, the room is small but cozy. One bed, one armchair, a door that probably leads to the bathroom. I stare at the furniture like it somehow betrayed me.

"There's only one bed," I mutter, stating the obvious because my brain is too slow to process anything else.

Lena tilts her head at me. "Of course, there's only one bed. What did you expect?"

Good question. What did I expect?

Before I can figure that out, she sighs. "Listen, we're both adults. We can be mature enough to sleep in the same bed without having…" She trails off, then dissolves into laughter again.

I smirk, shaking my head, and start to strip out of my shoes and pants.

"Why are you stripping?" she squeaks, covering her eyes.

I pause with fingers gripping the hem of my T-shirt. "Because I need to go to bed? I know it's early, but I really need to lie down right now. I'm not getting in bed fully dressed."

"Oh. You're right." She mumbles, grabbing her bag and practically sprinting into the bathroom.

I don't even bother getting under the sheets, just collapse onto the mattress with a sigh. The evening breeze drifts in through the open window, cooling my heated skin. At some point, Lena slips into bed next to me, but I don't even open my eyes. I'm too far gone to have any reaction.

PAIN SHATTERS THROUGH MY LEG, SHARP AND unrelenting, tearing me from sleep. A choked groan escapes me as I clench the sheets in my fists while my entire body locks up.

"Michele?" Lena's voice is thick with sleep but laced with concern. She shifts beside me. "What's wrong?"

I grind my teeth. "My leg."

There's rustling as she sits up, her silhouette outlined by the dim moonlight filtering through the window. "What's happening with your leg?"

"It hurts. A lot," I manage, my breath coming in ragged gasps.

She mutters something under her breath before fumbling to turn on the bedside lamp. The soft glow spills over us, and I see the horror in her face as her gaze drops to my leg.

The muscles are locked in a tight spasm, the scar standing out stark against my skin. I know it looks bad. I can feel how bad it is.

"What do I do? How can I help?" Her voice is small but steady.

"In the front pocket of my bag, there are painkillers. Can you grab them?"

She doesn't hesitate. In a blur, she's out of bed, rummaging through my bag. A moment later, she's back with the pills, a glass of water in her other hand. I toss back the medication, swallowing it down, then hand her the empty glass.

"Thank you," I whisper through clenched teeth.

"Is there something else I can do?" She's searching my face, looking for an answer I'm not sure I can give. This is my life, and I feel exposed letting her in when I'm so vulnerable. I've seen enough pity in everyone's eyes since the accident not to want to witness it on her face too.

I shake my head. "Not much. I just need the pills to do their job."

She frowns, unconvinced. "What if I try to massage the muscle? Stretch your leg?"

I hesitate. The pain is unbearable, but the thought of her hands on me, of her touch being the thing that helps, makes my breath catch in a silent gasp. She is worried, not pitying me, and this loosens my uncertainty a bit.

"It can't be worse than this," I admit.

She kneels beside me. Her touch is tentative at first, her fingers pressing gently into my calf. It hurts like hell. I suck in a sharp breath, but she doesn't stop. Slowly, carefully, she works through the tension, her hands moving with more confidence as she kneads out the knots. The pain shifts from unbearable to something I can breathe through, and eventually, she manages to stretch my leg out, letting it rest on the bed.

The worst of it passes, leaving behind the dull ache I've learned to live with. I exhale, my body sagging into the mattress.

Lena watches me. Her brows are pinched, and worry is still etched across her features.

"I'll be fine," I murmur, giving her a tired smile. "It's already way better than before."

She nods, but she doesn't look convinced. There's a question in her eyes, one I know she won't hold back for long.

"Go ahead," I say, preempting her. "Ask."

"Are you sure?"

I nod.

She hesitates for only a second before speaking. "What happened to your leg?"

"Motorcycle accident," I say simply. "Got crushed between two cars. My leg took the worst of it."

"Jesus Christ." Her voice is barely a whisper. "You're lucky to be alive."

I shrug. "Lucky to still have my leg. Injuries like this usually end in amputation."

Her eyes snap to mine, and I see the weight of my words settle over her. She looks almost terrified at the idea, and the sight softens something in my chest. Gone is the carefree Lena I've gotten used to lately, and I don't know how to feel about her worry. I've learned to deal with pity, but I still have a hard time reassuring people.

"When did it happen?"

"Six months ago. I was driving to my parents' place, and some idiot ran a red light, pinning me against another car."

She exhales deeply. "Is that why you're 'in between jobs'?"

I know this bothers her, but I'm grateful she didn't press until now. I'm still not ready to lay out the whole truth for her, but I can give her something.

A half-laugh leaves me before I can stop it. "Sort of. I'm an athlete, so..." I don't even know how to finish the sentence. I can see in her expression the realization of what I've lost. The horror, the sympathy. But not the pity, and I'm grateful for that.

"I get it," she says softly. "Can't you take more painkillers? Avoid getting to this point?"

This is the first time I haven't heard the dreadful words, "I'm sorry," coming from someone hearing my situation for the first time, and it's a refreshing feeling.

I shake my head. "They're strong. I don't want to rely on them too much. And they mess with my job… antidoping and all that stuff."

She nods slowly, then, without hesitation, she slides back under the covers and shifts closer. Before I can react, she tucks an arm under my head and pulls me against her, her fingers threading gently through my hair. The gesture is so natural that it throws me off guard.

I go completely still. I should pull away. I should make a joke. But instead, I let myself sink into her warmth, my arm wrapping around her waist. It feels so right, I can barely breathe. How is it possible I feel so safe with someone I barely know?

She presses a soft kiss to my temple. "Now sleep. And from now on, we take it slow," she says, turning off the lamp.

Warmth unfurls beneath my ribs. The heavy weight I've been carrying for months lifts, just enough to let me breathe again. In the dim light coming from the window, I bask in the comfort of her arms wrapped around me.

I've slept with countless women, but I've never felt as intimate with anyone as I feel with Lena right now. There is no amount of sex that can compare to the connection I have in the arms of this woman.

I don't want this night to end and reality to rise again with the fast-approaching sunrise.

9

———————

LENA

Michele stubbornly refuses to let me drive all the way to our next stop. We booked an old stone-walled house nestled in the rolling hills of Tuscany. We made one quick stop to pick up groceries and a couple of swimsuits, but other than that, it's been a straight shot here.

We don't have a time limit on this place, so we are staying as long as it takes until I'm sure he is fine. And I don't care how much he protests, he needs rest, and I can be more stubborn than him if I have to be.

The other night, when he woke up gasping through clenched teeth, his entire body seized by pain, I realized just how bad his injury really is. I'd seen the scar, but I hadn't known the extent of his injury, not truly. Now, I do.

And I also know that this tiny, vintage car he insists on driving isn't doing him any favors. Don't get me wrong, I love it, it's the quintessential Italian dream. But for him, being crammed in this thing for hours must be a nightmare.

Now, though, he looks completely at peace. He woke up with a smile on his face that matched mine, but I don't know if it's because we cuddled all night or if his leg is not bothering him as much.

Thinking about last night takes me back to the feeling of his skin against mine and our arms wrapped around each other. I wasn't thinking too much about the implications, just that it might be a good way to relax him, but the more we stayed like that, the more the thought of how right it felt kept nagging me. Because his body tangled with mine was absolute perfection, and I shouldn't think about him like *that*, considering I still have someone at home I need to talk to. Because yes, Preston still refuses to take my calls. Prick.

I sway gently in the hammock, hidden beneath the shade of a tree, watching Michele as he sprawls out on a towel under the sun. His sunglasses shield his eyes, but the satisfied curve of his lips tells me he's exactly where he wants to be.

I shouldn't be staring, but I can't help it. Not in view of such perfection.

He looks like he was carved from marble. Long, lean

muscles sculpted by years of training, not just gym work-outs, he is not the bulky type. I don't know what kind of athlete he is, but his body tells a story of long hours of practicing and honing his skills to reach higher and higher peaks. I mean, if it's his job, he must be good at it, or else he wouldn't be making money at it.

The dips and ridges of his stomach, the firm lines of his arms, the way the tendons flex subtly under his tanned skin, every inch of him screams something greater than simple aesthetics.

A dusting of dark hair covers his chest, just enough to make him look rugged. Untamed. Dangerous in a way that makes my stomach flip. I swallow hard and force my eyes back to my e-reader, but the words blur together. My skin feels too warm, even in the shade. And my lower belly buzzes with a building need to approach him and straddle his hips. I should really focus on my book.

A lazy ripple breaks the surface of the water beside him as he trails his fingers through it. The pool—it's not really a pool, more like an old stone basin once used for washing clothes—gleams under the sunlight, its surface disturbed only by the trickle of water spilling from a rusted iron pipe. I would like to be that water, grazed by his strong fingers making my skin ripple in pleasure.

I let out a slow breath. This is fine. Totally fine. I can keep my attraction under control. It's not like he can see me staring. I'm feet away, and my sunglasses are foolproof.

"I see you checking me out," Michele says, his voice laced with amusement.

Shit. *Not as subtle as you thought, eh, Lena?*

"I am not," I lie instantly, flipping a page on my e-reader as if I've been enthralled by it this whole time. "I was looking at the water." The excuse sounds lame even to my ears.

I don't know if it's the night spent tangled together, or the hot temperature of the Italian summer cooking my brain, but it seems I can't keep my thoughts strictly platonic when it comes to Michele. He has a glorious body, he is funny, and certainly knows how to flirt, but it's not like I haven't known men like him before. *Get a grip, Lena!*

He smirks, rolling onto his stomach and propping himself up on one elbow. "Sure."

I roll my eyes, even though he can't see them behind my shades. Or at least I think he can't, considering he caught me checking him out.

The silence between us stretches for a moment until his smirk deepens, he stands and dusts off his hands, then starts walking toward me with a little too much casual ease. He moves slowly and deliberately, like an animal preparing to attack its prey. And from the gorgeous, cocky grin on his face, he is sure he has already won.

"What are you doing?" My voice pitches higher as he reaches me, his hands sliding under my body before I can react.

I barely have time to yelp before he lifts me up, arms locking around my waist and knees as I instinctively clutch at his shoulders. His warm skin against mine sends pleasant shivers down my spine.

"Michele!" I squeak when I realize what he is doing.

Too late. He strides straight into the water, taking me with him. And then the cold hits me. Freezing, bone-deep cold.

I gasp as the water rushes up, swallowing me to the shoulders. My entire body jolts at the contrast between the summer heat and the icy pool, which is almost unbearable.

"You're insane!" I shriek, pushing at his chest. But I'm laughing. Goddamn him, I'm laughing. It was so unexpected that I'm not even mad at him. Considering where my thoughts were headed, I needed a cold bath to chill my overheated hormones.

He laughs too. A deep, rumbling sound that sends a sharp pulse of heat straight through me, in direct contrast to the water. It's not helping my cause that his hands are still on my waist, steady and firm, holding me close. Damn, not even the icy water is helping me. How can his skin be so tempting underneath my fingers? And those droplets running down his shoulders? They're *begging* my tongue to run over them.

"You needed a cold shower," he murmurs, his voice dropping an octave. He leans in just slightly so I feel the rough scrape of his stubble tantalizingly close to my cheek. "I saw you biting your lip while checking me out."

My stomach drops. He is totally right. I was biting my lip, trying not to moan, thinking about how he would feel between my thighs while I straddle him. I indulged way too long in that thought.

"I was not." My voice is embarrassingly breathless.

His grip tightens. Not enough to trap me. Just enough to make me feel it. The tension, the awareness sparking between us. There is an electricity running between us that is way too dangerous for two people submerged in water.

I suddenly realize how little space is left. My gaze flickers to his lips and my heart stutters. They're parted just slightly, with water glistening along their shape. His tongue darts out, catching a stray drop that slides down the corner of his mouth, and a traitorous thought slams into me: I want to do that. I want to chase every bead of water down his skin with my own tongue, follow the inked lines of his tattoos with my mouth, and feel the taut muscles beneath my hands.

His fingers flex against my waist, and I swear I feel the heat of them through the cold water.

I need to get out of here before I do something I'll regret. Now.

I abruptly push away, standing up so fast I nearly slip. "I'm freezing," I blurt, grasping at the excuse like a lifeline. "I need a hot shower."

I don't look at him. I can't. I just turn and rush inside with my pulse hammering, my skin burning, and the ghost of his touch still lingering on my body.

FORTY MINUTES. IT TAKES ME FORTY DAMN MINUTES IN the bathroom to get a grip, to wrestle my pulse back under control, and to focus on anything but Michele's hands on my waist, his lips parting ever so slightly, his breath warm against my face.

I can't do this. Not with Preston's name still making the rounds in the gossip magazines back home, his tongue practically down Ronan's throat in every new photo. Greta says not to worry, that the headlines will die down eventually. But Tabia is more honest, or better, not tiptoeing around the truth. She tells me the fire is still burning, fueled by every new sighting. They might not have found me in Los Angeles yet, but it's only a matter of time before someone blows my cover. Thinking about

Michele in *that* way right now is confusing and makes me feel guilty. Because, at the end of the day, I'm not like Preston, and if a relationship is still unclear, I don't dive into another one, even if it's just a summer fling.

I exhale sharply and push open the bathroom door. But the moment I step into the kitchen, everything I spent forty minutes suppressing comes rushing back with brutal, delicious intensity.

Michele stands at the stove, a glass of wine within easy reach, completely at ease in his own skin. And by skin, I mean *bare* skin because the only thing covering his body is a loose pair of linen pants hanging low on his hips, clinging to his butt in a way that makes my throat go dry.

The massive snake tattoo curling over his back shifts with every movement as he stirs the sauce in the pan. The flicker of the warm kitchen lights catches the lines of his muscles, making them stand out in sharp contrast. He looks like he belongs here, as if he's done this a thousand times before. Casual. Effortless. Devastatingly sexy. And maybe he has, considering how well he knows his way around the kitchen.

I should say something, but instead, I just *stare*. After a beat, he turns, catching me red-handed. His brows lift in amusement before his lips curve into a slow, knowing grin.

"Finally," he says, and damn, even his voice is as smooth as a caress. "I thought you were dead in there."

"No," I manage, stepping farther into the room. "Just needed to warm up a bit. The water out there is freezing."

A partial truth, but not the full story. Fortunately, he doesn't call me on it. Instead, he reaches for a second glass and hands it to me. The deep red liquid swirls inside.

"I'm making pasta with tomato sauce. Nothing fancy," he says. "You okay with that?"

The fact that he's cooking, that he already thought about dinner, makes my stomach stir in ways that have nothing to do with hunger. I love it when a man doesn't expect me to cook for him. I'm a nightmare deciding what to eat, and most of the time I end up ordering out.

"Hell, yes," I say, taking a sip of wine.

He chuckles, turning back to the stove. "Figured something simple was the best choice."

I admire the easy way he completes each task without thinking. He strikes me as someone who can make more than a simple pasta.

"Who taught you how to cook?" I ask, leaning against the counter, watching him.

His expression softens. "My mom. Typical southern Italian mother. She loved having us in the kitchen, but still believed it was a woman's job. Even so, she never turned me away when I asked questions."

"But you kept cooking," I guess, watching the way his hands move with practiced ease.

He shrugs. "Had to survive. I was out of the house by sixteen, chasing my dream. Picked it up from there."

A flicker of curiosity pulses through me again. *What exactly was his dream?* He always sidesteps the answer. Even now, he keeps it vague, as if he doesn't want me to know. By now I'm sure he's not a criminal, but why doesn't he tell me what kind of athlete he is? I can understand how talking about his job reminds him that his injury put a stop to that, but I don't need the entire story, just a bit to make me feel part of his world. I feel like I'm an open book, while he is a secret chest.

Before I can pry, he shifts the focus back to me. "What about you? How was life with your parents?"

I take another sip of wine, choosing my words. "I was homeschooled while my sister went to a normal school. My parents flew me to auditions and made sure I had tutors when I was filming on location. They didn't want to disrupt my sister's life for my career, so they found ways to balance both."

Being a child actress wasn't easy for my parents, but I was a stubborn little thing, and I knew that was my vocation.

His gaze sharpens. "Sounds harder than what I went through."

I smile. "I loved it. I knew by the age of eight that I wanted to act. My parents never let me lose sight of reality, though. They made sure I graduated on time, with flying colors. They were strict about that."

He nods approvingly. "We were both lucky. Some parents put everything on the gifted kid, pressure them until they break."

He's right, I've seen my fair share of stage moms to know how lucky I was to have parents who care about me.

"Oh, not my parents. Every penny I earned went into an investment account. By the time I was twenty, I was already rich, thanks to my dad's knack for investments."

Silence stretches between us, comfortable and warm, filled only by the gentle simmering of sauce. I watch as he scoops some onto a piece of sourdough bread, then turns to me.

"Here," he says, holding it up.

I lean in, my lips brushing against his fingers as I take a bite. The moment my mouth closes around it, I groan softly at the burst of flavor. I will never understand why Italian food tastes this good. It's a tomato, for Pete's sake!

"This is amazing," I murmur.

But Michele isn't looking at the food. He's looking at

me, at my lips. His eyes darken, and the heat behind them is unmistakable. A single drop of sauce clings to my lower lip, and before I can react, he reaches out, wiping it away with his thumb.

Time seems to slow while my pulse pounds in my ears and his thumb lingers on my lip, tracing the shape of it with agonizing slowness. The shiver of pleasure and anticipation goes straight down to my core, making me squirm. And then, *fuck*, he brings it to his mouth, sucking the sauce from his finger in a way that is entirely too sensual. Who would have thought cleaning food from your fingers could be so unbelievably sexy? My knees go weak.

His gaze flicks down to my parted lips. I can feel his unsteady breath on my skin. He is just as turned on as I am. My own intake of air is no better. His other hand slides up, his fingers threading into my hair at the base of my neck, gripping just enough to send a shiver down my spine.

His lips crash onto mine, and the world explodes. Heat sears through me as he kisses me like he's starving for it, like he needs this as much as I do. His tongue sweeps against mine, the taste of wine and tomato and something wholly *him* intoxicating me more than the alcohol ever could. The pounding of my heart in my ears is deafening, and everything disappears around us.

I press against him, my hands splaying over his chest,

feeling the heat of his skin, the steady pound of his heart. He groans into my mouth, the sound vibrating straight through me, pooling low in my belly. Everything I tried to suppress under the shower comes back with a vengeance. His lips are soft but firm, and they guide my mouth with the perfect amount of possessiveness. I'm not fond of men who think they have power over women, but Michele leads this kiss, guessing exactly what drives me insane.

His arm snakes around my waist, pulling me flush against him, and I gasp against his lips, arching into his touch. He takes advantage of the moment, deepening the kiss, his tongue stroking mine in a slow, devastating rhythm that makes me ache. If I thought he was craving me before, I was mistaken. Now he possesses my mouth like he wants to devour me.

I don't even notice when he backs me against the counter until I feel the edge dig into my lower back. He presses into me, and God help me, I want more.

I want his mouth, his hands on me, but at the same time, it's too much. I tear my lips away, breathless, my heart hammering in my chest.

"Wait," I whisper, my hands still pressed against his chest.

His brows pull together and concern flickers across his face, like he's worried he crossed a line he shouldn't have.

"I can't," I force out. "I'm not ready. I still need to talk to Preston. I need to close that door before I open this one."

His jaw clenches, but he steps back, giving me space, except for his hands, which remain on my waist, grounding me. I swear I see a glimpse of guilt crossing his gaze before hiding it.

"I understand," he says, his voice rough, but there is not a hint of doubt in that statement.

"It's not that I don't like you. God. I really like you." He smiles at my confession. "But I feel like it isn't fair for both of us if I don't solve my mess before dragging you into this."

He smiles and nods. "You don't have to explain. I understand, and I apologize if I took this too far."

I search his face for disappointment, for frustration. I find neither. Just patience and quiet understanding.

And that scares me more than anything. Because it makes me want him even more. I feel that pull at my chest tighten even more than before, and I'm scared that at some point it will snap, leaving me more broken than when I arrived in this country.

Shit.

10

LENA

One week.

Seven days of blissful peace in this house nestled in the rolling Tuscan hills. Days spent learning to cook under Michele's patient guidance, sipping exquisite wine, and indulging in lazy afternoons basking under the sun or swaying in the hammock with a book in my hands.

We never talked about the kiss. But somehow, nothing really changed. It isn't awkward between us. If anything, it feels natural. We still laugh and joke like we always did, even though the pull between us hasn't gone anywhere. I know I'm still drawn to him, and I'm fairly certain he feels the same way. There are moments, too many of them, when I catch him looking at me, when my skin tingles under his gaze, and I wonder what would happen if I closed the space between us.

And yet, we don't cross that line again. I often think about that kiss because, damn, it was a really spectacular one. The kind that makes your insides explode like a can of soda after you shake it. It was perfect on so many levels that if I think about it, I can still feel the tingling on my lips and his body pressed against mine. It would be so easy to slip into something more with Michele, but I'm not the kind of woman who goes straight for the next man, even if he is attractive and emotionally available.

But no matter how much I try to tell myself to slow down, Michele makes it easy to forget about the rest of the world. He's level-headed, effortlessly funny, and so damn considerate that I never feel the need to escape for some alone time. In fact, I crave his presence. More than once, I've found myself thinking about the moment I'll have to leave, and every time, an unfamiliar ache settles in my chest.

I don't want to think about what that means.

"I can't remember the last time I've been this relaxed," I muse, stretching out on the lounge chair as Michele passes by to refill our glasses with iced tea. "Actually, I don't think I ever have."

He hands me my glass and settles into the recliner next to mine. The sun kisses his tanned skin, highlighting the tattoos sprawled across his torso. My gaze lingers on the scar running down his thigh before I quickly glance away. He seems more relaxed these days, even though I know he would never tell me if he is in pain. He strikes me as the type who suffers in silence rather than worrying those around him. If I weren't in that bedroom that night, I would have never known the extent of his injury.

"Yeah," he says, exhaling deeply. "I know what you mean. I don't think I've ever had this much time to myself, not without the pressure to train or the constant rush to get back to work."

I tilt my head, studying him from behind my sunglasses. He wears his too, making it impossible to decipher what's going through his mind, but something in his tone tells me this conversation isn't just casual small talk. We skipped the awkward stage where you don't know how to make the conversation flow, or maybe it was never even there. Spending so much time with a person makes the small talk dry up fast, leaving space for more meaningful conversations.

I care about him, more than I should, more than I want to admit. And no matter how hard I try to suppress it, a part of me worries about what will happen when this brief escape ends.

"Do you have a timeline for your recovery?" I ask, my voice softer now. I don't know exactly what his injury entails, but I do know that for an athlete, something like this can be career-ending.

He shrugs. "Not really. I just have to keep working on it and hope it gets better."

I nod, even though his answer unsettles me. He's being deliberately vague, and I don't know if it's because he genuinely doesn't have answers or because he doesn't want to talk about it. Either way, I don't push. Whatever he's facing, I have no right to pry. When he is ready to tell me, he will.

"Does it still hurt?" I ask instead. Our bedrooms are right next to each other, and more than once, I've strained my ears at night, wondering if he needed help. But I never hear a sound.

He shakes his head. "Not this week. Being here, away from everything, helps."

That small confession tightens something in my chest. It's my fault if his leg is getting somehow worse. When he says he has to "work on it," I imagine that entails physical therapy and rest, something I haven't seen him do since we left Milan.

"Driving all this way couldn't have been good for you," I say, sitting up straighter. "I should go home and let you focus on recovering properly."

His head snaps toward me, and his jaw tightens. "Don't even think about it."

His words hold a weight that sends a shiver down my spine. There's something in the way he says it, something firm but almost desperate. It's like he is grasping for something I can't see.

"I don't want to make your injury worse," I insist, trying to keep my voice steady. "I don't need this trip. I can go back to Milan…"

"No." He cuts me off before I can finish, shaking his head as a small, knowing smile tugs at his lips. "You need this journey as much as I do."

I open my mouth to argue, but he presses on.

"This isn't just about my leg, Lena. It's not just about the physical injury. It's in here too." He taps his temple. "I need a distraction. I need to clear my head before I can figure out what comes next. This…," he gestures toward his leg, and his expression darkens momentarily, "changes everything. Whether I like it or not, I have to figure out a way forward. And if I don't change my mindset first, I'll lose my damn mind."

His words hit me like a punch to the gut. Because I get it, I don't even want to imagine what it would feel like if I suddenly couldn't act anymore. If the career I built, the one thing I've always known, was suddenly ripped away from me. What would I do then? Who would I be?

People like us don't have a Plan B.

When you dedicate your entire life to something, when you sacrifice everything to succeed, you don't stop to consider what happens if it all falls apart. You just keep going. You push harder. You chase the dream relentlessly because if you stop, even for a second, you might realize there's nothing else waiting for you.

I swallow hard, forcing down the lump in my throat.

Michele doesn't need my pity. He needs time. He needs this escape. And maybe so do I.

"Enough with the sad talk," he says suddenly, forcing a grin and shifting the conversation like he always does when things hit too close to home. "We should go into town and pick up some groceries for the next few days."

I nod, grateful for the reprieve. "I'll go get changed."

I stand, but as I walk away, I glance over my shoulder. He's staring at the horizon, lost in thoughts that are heavier than he lets on. And I wonder, just for a second, if I could be the distraction he needs. If I could be the thing that helps him forget. The problem is, I'm not sure I want to be just a distraction.

THE SMALL GROCERY STORE IN RADDA FEELS FAMILIAR now, like a place we've always shopped at together instead of just for the past week. Michele heads straight for the cured meats section, leaving me to wander through the fresh produce. My fingers skim over ripe tomatoes and fragrant basil. I take my time picking the best ones, enjoying the simple pleasure of it.

In Los Angeles, I'd grab a plastic container of pre-cut fruits and vegetables from the store without a second thought. Convenience always won out over freshness. But here I can taste the difference. The rich flavors and crisp textures are something I won't forget when I go home. I get the feeling that I won't forget a lot of things when I go home, not just the food.

I reach for a box of lemon tea bags and smile, remembering how Michele practically had an existential crisis when I grabbed bottled iced tea last time. His horrified expression still makes me laugh. He'd gone on about all the sugar and preservatives, insisting we had time to boil water and brew tea ourselves. And, of course, he was right. It does taste better this way.

By the time we meet near the registers, I've gathered everything we need.

"We should stop by the bakery for some fresh bread," Michele says, tossing a pack of prosciutto into our basket.

"Okay," I murmur, my attention snagged by a rack of gossip magazines near the checkout.

Something pulls my eyes toward one of the covers.

Maybe it's Michele's name in bold letters, maybe it's the slightly blurred background in the photo, but my stomach clenches as I reach for it. The moment I see the picture, my heart plummets.

It's us.

Sitting at a café, laughing over coffee, completely unaware that someone was watching. My name is printed in smaller text next to a boxed-out image of my face, but there's no mistaking it.

"What is this?" My voice is barely above a whisper as I show him the magazine.

Michele's expression darkens instantly. He doesn't answer. Instead, he starts unloading our groceries onto the conveyor belt, his movements sharper and faster than before.

"What is this?" I repeat, my voice tight with confusion. "Why is your name all over the cover?"

His gaze locks onto mine, pinning me in place. "I'll explain," he says in a low voice, "but not here."

I glance around. The cashier, a young woman, is sneaking glances at us. The man behind us in line is doing the same. Heat creeps up my neck, and I force myself to set the magazine down, flipping it face down.

We pack up the groceries as fast as possible and practically bolt out of the store. Michele throws the bags into the back seat, and the second I slide into the car, he peels out of the parking lot like we're being chased.

"Can you please explain now?" My voice is sharper than I intended, but my heart is still hammering from that headline.

Michele exhales heavily, gripping the wheel like he's bracing for impact.

I press on. "Why is your name on that cover? What kind of athlete are you?"

He hesitates. His jaw tenses, but then he finally says the words that drain the blood from my face.

"I'm a soccer player." He pauses, then he admits quietly, "I play for one of the biggest teams in Italy." His fingers flex on the wheel. "Or at least, I used to."

The weight of it sinks in. I don't know much about soccer, but I do know it's massive in Europe, like football in the U.S. My stomach twists.

"Are you famous?" I ask, even though I already know the answer.

His hands tighten on the wheel. "Yes."

And just like that, so many things click into place. The luxury hotels. The private boat rides. The vintage car. The fact that he never seemed concerned about money or time.

Holy shit.

By the time we reach the house, my mind is still racing. As soon as we step inside, I drop the grocery bags on the counter and pull out my phone.

I don't follow sports. I don't even Google people I

date. I avoid social media unless it's for work. But now I need to know.

I type his name into Instagram and immediately regret it.

"Twenty million followers?" My voice comes out as a squeak. I stare at the number, then at him, then back at the screen, like it'll change if I blink enough. "Are you kidding me?"

"They're just numbers," he says, brushing it off.

I scoff. "Just numbers? Michele, this isn't just local fame. This is international."

He leans against the counter, his expression shifting from serious to irritated. "So what?"

"So what?" I repeat, incredulous. "You know everything about me, and you kept this huge part of your life hidden from me. That's not fair." And, if I'm being honest, it stings. I trusted him. I let him in. But he held this back.

His jaw clenches. "Because, for the first time in years, someone didn't recognize me." His voice is rough, edged with something raw. "You didn't have any expectations. You didn't treat me like a star, or an investment, or a disappointment. You just…liked me. For *me*."

His confession slams into me, knocking the breath from my lungs. The tormented expression accompanying his confession is daunting.

"I was just Michele," he says in a quieter voice. "Not

the most promising soccer player of my generation who fucked up his career."

I watch the shift in him, the crack in the mask he always wears. The easygoing charm, the teasing smirks, the lighthearted jokes, they were all hiding this. The heartbreak. The fear. The loss.

"For the first time since the accident," he continues, his voice almost a whisper, "someone wasn't looking at me with pity." He swallows hard. "Do you know how many people bailed on me when I couldn't live up to their expectations? Even the team I gave everything to, ten years of my life, dropped me the second they thought I was damaged goods." His knuckles turn white as he grips the counter. "And my friends? One by one, they disappeared. I was no longer useful to them."

I feel it in my chest, the sharp ache of his words. I know how much fame can make you lonely. You never know who is there for you or just for what you represent. I can't blame him for basking in the moment of reprieve I gave him from all of that.

"What does your agent say?" I ask softly.

"He's working on it, but so far, only minor teams have made offers." His voice is hollow.

I don't know much about soccer, but I can tell by the way he says it that it's crushing him. Being at the top and then falling down. You feel like a failure.

"Are they that bad?"

"They're not bad," he admits, "but they don't have a shot at winning anything. And I know it sounds arrogant, but I still have another ten years in me." He stops himself. "Or at least, I did."

His voice breaks on that last word, and something in me cracks open. I don't think. I just reach for his hand, squeezing it gently.

"I'm sorry for how I reacted before," I murmur. "I didn't understand."

Michele shakes his head, a sad smile tugging at his lips. "It's fine. Honestly? I feel kind of…lighter. Now that you know." He searches my face. "I just hope this doesn't change anything."

I meet his gaze; I don't see the famous soccer player or the man running from his past. I see him. The real him. With all his insecurity and the weight he's carrying alone. It must be devastatingly tiring and incredibly lonely.

"I don't have a clue about soccer," I say with a teasing smile. "So to me? You're just Michele." And it's true. I have never watched a game or even thought about the game. It's something so far removed from the American lifestyle that it doesn't even make the news, unless it's the World Cup, and even then, it occupies just a small fraction of screen time.

He chuckles, the tension between us easing. But even as his lips curl into a smile, I see the lingering sadness in his eyes. And all I want to do is pull him into my arms and promise that he's more than his career, more than his fame, more than what he's lost.

But I don't know if I'm ready for that kind of intimacy yet.

11

MICHELE

We left the house in the Tuscan hills at midnight. Now that the paparazzi have caught wind of us, it's only a matter of time before they track us down. The only option is to keep moving. Keep them guessing.

So as soon as we got back from that ill-fated grocery run, we packed our bags, had dinner, and called around for a hotel willing to take us in Florence. Not an easy feat in the middle of July, but somehow, we pulled it off.

Now, we stand outside the Galleria dell'Accademia, and I'm ready to work my charm to get us past the massive line.

I step up to the ticket counter, flashing my most practiced, devastating smile. *"Ciao!"*

The woman behind the counter lights up, her polite

customer-service expression shifting into something warmer. "*Buongiorno.*"

"We'd like to buy two tickets." I switch to English deliberately, and as expected, the moment she registers Lena beside me, her eyes widen in recognition. Bingo.

"Of course," she says, fumbling at her computer, suddenly a little nervous.

I lean in slightly, resting my forearms on the counter. "Any chance we could skip the line? We're happy to pay extra." I flash the full force of my signature playboy grin, the one I know works.

From the corner of my eye, I see Lena roll her eyes. She's onto me. But she doesn't seem annoyed, just amused.

The truth is, I don't love using my fame to bypass normal inconveniences. But standing in line for hours, surrounded by people who might recognize us, is a risk I can't take. For me, it's an inconvenience. For Lena, it's a headline. And she's been through enough of those because of that jerk of an ex. I only made things worse when people recognized me and put me in the magazines with her.

The woman hesitates, shifting uncomfortably. "Do you have a reservation?" She already knows the answer, but she has to do her job.

"No," I admit, then grin. "But we can make one right now...for five minutes from now."

She giggles despite herself. "That's not how it works, but you know what? If you sign an autograph for my dad, I can call someone to take you through a different entrance."

I knew I could count on something like this. Everyone in Italy knows about soccer players, or knows someone who knows about us. It's almost a given that I can use my face to open doors. Which is why I never use it, unless it's an emergency. And considering how Lena is uncomfortable in crowded spaces, I say that this is an emergency. Or maybe I just want to spend as much time with her as possible, without being mobbed by fans. That's also a good reason to do it. A selfish one, but I don't linger too much on the guilt creeping into my stomach.

I barely resist the urge to pump my fist in victory. "Do you have a pen and paper?"

As she rummages around, Lena nudges my side. "You're bad," she mouths, her smile full of mischief.

I just smirk and shrug. She shakes her head, but she looks more amused than pissed about it. I sigh in relief.

After I sign the autograph and snap a quick selfie with her, on the promise that she won't post it for at least a week, a man arrives to escort us through a side entrance.

Lena glances up at me as we walk. Her expression is

teasing. "Do you always use your fame to get what you want?"

Her question is laced with more curiosity than annoyance.

"No," I say, feigning offense. "I usually take the conventional route. But let's be honest, most of the time, doors just open for me. What about you?"

Considering how famous she is, I have to believe there are places where she uses her fame to her advantage.

She tilts her head, considering. "Yes and no. If I go somewhere celebrities frequent, I get perks. But outside of those places, I'm just a regular person. No one's handing me a priority pass at the gym or at the grocery store."

"Never skipped the line at a club?" I ask because I did it a lot when I was younger.

She blushes slightly, and she is adorable. "Yeah. I did do that," she confesses

I chuckle, but my attention lingers on her. The more time I spend with her, the more I want to know about her life, her quirks, and her thoughts. It's unsettling. I don't usually linger on the personal details. And yet, with her, I do. I tend not to get too close to women I don't date. The whirlwind of people surrounding my life makes it impossible to know each one of them. It sounds arrogant and lazy, but that's the reality. I have little time for relationships, and I can't give everyone the attention they deserve, so I tend to surround myself with people that I know I want in my life longer than a night out.

But Lena is different. I shouldn't indulge in the comfort of a relationship that leads to nowhere. After this summer, we'll go our separate ways. But it feels like she's slipping under my skin in a way no one else has. This is not a summer fling, a relationship, but it feels like more than a friendship. Hence, my desire to know even the smallest detail about her. I have a feeling I'll regret my life choices when summer ends and reality slaps its ugly hand across my face.

We round the block following the guy who is talking about the recent soccer games and the championship that ended months ago. I tuned him out when he started dissecting the last game when my former team performed a miracle and won the championship. Without me. Lena seems to sense my discomfort, even though the guard is talking to me in Italian and she can't possibly understand, and she reaches for my hand, squeezing it slightly and giving me a small smile. This is why I can't ignore the pull between us, even though the most reasonable thing would be to not to get involved. She's someone you can't ignore.

We slip in through a service door, and the guy leaves us at the entryway to one of the exhibition's rooms. I sigh in relief when he goes away.

"Are you okay? You seemed a bit upset by the guard," she whispers to me softly, avoiding the people surrounding us, eavesdropping on our conversation.

I turn toward those beautiful blue irises that make me feel naked. I smile and nod. "He was talking about my former team as if I were still part of it, and that was a tough rant to listen through," I confess. I don't want to keep her out of my life anymore. The sense of relief to talk about these things with someone that doesn't pity me is both liberating and terrifying. What will I do when she's no longer here after this summer?

She frowns. "Don't people know that you're not part of the team anymore? I thought it was public knowledge."

I shake my head. "Yes and no. There are speculations, but nothing official. My team is taking their time, so I'm still on the roster. If I find another team, they can say that I wanted to change and not that they let me go because of the injury, which would mean facing public backlash about my forced departure."

She scoffs. "Do they have the same publicist as Preston? They sound a lot like a toxic ex." She raises an eyebrow to underline her statement.

I can't stop a laugh from bubbling up my throat. This is what I like most about her. She always seems to know how to make me feel better with a joke, without it sounding forced. She is genuinely a good person.

"I have to check, but at this point I think it's possible." I smile, putting a hand on the small of her back and guiding her toward the exhibit.

We wander through the gallery, admiring the artwork, the weight on my chest lightening every step we take and every smile she gifts me. But when we step into the sculpture hall, I'm surprised to see Lena light up like a kid on Christmas morning.

"I've always dreamed of seeing this in person," she breathes, practically vibrating with excitement.

She is so thrilled that I can't stop a smile from forming on my face. I probably look like a lovesick puppy looking at her like that, but who cares? She is irresistible like this.

I laugh. "What?"

She grabs my hand—actually grabs my hand and makes me shiver in pleasure—and drags me through the crowd, stopping in front of Michelangelo's David.

"Isn't it perfect?" she whispers, completely awestruck. The grip on my hand tightens, and I'm entirely aware of our closeness. Not that I'm complaining about it.

I force myself to drag my eyes away from her perfect face and toward the piece of art. I tilt my head, taking in the massive statue. It is impressive, more so than I expected. The detail is ridiculous, the veins on his hands so realistic it's almost unsettling.

"I have to admit, it's incredible," I say, though my gaze keeps flicking back to her instead of the marble masterpiece. It doesn't even compete with her beauty.

"And those abs?" she murmurs, her eyes shimmering with appreciation.

She is really into this dude, and I can't stop teasing her. I snort. "I have abs like that too. They're not marble, but they're solid enough."

She glances at me, her lips twitching. "I'll give you that. Your physique is…quite the sight."

A slow, satisfied grin spreads across my face. I've never cared much about my looks. My body is a tool, something I maintain for work. But hearing her say it like that? Yeah, I'll take it. I know she's checked me out plenty of times, but my ego is pleased that she is admitting it.

I smirk, letting my ego swell just a little more. "If the timing weren't against me, I'd say I was the model for this statue."

For a second, she just stares at me. Then, out of nowhere, she bursts into laughter, full, unrestrained giggles that shake her entire frame. Someone turns toward her to see what the fuss is about, and they smile, seeing her enjoying herself. I, on the other hand, am puzzled.

I blink, caught off guard. "What?"

She tries to compose herself, taking deep breaths, but

the giggles keep escaping. She laughs out loud to the point of bending over and putting her hands on her knees.

Finally, she places a hand on my shoulder and, between laughs, says, "I just hope, for the sake of all the women you've been with, and ever will be, that you're packing a little more…substance."

She gestures toward my crotch, then flicks her gaze back to David's.

It takes me a second. And then I follow her line of sight.

Ah.

Not the most flattering comparison, I admit that. That's what I get for strutting like a peacock in front of a woman.

For a moment, I just stare at her. Then, I lose it. A deep, gut-wrenching laugh bursts out of me, shaking my entire body. It's been so long since I've laughed like this, so long since I've felt this light and free.

And that's the problem. Because I already know when she leaves, she's going to take a piece of me with her. A piece no one else will ever be able to replace.

12

LENA

The Boboli Gardens look like something straight out of a fairy tale. Sunlight filters through towering trees, casting intricate shadows on the manicured paths. The scent of blooming flowers lingers in the air, mixing with the warmth of the mid-July stillness. Everything here feels slower, like time itself has softened its edges, allowing life to be savored instead of rushed through.

I stroll beside Michele in comfortable silence, the warmth of the sun kissing my skin. My cheeks are still sore from laughing so much back at the Accademia. That's the thing about him: being around him is effortless, like breathing. There's no pressure, no need to be the poised and polished version of myself that Hollywood demands.

With Michele, I don't have to be "Lena Sinclair, actress." I can just be me. Messy hair, no makeup, raw emotions and all. He doesn't judge. He never has. And every time I walk into a room, I catch his gaze burning into me like I'm something worth worshiping.

God, those eyes. Deep, dark, and molten, like rich, melted chocolate you want to drown in. They're maybe the part I like the most about him. Yes, his body is gorgeous, but his eyes make the world shrink down to just the two of us. There is no escaping the intensity of his gaze. Once he captures you with those irises, you're locked in, forgetting the rest of the world.

I inhale deeply, letting the moment settle into my bones. "I could get used to this," I murmur, stretching my arms above my head, tilting my face toward the sun. There is something magical about the Italian sun that makes you want to bask in it all day long. Or maybe it's the laziness that surrounds us these days. It's strange how a few months ago I didn't know how to live without planning my life down to the minute, and now I can walk carefree without knowing what we'll do the next hour. There is something powerful in knowing that anything is possible, we get to decide and nobody else. Coming to this country this summer, I realized how much my life depends on so many people. It's refreshing, for once, to do what I want without caring about pleasing other people.

Michele glances at me with amusement tugging at the corners of his lips. "What? Italy or being on vacation?"

I smile. "Both, I guess. I love the pace of life here. The food. The sun. The…" I trail off, biting my lip as I catch his smirk.

"The devastatingly handsome company?" he finishes, cocking an eyebrow.

I roll my eyes, but I can't help laughing. "You're alright, I guess." I've already admitted more than once that he's handsome, and he's caught me way too many times checking him out.

He clutches his chest in mock offense. "Alright? *Tesoro*, that's cruel."

I laugh at his dramatic response and bump my shoulder against his.

Before I can respond with some joke that will inflate his ego, my phone starts ringing. The shrill sound cuts through the tranquility, instantly dragging me back to reality like a slap in the face.

I sigh, already expecting to see Greta's name flashing on the screen. She's been calling almost every other day, demanding updates on my whereabouts and making sure I haven't thrown my phone into the Arno River. She is worried about me because of the news of a possible tryst between me and a mysterious soccer player, which made the headlines back home, and she wants to be on the same page about what I want people to know about it. I told her I don't care, as long as the paparazzi don't start following me around in this country.

But when I pull the phone out of my purse, my stomach drops.

Preston.

A month and a half. That's how long it's been since his affair blew up every gossip site in the country. For weeks, I've been desperately awaiting this call. For an explanation. An apology. Hell, even a half-assed excuse. But now, I just feel nothing. No anticipation. No sadness. Just a simmering irritation at the fact that he thinks he has the right to disturb my peace.

I should send him to voicemail. Give him the silent treatment, the way he did after I discovered the truth. But something inside me shifts. Maybe it's closure. Maybe it's anger. Either way, I answer.

"I have to take this," I say to Michele, noticing my voice turning somber.

Michele's eyes darken with concern, but he simply nods and takes a step away, giving me space. God, I wish more men were as considerate as he is.

I press the phone to my ear. "Finally, you decide to call," I say, letting my bitterness seep into every syllable.

Six weeks without being able to vent my frustration results in my fury raising its head in all its glory. And it feels good to direct these ugly feelings toward him.

Preston exhales sharply, already irritated. "Yeah, sure, whatever. Can we talk?"

His tone is so annoying I want to crawl out of my skin. I blink. Is he serious? *I* should be the one who's pissed, not him.

"Oh, so, you're finally ready to admit what you did and apologize?" My voice drips with sarcasm, and I don't even try to rein it in. I want him to feel every ounce of my disgust for him.

The silence stretches between us, thick and heavy. I can practically hear him calculating his next move, choosing his words carefully, just like always. I never paid much attention to this side of him; working in this industry teaches you to weigh each word carefully before someone takes advantage of you. But, now that it's being used against me, I realize how little he cares about me, or at least what we once had.

And then he speaks. "What? No! I want to talk about your Italian escapades."

I freeze. For a second, I think I must have misheard him. *He* cheated on *me*, got caught, and publicly humiliated me. But now he wants to police *my* life? Have I stepped into an alternate reality, without realizing it? I can't have spent four years of my life with this asshole.

"You can't be serious," I say, my voice flat.

"Of course I'm serious. The news reached the States, Lena. Your little European vacation is plastered all over the gossip sites." His voice is laced with barely restrained anger.

I knew that already, Greta told me, but the sheer audacity of this man still manages to stun me. He is so self-absorbed that he doesn't even contemplate *my* position in all this mess that *he* dumped on me. He could have told me he fell for another person, and I would have been heartbroken, but I would have understood it. Instead, he chose the easy way out without taking responsibility, and now he's making me out to be the bad guy.

I let out a sharp laugh, but there's no humor in it. "I caught you screwing another man because your *affair* was all over the magazines. And you're pissed at *me*?"

Michele's head snaps up at my raised voice, his brows knitting together in silent concern. I turn away, gripping the phone tightly. I don't want him to see me this upset over a man who doesn't deserve any of my time anymore.

"Don't make this about me," Preston snaps. "I called to tell you to come back and stop making me look like a fool, or else…"

I pause, and my breath catches in my throat. This man. This selfish, delusional *asshole*. How could I have been so blind to stay with him for four years?

"Or else what, Preston? Is that a threat? You think *you* look like a fool?" My voice trembles with fury. "You humiliated me in front of the *entire world* and didn't even have the decency to apologize. You deserve a lot worse than just bad press."

He scoffs. "Oh, don't be so dramatic. You're on vacation in Italy, Lena. How bad can it be?"

I swear, if he were standing in front of me, I would throw him into the nearest fountain. How dare he judge me? The nerve this man has is ludicrous. I want to end the conversation right now and tell him to go to hell, but I also feel he owes me an apology, even if I know it will never come.

"I'm in Italy because the paparazzi chased me out of the country *because of you,*" I spit.

I glance at Michele and see his worried face scrutinizing mine. I want to tell him that everything is okay, but he'll know it's a lie. Michele is everything but stupid and has a sixth sense for understanding when something is bothering me. And this time, there's nothing to guess. I can feel my face contorting in rage. I can't hide it.

"Well, it doesn't look like you're wasting any time getting over it. A *soccer player*, Lena? Seriously? That's such a cliché." His words are laced with venom. "I thought you had standards, but I guess a set of abs is all it takes to make you forget…"

I see red. Every ounce of humiliation, every shred of lingering hurt, dissolves under the weight of my rage.

"Oh, you're right," I say, my voice dangerously

sweet. "I *do* have standards. Which is why I finally realized I wasted four years of my life on a self-absorbed, cheating *worm* like you."

And with that, I hang up. I'm so furious, my heart pulses in my ears. My hands tremble as I unlock my phone and pull up my chat with Greta.

Bury him. Drag Preston through the mud. No more playing nice. I'm done being reasonable. He just called and threatened me, saying if I don't go home and play the good, heartbroken ex...well, I don't know what he'll do, but I don't trust him, not one bit.

It takes her all of five seconds to respond. I know she's usually glued to that phone, but this is a record even for her.

Say no more.

I exhale slowly, shoving my phone back into my bag.

Michele steps closer. "Are you okay?" he asks in a gentle voice.

I won't lie to him. I shake my head. "No. But I will be." I force a smile, even though anger still simmers beneath my skin.

I don't know if he understood what the phone call was about, but he seems worried nonetheless. That expression grounds me a bit, letting me regain a bit of composure after having the rug pulled from under my feet by Preston. It's strange how Michele can shift my entire existence just by asking how I feel. I'm so used to my answer being irrelevant to the men I've been with that the concern on his face feels huge.

He studies me for a beat. "Do you want to talk about it?"

I shrug and shake my head. Do I want to? Maybe, but I don't even know what to say without feeling like a complete idiot for being with my ex for so long. Now that all the hurt I felt when I discovered his betrayal has disappeared, I can clearly see just how gullible I've been. Preston is not the eccentric artist directing edgy movies I believed he was. He's just an entitled asshole adored by many because he can make or destroy careers in Hollywood.

"Just my ex being a raging asshole and me wondering why I wasted so much time on him." I grimace, wondering what he thinks about me.

Michele smirks. "Well, at least now you've got another reason to tell him to go fuck himself."

Just that. No excuses, no pity, no judgment.

I blink, then let out a startled laugh. "Yeah. No kidding."

He reaches for my hand, his fingers warm and steady against mine. A pleasant shiver races up my spine and dissipates the last of the anger still simmering under my skin.

"Come," he says. "The only cure for rage is gelato."

I arch a brow. "Do Italians solve *every* problem with food?"

He clutches his chest, gaping at me, feigning offense. "Of course not. We also use wine."

This time, the laughter spills out of me freely, warm and unburdened. Michele helped me discover a way of living that's nothing like what I was used to. I can't change what Preston did, and I can't change what people think about me, but I *can* trust the people who are important to me. And that is what matters most. Who cares if someone who doesn't know me thinks I'm an idiot for not understanding that Preston was cheating? Who cares if they think our relationship was fake? Greta believes me, and Tabia too. Michele shows only support for me, so why should I feel obligated to explain myself to strangers? Fuck them and what they think.

And just like that day in Milan, when I first said yes to this trip, I let Michele pull me forward, because somehow, I know he's leading me toward happiness.

13

MICHELE

Rome hums around us, chaotic, alive, and utterly magnetic. It's impossible not to get caught up in its energy, but beside me, Lena is quieter than usual. Her shoulders are a little stiffer, and her smile is not as quick. That phone call with Preston did a number on her, and I hate that he still has the power to do that. He's a prick. Not even man enough to have a real conversation. How do you not even apologize to the woman you've been with for the past four years? I didn't even consider ghosting when I was twenty, but at forty, his age, it just shows how emotionally immature he is.

I know Lena is trying to get over that phone call, and most of the time she seems to forget it, but I think sometimes she's worried about the repercussions of this situation. She told her publicist to speak up for the first time since the scandal, and things are heating up again on the other side of the ocean. She didn't hold back, explaining how Preston betrayed her and how she needed to take a break to grieve her four-year relationship.

Most people are on her side. Social media is trending on the side of support for her, but like every time something like this goes down, someone is pointing fingers, saying she's not so innocent if she's already moved on to someone else. Me. I'd bet my balls Preston's entourage is spinning this shit to save his image.

Prick.

I glance at her as we weave through the bustling streets, the afternoon sun spilling golden light over the ancient buildings. I've spent years under stadium lights, in the adrenaline-fueled rush of the game, but right now, nothing feels more important than seeing her smile again.

"You know," I say, nudging her arm playfully, "if you keep frowning like that, you're going to get wrinkles."

She rolls her eyes, but a smirk tugs at her lips. "Charming. Really, Michele, you sure know how to make a girl feel better."

The sound of my name rolling off her lips sends a shiver of pleasure down my spine. That accent will be the death of me. And she is smiling, something I'm proud of, considering I'm the reason she's getting out of her head.

"Just looking out for you," I say with mock seriousness. "Aging is a real concern, you know. Any day now, we'll be trading our nights out for early bird specials and complaining about back pain."

She lets out a laugh, small but genuine, and something eases inside me. That's better.

It's always been easy for me to make people laugh. I was always the class clown and someone who, in spite of having a career at sixteen, took his life lightly. I would have been squashed by the pressure otherwise. But with her, it's more than gaining a shallow laugh. I want her to be happy, really happy. And the thought unsettles me.

I want to keep that light in her eyes, so I grab her hand and pull her along without warning. It's becoming easier and easier to hold her hand in public. At first, I was unsure about what she thought, but then she let me do it, and sometimes she's the one reaching out for me. It helps that it's quite normal in Italy to display affection in public, and nobody gives us a second look if we hold hands. God, unless we're having sex in broad daylight, they don't even care if we kiss.

"Where are we going?" she asks, her tone suspicious but intrigued.

"You'll see."

We slip through the crowd, past buzzing cafés and tourists snapping photos, until the familiar sound of rushing water fills the air. The Trevi Fountain comes into view, breathtaking as always. The marble glows under the afternoon sun, and the water shimmers, catching every speck of light.

Lena stops beside me, eyes widening. "Okay, I have to admit, that's impressive."

The usual awe in her eyes has been missing since Florence a couple of days ago. I'm glad it's back, even if it lasts only a few fleeting moments. Baby steps, I tell myself. Easier said than done.

I cross my arms and nod, satisfied. "Of course it is. I wouldn't have dragged you here for anything less."

I have to say that it is easy to impress a woman in Rome. Any way you turn, there is some spectacular view or monument to discover.

She tilts her head, studying me. "You're really proud of your country, huh?"

She seems genuinely intrigued by this side of me, and I can't hide the excitement in my voice. I'm Italian, of course I'm proud of my country.

"Damn right, I am," I say. "But I brought you here for a reason. You know the tradition, don't you?"

She gives me a skeptical look. "Throwing money into a fountain and making a wish?" She gestures around to the dozen people doing exactly that.

I gasp in mock horror. "Lena, please. It's not *just* throwing money. You have to do it properly. Right hand over the left shoulder. Otherwise, it doesn't count."

Her lips twitch, fighting another smile. "Oh, well, I

wouldn't want to anger the wish gods," she jokes, and I finally start to see the old Lena, the one who laughs, smiles, and is happy.

"Exactly. Now, come on." I fish a coin out of my pocket and hand it to her before grabbing one for myself.

She holds it between her fingers, thoughtful. "So… what do I even wish for?"

She seems really concerned about messing this thing up, and I can't hide a small smile.

"They say that if you throw one, you will be back in Rome. If you throw two, you will find love, and three, you will marry in Rome," I explain.

She seems to think about it for a long moment, staring at the fountain like it can give her some answers. I find myself curious about what she'll choose. Considering she's just had her heart broken, maybe it wasn't the best idea to come here, but she doesn't seem too upset.

"I'm not ready for three, but coming back here would be fantastic, and two…" She lets out a sigh and looks at me with questioning eyes. "What should I choose? One or two?"

I don't have an answer for that because I don't have one for myself either. I always thought that finding love was more or less an obligation. If you're thirty and never married, a lot of people start wondering what's wrong with you. But now, beside this beautiful woman, I wonder if I've been missing something. I grab other coins from my pocket and open my hand in front of her.

"That's for you to figure out. But make it a good one. Once you throw it, there's no taking it back."

She grabs another coin from my hand, closes her eyes, and for a second, I just watch her. The way her brows furrow in concentration, the way her lips part slightly as if she's whispering her wish in her mind. There's something about Lena that makes it impossible to look away.

I force myself to turn toward the fountain, gripping my own coin. What do I wish for? One or two coins? I've never forced a relationship. I never needed to be in one to be satisfied, but love is entirely another story. I've never been in love with a woman. I cared about my exes, sure, but never to the point of thinking of spending the rest of my life with them. Maybe it's time to toss the two coins and make a wish while I'm here. You don't toss it for that reason, but you never know.

For the past year, my life has been a mess. The injury. The uncertainty. The constant question of what comes next. I take a slow breath and toss the two coins. *Let everything resolve. Let me finally find a solution for my life and my future...and maybe also love.*

I look back at Lena just as she flicks her coins into the fountain. She opens her eyes, catching me watching her, and for a second, we just stand there, the sounds of the crowd around us fading into the background.

I want to kiss her.

The realization hits me with the force of a freight train. It's not just because she's beautiful or because she's standing here in front of one of the most romantic places in the world. It's everything. The way she teases me like we've known each other forever. The way she doesn't take my crap. The way she can be sharp one moment and soft the next.

I shove my hands into my pockets, forcing myself to focus. *Walk, Michele, before you do something stupid.*

We start walking again, making our way toward *Piazza di Spagna*, the Spanish Steps rising before us in all their historic glory. Lena sighs, pleased, and I swear I can feel the tension from that phone call slowly fading from her.

After a few minutes of comfortable silence, she tilts her head toward me. "You're quiet. What's on your mind?"

I glance at her, then ahead again. There's no point in lying. It's what I'm thinking more and more these days, and I don't see the point of hiding it from her. We already kissed once; she knows how I feel about that.

"I want to kiss you," I admit with a certainty and a calm that surprises even me.

She stumbles slightly mid-step and whips her head toward me. "Excuse me?"

She seems surprised, like she is not sure she heard it right. While we never talked about that kiss, it doesn't mean that I've forgotten it. It was the most amazing kiss of my life. It's impossible to forget something that turned my chest upside down.

I chuckle. "You asked. I answered."

Her lips part like she's trying to figure out if I'm joking or not. "And you just...say things like that out loud?"

I shrug. "Why not? It's the truth. You should be used to the fact that I don't tiptoe around things."

She studies me for a long moment, maybe trying to figure out if I've gone mad or if I'm just joking, but there is no doubt in what I want to do with her. I have craved that kiss since I tasted her for the first time, and this desire is not going away anytime soon. And I'm almost certain she feels the same way. You can't not notice the tension between us.

She lets out a breath, shaking her head. "And when exactly were you planning to act on this grand revelation?"

My heart jolts. It's not a refusal. She is entertaining the idea as much as I am. Maybe she wasn't ready the first time, but a lot has happened since then.

I smirk. "Now seems like a good time."

She narrows her eyes at me, but there's amusement there too. "In front of all these people?"

I gesture around us. "Why not? The world already thinks we're having some kind of summer fling. If someone takes a picture, it's not exactly a shocking revelation."

She opens her mouth, then closes it again, like she's actually considering my point.

Finally, she sighs, shaking her head with an exasperated smile. "You're ridiculous, you know that?"

"And yet, here you are."

"Yeah," she murmurs, more to herself than to me. Then she exhales slowly and steps closer, tilting her head up. "Fine. But make it worth it, Moretti."

Oh, I intend to.

I reach for her, fingers brushing against her cheek before sliding into her hair. Her breath catches, and my pulse kicks up as I lower my head toward her.

The moment our lips meet, everything else disappears. The city moves around us, voices and footsteps, the distant melody of a street musician playing a violin. It all disappears in the background.

It's not some polite, testing kiss. There's no hesitation, no question about what we're doing. It's heat and urgency and something deeper that I can't quite put a name to.

Her hands grip the front of my shirt, pulling me

closer, and I'm drowning in her. The warmth of her, the way she tastes like the lingering sweetness of gelato, the way she sighs against my mouth like she's been waiting for this just as much as I have. Everything is pulling at my chest, tightening it in a vise that almost hurts.

My tongue moves with hers in a languid dance that heats me up from the inside. I want her. No, I need her. I need the way she makes me feel alive again, how she lights a spark in my chest and blows until it's a fire burning with passion and desire. It's been months since I felt this excited to live my life, and I'm starting to think that I was dying inside without realizing it.

She takes away the numbness the accident filled me with, and it's exciting and terrifying all at once. I don't know if my heart is ready for this, but I'm eager to try. In this moment, there's only her and the life she instills into my battered chest.

When we finally pull apart, she stays close, her forehead resting against mine.

"Well," she breathes, her voice slightly unsteady, "that was…thorough."

I chuckle, pressing a lingering kiss to the corner of her mouth. "I aim to please."

She laughs, and that sound, that light, carefree sound, is better than any wish I could've made at the fountain.

And for the first time in a long time, I don't care what happens next. I just know I want more.

14

―――――

LENA

I wake up slowly, wrapped in the hazy warmth of sleep, my body still buzzing with the memory of yesterday. The sensation is faint, like an echo reverberating through my skin, but it's there, the lingering imprint of *him*.

Michele Moretti. The soccer player. But for me, just Michele, the man who makes me forget everything else in my life.

My fingers brush my lips, and I close my eyes, exhaling softly. That kiss. It wasn't just a kiss. It was a shift, a crack in the carefully laid foundation I'd built around myself. I've been kissed before by men who knew they were handsome, who knew their touch could make me weak. Men who thrived on the chase, the power of the hunt, who saw seduction as a sport, and me as the trophy.

Michele is different. There was no selfish possessiveness in his kiss, no attempt to claim me as his prize. He seemed to claim me because he didn't want to let me go. He didn't push for more, didn't treat it as an invitation for something beyond that moment. And when we pulled apart, when my breath was still uneven and my heart pounded against my ribs, he just smiled. Easy, unbothered, like we hadn't just shattered a delicate boundary between us.

And then…we moved on. He didn't make it awkward. He didn't push or pull away. We continued exploring Rome as if nothing had changed, except everything *had*.

I shift under the sheets, stretching my limbs. The room is quiet, save for the distant hum of the city waking up. A sliver of sunlight spills through the curtains, painting golden streaks on the tiled floor. Outside, I hear the faint ringing of a bicycle bell, the occasional chatter of passersby, and the unmistakable scent of fresh bread wafting through the air.

I smile to myself, rolling onto my side, watching the light dance along the walls. Rome feels like a dream, like I've stepped into an old movie, playing the role of a woman who gets lost in a city of history and romance. Of kisses and whispered secrets.

A knock at the door pulls me from my thoughts. Frowning, I push the sheets away and pad toward the door, still in my nightgown, a silky, cream-colored thin layer of fabric that barely grazes my thighs. I should probably grab a robe, but curiosity gets the best of me.

I unlock the door and pull it open.

Michele stands there, holding a tray with two cappuccinos in delicate ceramic cups, steam curling from their surfaces. A brown paper bag rests beside them, slightly crinkled, and the scent of something sweet drifts toward me.

He looks at me, his eyes scanning over my face, down to my barely-there nightgown, and back up again. If he has any thoughts about my attire, he doesn't show it. His expression remains as calm and confident as ever, but I can see a glint of lust before he hides it behind his beautiful smile.

"Good morning," he says, his voice still tinged with sleep.

I blink at him, trying to shake off the fact that he's standing here, looking so effortlessly put together in a crisp white T-shirt and navy shorts, his dark hair slightly tousled. He looks like he belongs in an ad for *How to Be the Perfect Italian Man*. Damn, he is sexy as sin.

"Good morning," I murmur, stepping back to let him in. "You bring breakfast to all the women you kiss, or am I special?"

His lips curve into a smirk as he strides past me. "Depends. Do all the women I kiss look this good first thing in the morning?"

My stomach tightens, appreciating the compliment, but I roll my eyes, pretending he doesn't affect me so much, and shut the door behind him. "Flattery will get you nowhere, Moretti."

He sets the tray down on a small table by the open terrace doors. "That's a lie, and we both know it."

I shake my head, but I can't help the smile tugging at my lips. He is right, and if he keeps up his charming persona, I can't guarantee how I will react. Or do.

The morning air is cool as I step onto the terrace, the view stealing my breath for the hundredth time since we arrived. Rome stretches before me, rich in history and tales to discover. Terracotta rooftops bathe in golden sunlight, church domes pierce the sky, and streets are lined with flower-filled balconies. It feels surreal, like I've wandered into a Fellini film, where the city itself is a character whispering secrets to those who pause long enough to listen.

Michele follows, setting the cappuccinos and the bag on the small wrought-iron table. He pulls out a chair, gesturing for me to sit. I've lost count of how many times he's done this for me.

I arch a brow. "Are you always this much of a gentleman?" I like to tease him for his gestures that feel like another era, mostly because I'm not used to it, and I don't know how to react to them.

"Only when I'm trying to impress a woman in a nightgown," he says, winking.

And here we go—he's so candid in expressing what he thinks that sometimes he shocks me.

I laugh, sinking into the chair. "Well, points for honesty."

He sits across from me and pulls out two pastries from the bag. They are golden, pillowy soft, split open, and filled with thick, glossy cream.

I raise a brow. "That looks dangerously good. What is it?" My mouth starts to water just from the smell of it.

"*Maritozzi*," he says, handing me one. "A Roman classic. Sweet bun and whipped cream. Basically perfection."

I take a bite, and my eyes nearly roll back in my head. "Oh my God." I moan like an orgasm just hit me. And from how my body is tingling for this delicacy, I might have just come and don't realize it.

He chuckles. "I'll take that as a good sign."

"It's a *very* good sign," I say around another bite. "This is…unreal." How is it possible someone came up with something so good?

"See? You're getting the full Italian experience."

I sip my cappuccino, letting the creamy foam linger on my lips before licking it away. Michele watches me, something unreadable flashes in his gaze, like there is some worry in his chest that he is deciding to share with me, but he is not sure. I study him from behind the rim of my cup.

He leans back in his chair, crossing his arms. "You said last night that we were lucky we walk a lot. What did you mean?"

He goes straight for what is bothering him, I can see it in his tight muscles and frowning brows. I appreciate this side of him.

I wave a hand. "Just that if we keep eating like this, I'll need to live on a treadmill when I get back to LA."

I realize it's the wrong thing to say when his face darkens, leaving me puzzled.

His expression shifts slightly, his brows drawing even more together. "You worry about that?"

I shake my head. "No, not really. I mean, yeah, Hollywood has its expectations, and I do need to stay in shape, but I don't obsess over it. I love staying active. I feel better when I exercise. But I also love food, and I'd rather enjoy what I eat than spend my life counting calories."

He let out a sigh of relief that surprises me. Was he worried about my approach to food? I know most people think Hollywood has the highest rates of eating disorders, but I'm not part of that statistic. I value my health.

He studies me for a moment, then nods, seemingly satisfied with my answer. "That's good."

I tilt my head. "Why do you look so concerned?"

"Because too many people, especially women in your industry, don't see it that way," he says simply.

Is he worried about me? The realization hits hard in my chest. It's a kind of confirmation of the feeling I have that our relationship is far more complicated than we want to admit.

I purse my lips, nodding. "Yeah. It's a weird world. Sometimes, it's exactly like people imagine: glamorous parties, designer clothes, eccentric rich people with ridiculous habits. And sometimes, it's just…work. Waking up at four a.m., sitting in a makeup chair for hours, shooting until midnight, then going home and collapsing into bed like any other exhausted person. And this applies to food too. I see way too many actors and actresses, killing themself in the gym for a part, eating ridiculously tiny portions, but others just live a healthy life. We're lucky enough that we have access to the best food and the best trainers to help us with that."

He seems to think about it for a long moment before smiling and nodding.

"You don't sound like you mind working your ass off for it." He takes a sip from his cappuccino, studying me.

I smile, shaking my head. "I don't. I love what I do.

I'm lucky. I get to live my dream, and I don't take that for granted."

Michele nods slowly. "I get that."

I look at him, suddenly curious. "What about you? What's life like for you outside of…well, everything that happened?"

He exhales, looking out at the city for a moment before answering. "It used to be fast. Always moving, always training, always preparing for the next game. Now…it's different. Slower. And I thought I'd hate it, but…" He looks at me, his gaze soft. "I don't."

A warmth spreads through my chest. There's something incredibly *real* about this conversation, about sitting here with him, drinking cappuccino and talking about life like we aren't two people who just had a kiss that could've set the world on fire. We are taking our time getting to know each other, and the feeling is so surreal it feels like I'm dreaming it.

The slow life. Michele is giving me that. Letting me exist in it, without expectations, without pressure. And I don't know what that means yet, but I do know I don't want it to end.

I know what he means, that he doesn't hate it, because since coming here, I've discovered part of myself that I didn't know existed in the frenetic chaos of my life. Things that you have to slow down to savor, such as taking your time to go to the grocery store and think about what you want to eat based on what you find, rather than rushing through the shelves and grabbing the first thing you see.

It sounds stupid and insignificant until you find yourself anticipating a meal because you notice the ingredient you didn't even know you were craving. I've learned to listen to my body more, and this is reflecting on my mental health too.

I reach for another bite of my *maritozzo*, flashing him a grin. "So, Moretti…what's the plan for today? More sightseeing? More attempts to seduce me with food?"

He smirks. "You say that like it's a bad thing." His usual playfulness hits me full force.

I laugh, and just like that, the morning feels even lighter. This moment, this slow, easy peace, it's something I never knew I needed. And something I might not be ready to let go of.

THE AIR SMELLS LIKE SUMMER, WITH ITS WARM EARTH, sun-drenched leaves, and the faintest hint of blooming flowers drifting through the breeze. Villa Borghese stretches before us like an oasis of green in the middle of Rome, with wide gravel paths winding through towering cypress trees and ancient statues peeking out between the hedges. There's a quiet hum of life here, birds chirping in the branches, the distant laughter of children, the occasional swish of a bicycle rolling past.

I take a deep breath, letting the tranquility settle in my bones. Rome is full of breathtaking places, but this feels like a hidden pocket of magic.

Michele walks beside me, hands tucked into the pockets of his navy shorts, his steps lazy and unhurried. The morning light catches in his dark hair, giving it a golden sheen, and I find myself glancing at him more often than necessary. He looks…relaxed. Like he belongs here, like this version of him, carefree and unburdened, is who he was always meant to be.

"How is it that you're Italian, and yet I'm the one who suggested Villa Borghese?" I tease, bumping my shoulder lightly against his.

Michele smirks, tilting his head toward me. "Because I don't usually play tourist in my own country. But I have to admit, it's not a bad suggestion."

I feign shock. "Is that a compliment?" My stomach flips in response.

"Don't let it get to your head," he quips. "It's already big enough."

I gasp in mock offense, placing a hand over my chest. "Rude."

He chuckles, the sound warm and deep, and I can't help but smile. I want to record that laugh and bring it with me. I would listen to it every time I'm sad.

We continue strolling, the gravel crunching beneath our feet, the sun filtering through the trees in golden patches. I glance around, soaking it all in: the Renaissance fountains, the grand sculptures that seem frozen mid-motion, the endless greenery stretching before us like something out of a painting.

And then, out of nowhere, I feel his fingers brush against mine. It's the lightest touch, almost accidental, but then, without hesitation, without even looking down, he links our fingers together. My breath catches in my throat.

I glance at him, my pulse stuttering, and my breath hitching just slightly. He doesn't seem to notice what he's done. Or maybe he does, and he just doesn't care. His grip is easy, casual, like it's the most natural thing in the world to be holding my hand. It feels so natural that the thought throws me off.

I don't pull away. Instead, I let my fingers settle into his, warm and firm and steady, and something in my chest flutters wildly at the intimacy of it. I will never get used to it, but we're just holding hands, for Pete's sake. It's not like I'm fourteen with my first crush, even if it feels exactly like that.

"Lena."

His voice is teasing, and I blink up at him, realizing I've been staring at our joined hands instead of watching where I'm going. I feel my cheeks heat up, and not because of the sun.

"Sorry," I mutter, forcing my gaze forward.

"You're getting all flustered," he teases, but there is something else in his tone. Something that sounds a lot like an unspoken question.

"I am not." I blush even harder.

"You so are." His smile threatens to split his face in two, it's so wide.

"Shut up," I huff, but my lips twitch, betraying me. I'm totally getting sentimental over holding hands, but I can't admit that, not even to Michele, because it would mean admitting there is something stirring in my chest that I should nip in the bud before we go way too far.

Michele grins but says nothing else, just keeps walking, his fingers still wrapped around mine, like we've done this a hundred times before. It *feels* like we have done it hundreds of times before.

We wander deeper into the park, past clusters of people lounging, past a pair of kids playing with plastic swords. It feels like we've stepped out of reality and into some golden, slow-moving dream where nothing exists but the two of us.

"Did you know Villa Borghese was once a vineyard?" Michele says, glancing at me.

I arch a brow. "Are you about to drop some Moretti-approved historical knowledge on me?"

I love it when he talks nerdy to me.

He smirks. "I might."

"Okay, professor. Hit me with it."

He squeezes my hand lightly, and that simple gesture, playful, easy, and intimate, sends a thrill down my spine.

"This whole park used to belong to the Borghese family," he explains. "They built it in the seventeenth century as a private retreat with fountains, sculptures, and even their own little zoo. Obviously, they also had a vineyard, like most rich people during that era. Eventually, they lost it, and the city took over."

"Huh." I glance around, taking in the grandeur. "Rich people really do love their extravagant backyard projects." I'm glad it's not just a Hollywood thing.

"Oh, absolutely." He grins. "You should see the inside of the Borghese Gallery. Paintings, statues, marble everywhere. It's ridiculous." He's so excited about this that I feel like there's more behind his passion for historical facts.

I hum thoughtfully. "And here you are, impressing me with your knowledge of the place. Are you secretly a history nerd?"

He scoffs. "Please. I just had an Italian education, which means I had this stuff drilled into my head whether I wanted it or not."

I feel he's downplaying it. Nobody knows so many

facts about a topic unless they're deeply interested in it, even if they are forced to study it in school.

"Right." I nod teasingly. "So you're just a reluctant history geek?"

"Exactly." He grins, but I can see in his eyes that he's just messing with me.

"You are not fooling me, Moretti. You like history." I playfully bump my shoulder against his.

"Damn! I chose the smart girl, didn't I?" He raises a questioning eyebrow at me.

I shrug. "I've just learned to read people, and you are definitely a history geek."

He chuckles, but he doesn't deny it. He seems almost shy about it, and it's a reaction that surprises me. I've never seen him embarrassed about anything, and I feel honored that he shared this vulnerable side with me.

I'm so absorbed looking at Michele that I don't realize we've reached the lake, and I stop in my tracks, my breath catching.

The water is still and glassy, reflecting the perfect blue of the sky. Ducks drift lazily across the surface, while weeping willows dip their branches into the ripples. And there, standing like something out of a myth, is the Temple of Aesculapius—a pale, elegant structure with towering columns, its reflection shimmering in the lake like a mirage.

"Wow." I exhale. "This is…"

Michele smirks. "You're running out of words, *Hollywood.*"

I elbow him lightly. "Shut up. I'm having a moment."

He laughs, then tilts his head toward a small wooden dock where a handful of rowboats are tied up. "Come on. Let's take one."

I raise a brow. "You're volunteering to do manual labor?"

"I am very strong, you know." He flexes his pecs under the T-shirt and I have a hard time not drooling over him.

I snort. "Is that so?"

"You've seen my arms," he says, completely deadpan. "You tell me."

I roll my eyes but let him lead me toward the boats. A few minutes later, we're drifting across the lake. The gentle lap of water against wood is the only sound around us. Michele rows effortlessly, his movements steady, powerful, and I try *very hard* not to stare at the way his forearms flex with each stroke.

He catches me looking and smirks.

I scowl. "You're enjoying this too much."

"Enjoying what?"

"Showing off."

He leans forward slightly, his voice dropping just enough to make my pulse stutter. "You think I'm showing off?"

I purse my lips. "I *know* you are."

His grin is pure mischief. "Well, at least I have an audience who appreciates it."

I shake my head, laughing, and lean back against the wooden bench, letting the moment wrap around me like a warm breeze. It's perfect. Stupidly, ridiculously perfect. And way more romantic than I anticipated.

I glance at Michele, at the way the sunlight glows against his tanned skin, the easy way he watches me, like there's nowhere else he'd rather be. And the strangest thing is, I believe it.

It feels like a date.

He hasn't said it. I haven't said it. But it *feels* like one. And I'm excited and terrified all at once.

15

MICHELE

"**Y**ou realize you just screamed louder than you did in that horror movie you starred in, right?"

Lena huffs, gripping the Vespa's handlebars with a death grip like the machine might suddenly come to life and throw her into the sea. "That's because ghosts aren't *real*, but me crashing this thing into a car? *Very* real possibility."

Her voice is high-pitched, and I can feel the tension in every muscle of her body. We are standing still right now. Nothing can happen.

I bite back a laugh. "You're not going to crash into anything," I say in her ear, and she stiffens even more. I don't know if it's because she's scared or because she's nervous, given my body pressed against hers. I hope it's the latter.

She shoots me a glare over her shoulder. "You don't know that."

Nope, she is definitely scared.

"Lena, *tesoro*, it's a Vespa, not a wild stallion." I pat the seat behind her. "Just ease into it. Feel the balance." Easier said than done, considering it's her first time driving something on two wheels, but I trust she can do it.

She exhales dramatically, her shoulders rising and falling. "Okay. I can do this. I'm a strong, independent woman. I…" The Vespa wobbles slightly, and she lets out another high-pitched squeal. "*Michele!*" We are still in the same spot. We haven't moved an inch.

I chuckle and tighten my grip on her waist from where I'm seated behind her. "I'm right here. You're fine."

I want her to at least reach the end of the small space where we stopped. It's not like she's driving this thing around southern Italy. It's literally less than ten meters.

"I am *not* fine," she mutters. "I'm about to become a statistic."

I shake my head, suppressing a grin as she slowly, *very* slowly, twists the throttle. The Vespa inches forward, barely moving, and I swear the tires haven't done a complete turn. I have never seen this side of Lena, and it's cute seeing her out of her comfort zone. She is always so put together and confident that I love seeing some vulnerability in her. She becomes more real and less of a Hollywood star.

Lena glances over at me, triumphant. "See? I got this."

"You're going *negative* miles per hour, Hollywood." I tease her.

"It's called *safety*, Moretti." She side-eyes me, and I grin.

I smirk. "It's called *stopping traffic*." I push her buttons in the way I discover I love.

She scoffs but twists the throttle a little more, and suddenly, the Vespa lurches forward like a caffeinated Italian grandmother late for Mass. I swear I saw my death, journalists all over Positano documenting our sudden departure from this earth. My heart hammers in my chest, and the doubt that we are going to die right here and now creeps into my guts. Maybe she's right, we are becoming a statistic.

I grip her waist tighter. "Whoa, okay!"

Lena shrieks, veering wildly toward a line of parked cars. "Oh my God, oh my God. *Michele, do something!*"

I reach around her, grabbing the handlebars just before we become one with someone's overpriced sports car. With a quick correction, I steer us back toward the road. Jesus. I really underestimated the danger of this idea.

Lena lets out a breathless laugh. "That was *not* my fault."

"Really?" I arch a brow. "Because I think the Ferrari owner behind us would disagree."

She twists around, wide-eyed. "Is it scratched? Oh my God, am I about to owe someone a quarter of a million dollars?" She sounds really concerned.

I laugh. "Relax. We didn't touch it." Luckily, or I would be nursing an injury on my right leg as well.

She groans, slumping against me for a second. "This is impossible. My balance sucks."

The warmth of her body against mine drives my mind down a very sexy and dangerous path. I have a hard time focusing on what is happening, and I can't afford distractions right now.

I nudge her lightly. "It's not impossible. You just need to trust yourself."

She tilts her head back. "Says the guy who can probably drive this thing blindfolded."

Her lips are so close I just need to turn my head a bit more to reach them and kiss the hell out of her.

"Maybe," I say, grinning.

She grumbles something under her breath before sitting up straighter. "Okay, let's try again."

I adjust my hands around her waist, and she revs the

throttle, this time moving forward at a somewhat acceptable pace. Fast enough not to lose balance, at least.

"There you go," I encourage. "Now just keep your shoulders loose, and…"

The Vespa jerks forward again.

Lena yelps. "Nope! Nope*!*"

We swerve dramatically, and I burst out laughing, clutching her tighter as I feel the tires skid a bit on the asphalt.

"Stop laughing!" she cries, but she's laughing, too, her body shaking against mine.

I can't help it. The sight of her, all wide-eyed and panicked, gripping the handlebars like they're her last hope for survival, is hands down the funniest thing I've seen in years.

"You should see your face right now," I tease.

"I hate you," she says, breathless and giggling.

"You *love* me," I correct, still laughing. When the word leaves my lips, my heart clenches and I ignore it.

She turns her head slightly, a mischievous glint in her eyes. "If you're not careful, Moretti, I'll let go and let *you* drive this thing."

I smirk. "Go ahead."

She makes a move like she's actually going to let go, and I react instinctively, tightening my grip and pressing closer.

"Okay, okay, no funny business," I say, grinning against her ear.

She huffs but doesn't pull away, and for a moment, we slowly inch forward through the winding roads of Positano. The salty breeze ruffles through her hair, and the pastel-colored buildings spill down the cliffs like something out of a painting.

The laughter fades, but the warmth doesn't. I don't know when it happened. Somewhere between teasing her in Rome, holding her hand in Villa Borghese, and this—holding her steady on a Vespa while she laughs like the world isn't watching—I've started feeling something I *shouldn't* feel. Something that digs under my skin, warm and insistent, curling around my ribs.

I like this. Not just the teasing or the chemistry.

Her.

I like *her*.

And that should be a problem. But right now, it isn't. Right now, it's just us on a Vespa, without knowing what the future looks like and not caring a bit about it. I don't feel scared when I'm with her.

She twists the throttle again, trying to keep a steady speed, and I swear we might actually survive this…until she nearly crashes us into a parked Fiat.

"*LENA!*" I shout

"*I GOT IT, I GOT IT!*" she screams

She does *not*, in fact, got it. I react fast, reaching for

her wrists and yanking them left just in time to avoid disaster. The Vespa wobbles, and Lena shrieks, and I finally do what I *should* have done from the start. I slide forward, gripping the handlebars myself and bringing us to a smooth, controlled stop.

Silence.

Lena pants, gripping my thigh so hard it almost hurts.

I lower my forehead on her back and exhale a breathless laugh. "That was close."

She groans, dropping her head against my shoulder. "I almost killed us." Her voice is still shaky.

I rub soothing circles on her arms. "Only a little."

She snorts. "New rule: I don't drive."

"Agreed." I shift slightly, and a sharp ache shoots through my injured leg.

I grit my teeth, ignoring it. It's fine. I've gone more than a month without physical therapy, and yeah, I feel it, but I refuse to let it ruin this moment. It doesn't help that all the weight of the Vespa is on my left leg.

Lena lifts her head. "You okay?"

I force a smirk. "I'm more worried about your ego than my life expectancy right now."

She smacks my arm lightly. "Ass."

I chuckle, then swing my leg over and take my rightful place in the driver's seat. Lena instantly relaxes, and the smile appears less forced on her lips.

"Hold on tight, Hollywood," I say.

She doesn't hesitate. Her arms wrap around me, her hands splaying across my stomach, and it's enough for everything to shift. I feel her heartbeat against my back. The way she fits against me, like she's *meant* to be there. I swallow hard, then rev the engine.

"Ready?"

She exhales, laughing softly. "Not even a little."

I grin. "Too bad."

And with that, we take off, winding through the sunlit cliffs of Positano, her laughter mixing with the breeze. And for the first time in a long, long time, I don't think about the past. I don't think about what's coming next.

I just think about *her*.

THE ENGINE HUMS BENEATH US AS THE BOAT CUTS through the impossibly blue waters of the Amalfi Coast. The sun is high, its golden reflection shimmering over the gentle waves, and the scent of salt and citrus lingers in the air. Lena leans against the railing, her hair whipping in the wind, looking every bit like the Hollywood star she is. She is untamed, radiant, and completely captivating.

"You're staring," she says without turning around, with a knowing smirk tugging at her lips.

I don't even bother denying it. "I am."

She tilts her head, glancing at me over her shoulder. She studies me for a long moment, biting her lower lip like she always does when she is thinking about something, and that drives me crazy.

"Something on my face?"

I slowly scoop closer, resting an arm beside her on the railing. "Just the sun," I murmur. "And maybe a beautiful smile."

She huffs out a laugh. "Smooth, Moretti."

"Always."

The captain, Matteo, clears his throat behind us, clearly amused. "We're almost at *Li Galli*. You two planning on staying dry, or are you actually getting in the water?"

Lena turns fully to face me, arching a brow. "Depends. Are you scared of the sirens, *professore*?"

I love it when she calls me teacher. She teases me about my passion for historical facts, but I know that she likes it when I go on one of my rants. She is a curious person and she asks a lot of questions.

I smirk. "Scared? *Tesoro*, I grew up on these myths." I gesture toward the rocky islets in the distance, their rugged beauty rising from the sea like something out of a mythology book. "Li Galli. According to legend, this is where the sirens lived, luring sailors to their doom."

She presses a hand to her chest in mock horror. "Doom, you say? And yet, we willingly came here?"

"Reckless of us," I agree.

She grins, stepping closer, her voice teasing. "So tell me, history geek, if you hear them, will you tie yourself to the mast like Odysseus? Or will you give in?"

I pretend to think it over, then lean in slightly, letting my lips hover near her ear. "You're the only siren I'd listen to."

Her breath hitches. I pull back just enough to see the way her lips part, the way her pulse flutters at the base of her throat. The temptation to kiss that skin is way too strong right now. She is the siren that captured me, and honestly, I don't want to be rescued.

Matteo, clearly enjoying himself, claps his hands. "Well, if we're all done flirting, let's get you in the water before the sirens steal your soul."

Lena clears her throat, scooping back. "Right. Swimming. Yes."

I chuckle, peeling off my shirt as she turns toward the water. She sneaks a glance at me, her eyes lingering on my chest before she looks away too quickly, pretending not to notice.

Amused, I watch as she strips down to her swimsuit, black, simple, but somehow more alluring than anything overly elaborate.

She catches me staring this time and smirks. "Something wrong?"

I shake my head. "No, just debating if I should warn the sirens about you."

She laughs, rolling her eyes before stepping onto the edge of the boat. With a graceful leap, she dives into the clear, turquoise water.

She surfaces with a gasp, pushing her hair back. "Oh my God, this feels amazing!"

I follow. The cool water is a sharp contrast to the heat still simmering between us. When I come up, she's already floating on her back, eyes closed, her face turned toward the sun.

I swim toward her, the water lapping against my skin, until I'm close enough to touch, but I don't.

"This is perfect," she sighs.

I watch her, the way the sunlight kisses her skin, the way the gentle waves carry her. "Yeah," I murmur. "It is." She is perfect in every way, from her physical appearance to her smart brain, her kindness, and her sense of humor. I could watch her for the rest of my life.

She catches me staring, and her lips tilt up in a knowing smile. "Is that a confession, Moretti?"

"Maybe." I shrug. I can't deny my attraction to her, and I'm pretty sure she already knows I like her.

She treads water again, tilting her head. "You never

answered my question. If you hear the sirens, what would you do?"

I smirk. "I already told you. You're the only siren I'd listen to."

She watches me for a long moment, and I can see the shift in her eyes, the teasing edge softening, and something warmer settling in. Something dangerous. Because if I let myself sink into her soul, I won't resurface.

She reaches out suddenly, skimming the water between us with her fingers, sending ripples that touch my skin. It's barely anything, just a graze, but it feels like more. Like an invitation. And I want to take it. I want her hands tracing a scorching path down my skin.

I swim closer, the distance shrinking until there's nothing but the sea and the sound of our breath. She's looking at my mouth now. I should pull away. I should say something light, make a joke, steer us back into safer waters, but I don't.

Instead, I lift my hand, brushing a stray drop of water from her cheek with my thumb. Her skin is warm, soft, and when she exhales, her breath fans against my lips. My body tightens in response, ready to reach out and drag her into the right place, between my arms.

I can't tell if I move first or if she does, but suddenly, the space between us is nearly gone. Nearly is the key word here.

Because Matteo chooses *that* exact moment to yell

from the boat, "You two planning on breathing anytime soon, or should I start CPR drills?"

The asshole has every intention of ruining this moment; if he wasn't a friend, I would have flipped him off. He's getting revenge for the time I ruined his chance with my sister, telling her he just dumped his girlfriend. He's a friend, but I know how he jumps from one woman to another without a second thought, and I'm the kind of asshole brother that doesn't want *that* kind of guy for his sister. Perhaps not my best move, but I don't regret doing it.

Lena jerks back with a laugh, cheeks flushed. "We're fine!" she calls, glancing at me with sparkling eyes and a bit of lust lingering in her gaze.

I exhale, dragging a hand through my hair, chuckling. "He's got great timing." That asshole was watching and waiting for this exact moment.

She grins. "Yeah. Fantastic."

Almost as if he knew *exactly* what he was doing.

We swim for another moment, letting the tension settle before she nudges me playfully. "Race you back to the boat?"

I smirk. "You sure you want to lose that badly?"

She gasps, mock-offended. "Oh, it's *on*, Moretti."

And with effortless ease, the moment shifts again, back to laughter, teasing, back to whatever *this* is between us.

Lena flops onto the cushioned bench at the back of the boat. Her hair is still damp from the swim, and her skin is glowing under the midday sun. I sit across from her, leaning against the side of the boat, stretching my legs out. Matteo has already set up a small spread for us: platters of fresh fruit, caprese sandwiches, and a bowl of lemony seafood salad. A bottle of chilled white wine sweats beside it, the condensation rolling down the glass.

"You didn't tell me this was a luxury cruise," Lena teases, reaching for a strawberry. She bites into it and her lips stain red. I watch as she licks them, my body lighting up in response.

I shrug, watching her too closely. "What can I say? I have connections."

She smirks, chewing thoughtfully. "And by connections, you mean Matteo?"

"Exactly." I grin.

Matteo chuckles from his spot near the helm, where he's pretending not to eavesdrop. "Don't worry, *bella*. Moretti only calls me when he wants to impress a woman."

I throw a friendly shut-up glance at him.

Lena raises a brow, turning to me. "Oh? Should I be flattered or suspicious?"

Her teasing tone hides a bit of curiosity. I wonder if she wants to know how many women I've brought here.

I pick up my wine glass, holding her gaze as I take a slow sip. "A little of both."

She raises an eyebrow, taking in my comment. She doesn't prod further, and I crave being alone with her to see where this teasing will go.

She laughs, shaking her head as she reaches for a sandwich. "God, I'm starving. Swimming is exhausting."

I grab one, too, taking a bite. The bread is still warm, the mozzarella soft, the basil fresh. This tastes like home, like summer, like something simple and perfect.

Lena sighs in satisfaction, closing her eyes. "Why does everything taste better in Italy?"

"Because it actually does."

She hums in agreement, swinging one leg over the other, and her foot brushes against my shin. It's nothing, an accident, but I feel it anyway. Like every small touch from her that sinks into my skin, leaving something behind. The image of her sprawled over that bench, completely naked, while I savor every inch of her skin, makes a surprising appearance in my head. If I keep going down this path, I'll need to swim to the hotel to soothe the ache in my groin.

"So," I say, resting my elbow on the back of the bench, "what's the plan when summer ends?" Something I've been dreading asking for days now, but can't ignore anymore.

I don't expect her face to fall, just for a second, like

she hadn't considered it. She places her sandwich back on the plate, wiping her fingers on a napkin. "I guess I'll go back."

"To Los Angeles?"

"Yeah." She pauses, twisting a ring around her finger. "I mean, that's where my life is. My home, my career…"

I watch her carefully. "But?"

She exhales, glancing out at the open sea, as if the horizon holds the answer. "I don't know. I haven't really made plans. No auditions lined up yet. No projects in the works."

I lean forward, resting my forearms on my knees. "Is that normal? The waiting?"

She nods. "Oh, yeah. There's always waiting. Always uncertainty." She twists her lips in a wry smile. "Some actors fill the gaps with small projects, commercials, voiceovers… Some just hold their breath and hope something comes along."

"And you?"

She hesitates, then shrugs. "I guess I'm somewhere in between. It's weird. I should be panicking by now. You know, like Hollywood forgot about me while I'm here enjoying my life. But for some reason, I'm not."

I watch the way her fingers trace the condensation on her wine glass. "Because of this summer?"

She nods, looking almost guilty. "Yeah. It's like… everything outside of here doesn't feel real. I haven't had to think about press, auditions, industry bullshit… I've just been *living*." She gestures to the boat, the water, and the coastline beyond us. "And now that I'm thinking about it, I don't want it to end."

Her confession surprises me, and something heavy settles in my chest. I shouldn't let that happen. I shouldn't be thinking about what it would be like if she didn't leave. That's insane. We've known each other for barely two months.

But the idea of her getting on a plane and going back to Los Angeles, back to a world where I don't fit, where I'd be nothing more than a summer fling she remembers fondly, makes my stomach twist. And the worst part is that I have no right to feel this way.

I clear my throat, pushing the thought away. "Then don't go."

Her head snaps up. "What?"

I force a smirk. "Stay in Italy. Start a new career. Maybe Matteo needs a deckhand."

Matteo barks out a laugh. "She'd bring in more business than you ever did, Moretti."

Lena snickers. "Oh, I'd *love* to see that. Me, working on a boat, pretending I know anything about tying knots or…what do you even call the parts of a boat?"

I grin. "The bow, the stern…"

She waves a hand. "Yeah, yeah, all that. The point is, I'd be terrible at it."

"But you'd be terrible in Positano, which is better than being miserable in Los Angeles."

She laughs, shaking her head. "Tempting." She sips her wine with a thoughtful gaze. "But that's not real life."

"Maybe it doesn't have to be." I don't know why I'm pushing this idea, perhaps because I don't want to feel alone in wanting this summer to last forever.

She looks at me then, really looks at me, like she's trying to figure out if I mean it. And the truth is, I don't know. I just know that being here with her is the first time in a long time that I haven't felt like I'm waiting for something to go wrong.

The boat rocks gently, and the waves lap against the hull. The scent of salt, citrus, and sun-warmed skin fills the air between us.

Lena exhales, leaning her head back against the seat. "It's nice to pretend, though. That this could last forever."

I stare at her, at the way the sunlight catches in her hair, turning it gold at the edges. I want to tell her that maybe it doesn't have to be pretend. That maybe what we have, whatever it is, doesn't have to end when summer does.

But I don't. Because that would be stupid.

Instead, I pick up a piece of watermelon and hold it

out to her. "Here. Before you start getting all *too* existential on me."

She grins, biting into it, juice dripping onto her chin. I reach out instinctively, swiping it away with my thumb before I can stop myself. She freezes. I should move my hand. I should pull away, but I don't.

Her breath hitches, her lips part slightly. Something thick and electric settles between us.

And just as quickly, she clears her throat, laughing lightly. "Well. That was very *Titanic* of you."

I smirk, leaning back. "Would you like me to sketch you next?"

She snorts, tossing a grape at me. "Behave, Moretti."

I catch the grape easily, popping it into my mouth. "No promises."

She laughs, shaking her head, shifting the moment back to something easy, something light. But the weight in my chest remains because summer *will* end. And when it does, I don't know if I'll be ready for that.

16

LENA

The sun is a thick golden blanket over Positano, warm and heavy against my skin. I lie back on the rented sunbed. The woven fabric is hot beneath my bare legs, and I close my eyes for a second. The sounds around us are the symphony of summer with the waves lapping against the pebbled shore, kids laughing somewhere behind us, and the faint buzz of a scooter echoing from the cliffside roads above. It's all softened by the sound of Italian voices, smooth and lyrical like a lullaby. I realize that I really love the sound of this language, even if I can't understand a single word. And it's sexy as hell rolling out of Michele's lips.

I tilt my head toward him. He's beside me on the next lounger, one hand behind his head, the other holding a spoon as he lazily scoops out a bite of the cold *delizia al limone* we're sharing. The small glass bowl rests on a plate between us, the creamy dome of sponge cake and lemon cream already halfway devoured. It's cold and tart, with just enough sweetness to make my toes curl in happiness.

"Okay, you were right," I say, scooping a bite for myself. "This is better than any overpriced vegan gelato in LA."

Michele smiles without opening his eyes. "That's because it has actual flavor. And dairy. And joy."

I poke his bare shoulder with my spoon. "Hey! Vegan food can be joyful."

He cracks one eye open. "Can it, though? The cauliflower pizza you described is the epitome of joyful, I believe you." His words drip with amusement.

I stifle a laugh and stretch, my limbs buzzing with residual energy from yesterday's boat trip. The water, the laughter, the near-kiss that still tingles on my lips when I think about it. It's all simmering beneath my skin like a dream I don't want to let go of.

Still, I can't just lie here all day. I've had a morning nap, a dip in the sea, and two desserts. My body is starting to itch for movement, for streets to explore, corners to turn, photos to snap, and treasures to discover.

I push my sunglasses up onto my head and glance over at him. "So…what do you say we go explore a bit?

Just a walk up to the shops? I saw this boutique yesterday with the cutest linen dresses, and I bet there's more…"

Michele doesn't move. "Lena…"

I sit up a little. "What? I'll let you pick the next pastry shop. Deal?"

He sighs, not irritated exactly, but there's a tightness to it. "Why don't we just stay here a bit longer? Relax. That's what people do in Positano."

I blink at him. "I am relaxed. I just want to walk around. See the town."

He finally turns his head toward me, the corners of his mouth quirking like he's trying to hold on to his patience. "You've been bouncing on that lounger for the past fifteen minutes like a kid waiting for recess."

I open my mouth, then close it again, suddenly aware that yeah, I might be doing just that. But still, I don't understand his reluctance.

"You're not on a Hollywood set, Lena," he says, his voice gentler now. "There's no schedule to meet. No director yelling 'cut.' You can just…enjoy this moment."

I plop back onto the sunbed with a dramatic groan. "But there's so much to *see*. I don't want to miss any of it. Who knows when I'll be back here?"

"That's exactly why you should slow down. Take it in. *Breathe*."

I glance sideways at him. His skin has gone golden

under the sun, his curls drying into lazy waves, and there's a quiet, steady rhythm about him I still don't fully understand. It's like he belongs here, carved into this place as if even the waves adjust their rhythm to match his.

But something's off. His words are calm, but there's a stiffness to his body. I watch as he shifts on the lounger. Once, twice. Then again. And that's when I notice it. His injured leg is trembling ever so slightly. I sit up a little straighter. My stomach drops. He's in pain.

How did I not notice earlier? I was too busy going on about linen dresses and lemon tarts and dragging him from one corner of Italy to the next. What an idiot I am. Michele is the one dragging me around to see places and fill my heart with the beauty of this country, but not today. I should have guessed sooner that something was bothering him.

"Are you okay?" I ask carefully, pretending to adjust the umbrella shade.

"I'm fine." The answer is automatic. Way too quick to be sincere.

I glance at him again, and I realize the set of his jaw isn't from my enthusiasm. It's from discomfort. His fingers are pressed against the edge of the lounger, gripping the wood tightly like he needs the anchor.

I shift my tone, light and casual. "We don't *have* to go. I was just saying."

"You should go," he says, not looking at me. "Go explore. I'll be here when you get back."

A tiny flame of guilt sparks in my chest. "Nah." I wave a hand dismissively and plop back on my lounger. "Too hot. I'll just melt on the cobblestones and get run over by a Vespa or something. Besides, I want to see if you're secretly hiding the rest of that lemon cake under your towel."

He glances at me, brow lifted. "You're staying because of the cake?"

"Of course," I say with a straight face. "You think I'd give up my shot at the last bite?"

He snorts, but I see that his shoulders relax. He adjusts the pillow behind his back, loosening up an inch or two.

I don't mention his leg again. I don't tell him that I noticed. I don't want to embarrass him or make him feel like a burden. Even if it does worry me, the worsening of his injury. I'm certain he should be working on it and not traveling with me, not overexerting himself to make me happy.

Instead, I lean back, pick up my sunglasses, and slide them on again. The sun is high now, warm and heavy and rich. The sound of the sea rushes in steadily and comforting. I pull the edge of my towel over my stomach, tucking it in like a blanket.

He doesn't know I'm staying for him. That I'd rather

sit here in the heat and sweat through my swimsuit than leave him alone to grit his teeth against the pain. Though I'm pretty sure he's guessed it. He's too smart to ignore my sudden change of heart.

However, the truth is that I enjoy being near him. I like watching the way his brow furrows when he's lost in thought or how he always seems to know when I need a sip of water before I do. I like that he can tease me about my tourist energy one second and then make sure I have the softest spot on the towel the next.

There's a rhythm between us now. Something unspoken. We gravitate toward each other, anticipating what the other needs without even needing to speak.

And if that means skipping a stroll through linen boutiques, then fine. I'll stay. I'll sit in the sun and eat lemon pastries and let the sea lull us into this strange, perfect stillness.

Besides, it's not like the town's going anywhere. But this moment? I'm not willing to miss the quiet closeness between us.

THE SUN IS JUST BEGINNING TO DIP BEHIND THE HORIZON when we find ourselves climbing a narrow stone path that winds along the edge of Positano. The air smells like sea salt, grilled fish, and blooming jasmine. My hair is still a little damp from the beach, curling from the salty breeze, and every few minutes, Michele reaches out to tuck a strand behind my ear like he can't help himself. Not that I mind, honestly.

He doesn't say where we're going. He just gives me that slow, secretive smile that sends heat curling low in my belly, and I follow him willingly. I would follow that smile down a cliff, if I'm being honest. When we reach a quiet restaurant perched above the sea, I understand. There's only a handful of tables, and none as magical as the one waiting for us in the farthest corner of the terrace.

It's tucked beneath a flowering pergola, candlelight already dancing across the small tablecloth, the view stretching wide and infinite beyond the cliff. The sea below glows with the last amber light of the day, and the sound of waves echoes gently up the rocks.

The owner greets Michele like an old friend. They exchange a few fast words in Italian before he turns to me with a proud smile and says, "For *il campione*, I give the best seat. No one will bother you here."

I glance at Michele, who is smiling almost shyly. I don't know how he referred to him, but I've learned that they call him different variations of *the greatest soccer player* or *the champion*. And behind that cool facade, I can see the embarrassment creeping up to tinge his cheeks slightly.

The table is so small that our knees brush beneath it, and when we sit, we naturally lean closer. There's no space between us, not really. Just heat. And something unspoken that grows more impossible to ignore with every breath.

The candle between us flickers, illuminating his curls, his lashes, his perfect full lips. Those lips, the ones that drive me insane, just remembering our kiss. The golden glow softens him in a way that almost hurts to look at. He's more relaxed now, the tension from earlier at the beach melting away in the warmth of the evening, the wine, the quiet. His leg doesn't tremble here. Or maybe I just don't see it in the dim light. Either way, I don't ask.

We order seafood, fresh pasta, and lemon risotto for me, with a bottle of local white wine. Our conversation starts off light, teasing, and flirtatious. Our hands brush again and again, and neither of us pulls away.

The air between us is charged, like something could spark at any second, completely forgetting the other tables around us. He shifts his leg slightly, and the pressure of his knee presses into mine. He doesn't move it. I don't either.

"This view is ridiculous," I murmur, looking at his profile while he gazes into the horizon.

"You're not even looking at it," he says, turning around and meeting my eyes.

His deep chocolate eyes lock on mine, and it's impossible to look away.

My heart skips. "Caught."

"You are," he says softly with a low and teasing voice. "But I don't mind."

He's flirting without even trying, and I don't know how he does it so effortlessly. Like my presence across this table is something he's waited for, something he's savoring.

"I have a question," he says after a sip of wine, his gaze still locked on mine. "What happens after the summer?"

The words catch me off guard. "You mean when I go back?"

He nods, fingers toying absently with the stem of his glass.

I exhale slowly, looking back at the water. "I don't know. I don't have any auditions lined up yet. LA feels far away right now. I guess I've been pretending it doesn't exist."

There's a pause, heavy and thoughtful. I glance back at him and find his brow creased, like he's trying to solve a puzzle without all the pieces.

"Sometimes," he says slowly, "far away is exactly where it should stay."

I smile at that, but there's something tender inside me cracking open. Something that whispers I don't *want* this to end. The idea of leaving this little pocket of a world we've created with sun-drenched days, boat rides, and shared laughter, makes my chest ache.

He looks at me like he feels the same thing. I don't say it, and neither does he, but it's there. The heavy weight of reality looming over us like a storm cloud on the horizon you can't outrun.

We eat slowly, more for the company than the food. Every moment feels suspended. Sacred. Our conversation changes direction, wandering from favorite books to embarrassing childhood stories. He tells me how he used to sneak out of bed as a kid to watch late-night matches on TV and how he nearly got expelled from school for skipping too many days to attend a youth league tournament.

"And now look at you," I say, "Italy's golden boy."

He snorts softly. "That's what the papers say. I don't know about golden."

"You're humble," I reply, watching him. "It makes it worse."

"Worse?" he raises an eyebrow, amused.

"Harder to resist."

The words leave my mouth before I can stop them. His eyes darken just a fraction, and I see the shift in him, subtle, but unmistakable. His hand finds mine across the table, fingers brushing and lingering against my skin.

Every breath I take feels suddenly shallow, like my lungs forgot how to function.

My confession is merely the culmination of the turmoil within my chest that has begged for release for days. Because this tension between us, even if we don't speak of it, is impossible to ignore.

He leans in, his voice is husky and quiet. "You're not so easy to resist yourself, you know."

I feel it like a ripple down my spine. The air between us crackles. *This is the moment. He's going to kiss me.* And I don't mind it at all because I've been craving his lips on mine since that kiss in Rome, the one that made me forget every other kiss in my life.

"*Scusa?*" A small voice interrupts us.

We both blink. Like we've been pulled underwater and dragged up for air, a return to reality neither of us saw coming or was ready for.

A boy, maybe six or seven, stands at the edge of our table, wide-eyed and clutching a well-worn soccer ball. His cheeks are flushed, and his voice is shaking with excitement. "*Tu sei Michele Moretti, vero?*"

Michele blinks, then nods and smiles gently. "*Sì, sono io.*"

"My dad says you're the best striker Italy's ever had! And that goal you scored at the Euro final..."

The kid's eyes light up like stars. His dad hovers

nearby, clearly trying not to interrupt but watching with a proud, hopeful expression.

Michele stands slowly, just a little stiff, but he masks it well, and crouches beside the boy, taking the ball and signing it with a steady hand. They talk for a few minutes, Michele asking questions and the kid answering shyly. They pose for a picture, Michele ruffling the kid's hair afterward with a wink. "Keep practicing, Luca. I'm sure one day you'll wear the jersey."

"*Davvero*?" the kid's voice cracks with joy.

"Really." Michele nods.

When they finally leave, thanking him profusely, we're left staring at each other across the table, both a little breathless.

For the first time tonight, I remember where we are. That he's *him*. That I'm not just here with the beautiful, infuriating man I've spent the last weeks falling headfirst for, but with a national treasure. A face that lives in stadiums, in headlines, in highlight reels. And suddenly, we are no longer just two people sharing candlelight. Our lives are too complex and too public to pretend to be normal people. We are not, and we should remember that.

Michele runs a hand through his curls, lets out a long breath, and gives me a crooked smile. "Well. That killed the mood."

I smile back, my heart still thudding. "Only a little."

He reaches across the table again, and this time, he doesn't pull his hand away. "They never forget. Kids like that. You should've seen me at his age. All I wanted was someone to believe I could be more."

I squeeze his fingers. "Now *you're* that someone."

He looks at me, quiet for a beat. "Yeah," he says. "But tonight, I just wanted to be *this* someone." He says softly, stroking my hand with his thumb, never leaving my gaze.

And I know exactly what he means.

THE WALK BACK TO THE HOTEL IS QUIET.

It's not awkward, but we don't feel the need to fill the silence with small talk. As if the sea stole our words and carried them out with the tide.

Michele walks beside me, his arm brushing mine now and then, but he doesn't reach for my hand like he did earlier. He's quiet, lost in thought, and the easy touches from dinner are gone, as if the moment with the little boy reminded us both of something we were trying to forget. That outside of this bubble, there's a world that still sees him as *Michele Moretti*, the star. Not just a man who smiles at me across a candlelit table and makes my heart race without even trying.

His limp is subtle, but it's there. I only catch it when

he thinks I'm not looking, when his steps falter for a split second, or when he presses his fingers to his thigh like he's trying to chase away the discomfort. He hasn't done his physical therapy in almost two months; I'm aware of that. I've watched him push through the pain like it's just another opponent he has to beat, but tonight, he's tired.

I slow my pace until we're walking in sync again. I don't say anything. He doesn't either.

When we reach the hotel, I turn to him in the elevator, trying to keep my voice light. "I think I'm calling it a night. I'm kind of beat."

He nods. "Yeah, me too."

But he doesn't press the button right away. We just stand there for a moment, the space between us charged, like something's still hanging in the air from before. His eyes drop to my mouth. Mine linger on the curve of his jaw, the way the light shadows his cheekbones. He smells like sea salt and lemon and the faintest trace of the cologne he wore to dinner. I want to lean into him. I want him to lean into me.

But he doesn't.

Instead, when we reach our hallway and stop in front of our separate rooms, he hesitates. His gaze lingers, soft and unreadable.

"*Buonanotte*, Lena," he murmurs, his voice low and rough around the edges.

Then he leans in and presses a kiss to my cheek,

warm, slow, lingering just long enough to make my breath catch. His stubble brushes my skin. I close my eyes without meaning to.

"Sleep well," he adds, so quietly it could almost be a figment of my imagination.

And then he's gone.

I stand there for a moment, heart thudding in my chest, his warmth still burning against my skin. My cheek pulses where his lips touched it, like it's trying to memorize the shape of his mouth.

Inside my room, I close the door and lean against it for a beat before pushing away and walking toward the bathroom. The tile floor is cool beneath my bare feet, the hotel lights dimmed to a soft glow. I let my dress fall to the floor and step into the shower, turning the water as hot as I can stand it.

The steam fogs the mirror, curls around my body, but it doesn't melt the thoughts spinning through my head.

I should be tired. I *said* I was tired. But now I'm wide awake. All I can see is Michele. The way he smiled at me at dinner. The way his voice dipped low when he leaned in. The gentle way he held that little boy's soccer ball and the way his eyes lingered on mine like I was the only thing in the world he could see.

And then, the limp. The flicker of pain he tries so hard to hide.

I press my palms against the shower wall and lower

my head under the stream of water, trying to make sense of the knot in my chest. I'm not just worried about him. It's more than that.

I *care* about him.

Not as some guy I've been flirting with under the sun, not as the man who makes my stomach twist every time he touches me, but as *him*. The man who makes me laugh until I cry. The one who watches the sea like it's speaking to him. Who teaches me how to drive a Vespa even when he's injured. Who kisses me on the cheek instead of taking what we both clearly want because he's thinking of *me*.

And that terrifies me.

Because I don't know what will happen after this summer. I don't know where I'll go, or what I'll do, or where he'll end up if his leg doesn't heal. I don't want to imagine a world where he can't go back to the soccer field, the place that gave him everything. The place he loves.

But part of me is just as scared of going back to *my* world, where things are shallow and uncertain and exhausting, and leaving behind this strange, golden bubble we've created together.

I lean my forehead against the tile and sigh. When I close my eyes, I see him again.

Michele.

The curve of his mouth, the heat in his eyes, the mess

of curls I want to sink my fingers into. I imagine his hands on me, his mouth finding mine, slow and deliberate. I imagine what would've happened if that kiss hadn't landed on my cheek but lower. Real. Hungry.

My breath stutters.

I can't stop thinking about him. About his deep, chocolate-brown eyes and the light dusting of hair on his chest that I wanted to touch one morning in Tuscany when he walked out of his room in nothing but a towel, scratching his jaw and smiling at me like he didn't even realize how wrecked he made me.

I exhale a soft sound, cheeks flushing hot, and wrap my arms around myself beneath the water. My skin is sensitive, tingling, like it remembers his touch even though he's never really *touched* me like that.

But I want him to.

God, I want him to.

I lower my hand between my thighs, slipping my fingers between the soaking folds of my core. Wet from the arousal I have carried since dinner, and that demands a release. I flicker the bundle of nerves at the apex of my thighs and moan softly. I pinch my nipple with one hand while the other plunges two digits deep inside my hot core. I pump into my opening hard and fast, pressing my palm against my clit and feeling the pleasure building fast inside my lower belly.

I imagine Michele's fingers filling me, curling deep

inside me, while his luscious lips pull my nipple into his mouth and suck. Hard.

The pleasure washes over me like the waves outside this room, lapping against the rocks and making it impossible to resist moaning Michele's name while I come undone under the hot shower, thinking about how he would feel here with me. I breathe hard with my forehead pressed against the cold tile walls, my legs struggling to keep me up.

I step out of the shower and wrap a towel around myself, sitting on the edge of the bed with water still dripping from my hair. The sea breeze floats in through the open window, cooling my overheated skin.

The ache in my chest is more than desire. It's longing. Deep and raw and unexpected.

I've known him for barely two months, but I already know this isn't something I'll be able to walk away from easily.

I lie down, staring at the ceiling, listening to the waves in the distance.

Somewhere down the hall, Michele is in his room. Probably lying in his own bed. Probably not thinking about me the way I'm thinking about him.

Or maybe he is, and somehow, the idea of that is the only thing that finally lets me fall asleep.

17

I don't think I've ever been this quiet in my life. Not on purpose, anyway.

I'm standing at the edge of the *Belvedere*, the wind ruffling my hair, staring at the carved-out honey-colored cliffs in front of me as if I've accidentally stepped into the pages of a fantasy novel. The ancient dwellings rise in layers, stacked one above the other like some magical creature took a chisel to the hillside and carved an entire city from stone. The warm light of the late afternoon paints the rooftops in amber, and the shadows stretch long in the crevices of the old streets.

"I…" My mouth opens and closes. "I don't even know how this is real."

Michele chuckles beside me, amused. "It's real. Very

real. That's Matera. Or more precisely, *I Sassi di Matera.*"

"The Sassi," I repeat, the word soft and strange in my mouth. "Like…the stones?"

"Exactly. They're ancient cave dwellings. People have lived here for thousands of years. They say it's one of the oldest continuously inhabited settlements in the world."

I blink at him, then look back at the view, my brain struggling to connect the dots between something *this* old and the world I come from, where everything gets knocked down and rebuilt every ten years.

"And people actually lived in *those*? In the rocks?"

"Still do, in a way. Many of the Sassi have been restored. Some are houses, others are restaurants or hotels now. However, people did live in those caves, generation after generation. Whole families. With their animals, their tools, everything. Until the 1950s, when the government forced evacuations because of poor sanitation and poverty."

"That's…insane. And beautiful. And kind of heartbreaking," I murmur, squinting at the twisting, narrow alleys between the stone homes. "It looks like it belongs in Narnia. Or…*Game of Thrones*. Did they film here?"

"They did, actually," he says with a crooked smile. "Not *Games of Thrones*, but *The Passion of the Christ.*

Matera has doubled as ancient Jerusalem more than once."

I let out a breathy laugh, still stunned. "I can see why."

I step closer to the railing, bracing my hands against the warm iron. "How does this even exist? Why don't people talk about this more?"

"They do," he says gently. "Just not in LA."

That earns him a side-eye glare. "Touché."

But when I glance at him, he's not laughing. He's watching me.

His expression is soft, almost reverent, like I'm the marvel here and not the ancient stone city unfolding before us. His dark hair curls slightly in the breeze, and there's a hint of sun still lingering on his cheekbones, lighting up the specks of gold in his eyes. He doesn't say anything. He just looks at me like I've given him something. Like my wonder is something sacred.

And that's when I feel the little flip in my chest. The one that doesn't just flutter but settles, warm and deep.

"You're staring, Moretti," I tease, trying to lighten the moment before it gets heavy enough to change everything.

"I like watching you fall in love with Italy," he says simply.

Oh.

I turn quickly, pretending to examine a rock nearby

like it's the most fascinating geological feature in the world, because if I keep looking at him, I might say something dumb. Or honest. Or both.

We start walking down toward the old part of the city, winding through dusty steps and uneven cobblestones. The buildings are built right into the mountain, with stone archway doors and stone window sills. Even the air feels like it's tinged with the memory of centuries. It's like the walls are still holding secrets of past lives.

I keep touching things. The stone walls, the low wooden doors, the plants and flowers growing straight out of the cracks in the walls and roofs. It feels almost forbidden to be here, like I've trespassed into a storybook.

"I swear," I whisper, "this place has put a spell on me."

Michele grins. "It kind of does. The Sassi were abandoned for years. People thought they were a shameful symbol of poverty. But then they started being restored, repurposed. Now they're a UNESCO World Heritage Site."

"So they came back to life."

He glances at me, something unreadable flickering in his eyes. "Yeah. Exactly."

We stop in front of an old stone archway leading to a shaded alley. The temperature drops slightly, the air cool and damp as if the stones themselves breathe. I run my fingers along the wall, feeling the grooves time has etched into it.

"It's insane to think people slept here," I say quietly. "Like…real people, with lives, and stories. They cooked dinner and laughed and cried and grew old inside this rock."

Michele nods. "Sometimes, entire extended families shared one dwelling. There were no proper bathrooms, no ventilation. Kids and animals lived together. But they also had a strong sense of community. They lived close to the land. To each other."

I glance at him. "You know a lot about this."

He shrugs, one shoulder lifting. "I like history. Especially places that have seen everything and survived."

I let that sit for a second.

"Do people *still* live in the Sassi?" I ask after a pause.

"Some, yes. A few locals moved back. But they're mostly tourist spots now. You can even sleep in one."

"Wait! *We* can sleep in one?"

His eyes twinkle. "If you want. I can see if there's a hotel with a room open. Some of them are really beautiful. All restored inside. Still part of the rock, but with modern comforts."

My heart skips a little. Not because of the novelty of staying inside a cave, but because of the way he looks at me while he suggests it, like he would do anything to make me happy.

I nod slowly. "Yeah. I'd like that."

Michele smiles, and it's that smile again, the soft one that makes my chest ache in a way I don't entirely understand. I want to hold onto this moment, bottle it up. The stone city glowing under the fading sun, the smell of old earth and rosemary in the air, and Michele beside me, looking like he belongs to this place in a way I never could, but somehow still makes me feel like I belong too.

We walk on, slowly, our footsteps echoing off the old walls. The silence between us now is the good kind that doesn't need to be filled with shallow chatter.

Maybe some places are meant to be rediscovered.

And maybe some people are too.

BY THE TIME WE STEP INTO THE FOURTH HOTEL CARVED into the cliffs of the Sassi, my feet are beginning to protest. The air is cooler down here in the winding alleys, shaded by the way the old stone buildings stack over one another, but it's still August. Still southern Italy. Still a hundred degrees and climbing.

"I'm starting to think we should've booked ahead," I mutter, wiping the sweat from my neck with the back of my hand as we step inside the arched entrance.

Michele smiles faintly, though there's a sheen of heat on his forehead too. "Where's the fun in that?"

The lobby is small and intimate. More like someone's living room than a hotel reception. Worn terracotta tiles, low-beamed ceilings, and an old wooden desk where a woman with silver-streaked hair greets us with a warm, knowing smile.

"*Buongiorno*," she says cheerfully. "You're lucky, you know. Everyone's booked, but I've just had a cancellation."

Michele's brows lift. "Really?"

She nods. "Our best room. The honeymoon suite. Very romantic." Her eyes twinkle between us. "It's perfect for a couple."

I feel my face flush. A pulse of something I don't have a name for ripples through me.

Michele glances down at me with a small, silent question in his eyes. Do we correct her? Do we keep going? Do we share a bed?

And I don't hesitate.

I give him a grin and nod, maybe a little too enthusiastically. "Sounds perfect."

The woman gives us the key and points us toward a narrow stone stairwell that leads down into the earth, where the cool, damp air kisses my skin the deeper we go. We're quiet as we descend, but my mind isn't. It's racing, with the echo of her words, with the realization of what I just agreed to.

Michele breaks the silence as we near the end of the hallway. "Just to be clear…we're adults, right?"

I glance at him, smirking. "Painfully."

"So sharing a bed doesn't mean anything unless we want it to."

I laugh softly. "Are you trying to reassure me or yourself?"

He gives me a half-smile. "Bit of both."

I stop in front of the room and tilt my head toward him. "We'll be fine. We can keep our hands to ourselves."

But even as I say it, I'm not entirely sure I believe it. The key slips into the old brass lock with a soft click, and we step inside. Then we both go silent.

The room is bathed in warm light from sconces nestled into the rock walls. It's like walking into a dream, or maybe the heart of the earth itself. The bed stands in the center, cast iron, elegant, and just wide enough to make my thoughts wildly inappropriate. The back wall is the real cave, honey-colored and textured, like the surface of the moon or a piece of Swiss cheese, pocked with small holes and deep indentations. It's breathtaking. Ancient and intimate all at once.

There are no doors. Instead, curved walls carve out a sitting area, a bathroom, and a bedroom space, each tucked into the natural shape of the cave. The shower is in the middle of the bathroom, made of glass on three sides, with the fourth built right into the rock. Above it, the vaulted ceiling dips low, giving the whole thing a secret, forbidden feel.

Michele lets out a low whistle behind me. *"Porca vacca."*

I blink slowly, still staring. "Okay…yeah. We're definitely not giggly teenagers, but this room is straight out of a sex dream."

His laugh is quiet and close. Too close. When I turn, he's just a foot away, his hands in his pockets, his body still and tall in the low cave light. His eyes are darker than usual, deeper somehow, and the flicker of a smirk on his lips doesn't hide the heat behind them.

"You sure you're not the one who needs reassurance now?" he says softly.

My breath catches. Because no, I'm not sure of anything in this moment except how aware I am of him. The closeness. The memory of his hand brushing mine on the boat. His thigh pressed against mine at dinner. His scent—sun, and soap, and something inherently *him*—makes the air feel thicker in my lungs.

I swallow. "We'll be fine," I say again. But this time, it comes out breathless.

He lifts a brow, not saying a word, but his eyes drop to my mouth for half a second too long.

I step away, pretending to admire the cave wall, pretending I'm not seconds away from combusting.

"So…should we unpack or just strip down and use that fantastic shower?"

Michele laughs again, but there's an edge that sounds a lot like nervousness. "You first. I'll just be over here… trying to remember that we're keeping our hands to ourselves."

With just those few words, the tension rises again, curling around us like the warm light in the room. It buzzes beneath our itched breaths, coils in the space between our glances, and lingers in every brush of silence.

This place is too beautiful. Too intimate. Too perfect.

And suddenly, I'm not thinking about the heat or the caves or even the day. I'm thinking about *tonight,* and the way this room was made for everything we keep trying not to say.

BY THE TIME I STEP OUT OF THE SHOWER, MY SKIN IS flushed, and not just from the heat. The water didn't help. If anything, it made everything worse. I spent way too long thinking about Michele's hands, the flex of his muscles, the way his voice drops when he teases me, the way he kissed my cheek last night like he wanted more but was holding back.

Now, wrapped in nothing but the hotel's impossibly

soft white robe, I feel the fabric cling to the damp curves of my body. It's a poor excuse for armor against the storm brewing inside me.

I pad barefoot into the bedroom and then stop in my tracks. He's on the bed. Sprawled across the mattress like he owns the whole damn thing. His legs hang off the edge, his arms are stretched above his head, and he's wearing only a pair of black boxers. The rest of him is glorious. Sun-kissed skin, sculpted abs, that line of muscle that dips beneath his waistband in a perfect V.

He looks like sin in human form. And he's staring at the ceiling like he's trying *really* hard not to look at the bathroom. Or maybe he's trying to talk himself out of something.

But then he *does* look at me

And I see it—all of it—in his eyes. The hunger, the heat, the wild, burning *want*. His gaze drags over me like a touch, dark and slow, and I feel the throb between my legs pulse harder.

I don't think. I don't speak. I just *move*.

"Fuck it," I whisper.

He sits up slightly, like he thinks I might say something else, but I don't. I cross the room in a few long strides, my robe parting just enough to make him swallow hard. His eyes stay locked on mine until I'm climbing onto the bed and straddling his hips.

He opens his mouth—maybe to speak, maybe to stop me—but I kiss him before he can say anything.

And God, the *way* he kisses me back. It's all fire and tension and the crash of something we've been holding back for far too long.

The world disappears. The cave, the bed, the quiet buzz of life beyond the thick stone walls. They all fall away. There's only us. The sound of breath, of skin, of his voice as he groans softly into my mouth when my hands rake through his hair.

He cups my ass firmly with his big, strong hands and drags me toward his hardening shaft. My sensitive clit presses against the fabric, and I moan when a shiver of pleasure runs up my spine.

Michele's mouth is a piece of art. Made for kissing and nipping and devouring mine by God himself. His soft full lips suck on my lower one, and when his tongue slips into mine his long, sensual strokes make me dizzy. He takes his time savoring me, exploring the sensation of this kiss. It's different from the previous ones. It's more deliberate, dirty, and driven by a goal that we're both craving. There is no going back from here.

His long fingers slip from my buttcheeks to my core, stroking the seams with lazy exploring movements. When his digits go deep, tentatively stroking my opening, he breaks our kiss to lean back and look me in the eyes.

"You are soaking wet," he states in surprise.

He is so serious that he knocks the air out of my lungs.

I let out a disbelief-filled giggle. "You're here, your whole glorious body on display, what did you expect? I'd have to be blind not to get turned on by you."

He chuckles, stroking his fingers on my sensitive parts and making me quiver. "I was only trying to cool down, I swear."

I roll my eyes. "Yeah, sure. Keep telling yourself that."

His chuckles fade into a deep groan when he grabs a fistful of my hair and sinks his tongue into my mouth again in a frenzied, ravenous kiss that takes my breath away.

This is the Michele I always imagined behind the gentleman who accompanied me on this journey. Possessive, passionate, and entirely uninhibited. Gone is the respectful touch, his wild side takes over as he tilts my head to the side to deepen the kiss. I have never been kissed like this, like he's trying to mark me so deep I'll never get rid of his imprint.

His hips push hard against my core, making me feel the entire length of his now hard and glorious cock. I whimper when one of his hands wraps around my waist and pushes me down while he raises his hips.

"I need to taste you," he whispers frantically against

my lips while he easily gets rid of my robe, letting it pool on the floor.

"First, I want your boxers out of the way. Now," I order, pushing myself up on my knees, giving him the space to slip his underwear down his muscular thighs and to the floor.

He chuckles. "I like it when you're needy and bossy at the same time."

A groan cuts off his words when I grab his hot, hard shaft in my hand and stroke it, lowering myself on his lap again and grinding my clit against it.

"Fuck," he grits out, putting his hands on the bed behind him and tilting his head back.

A grin escapes my lips as I lower my gaze to his taut body, his abs clenching hard with every stroke of my hand. He is so gloriously perfect, and I can't believe he is mine to cherish and enjoy.

"I need to taste you," he says again, pushing himself up and grabbing my hips.

He lies on the bed and guides me to straddle his face. He thrusts me down until I'm in his mouth, moaning when his tongue traces my seam from ass to clit and my legs tremble in pleasure.

"God, I don't know how much I can resist if you keep doing that." I let out a desperate whimper.

I don't know if I want him to make me come fast or take his time dragging out this blissful sensation forever.

He licks a second time, and I quiver.

"Trust me, this won't be the only time I will make you come tonight. You taste so good I'll be licking this pussy all night long."

He sucks on my clit, and I let out a desperate moan while I fall forward and put my hands on the bed to hold myself up.

"I want to taste you too." I whimper in response while I push up, gaining a disappointed groan from Michele.

He doesn't complain too much when I shift and position myself again over his face, but this time facing his magnificent cock. It's long and hard, and the veins climbing up his length are pulsing, making it twitch. A bead of precum is taunting me, and when I bend to lick its salty taste, Michele lets out a groan that reverberates on my clit and sends waves of pleasure straight to my core. I'm so close to coming, I almost can't breathe.

I circle the head of his cock with my tongue once, twice, three times, until his hips shoot up in need to sink into my mouth. I take him out of his misery and suck him in. Using the right amount of suction to take him deeper, but slowly enough to drive him crazy.

"Fuck. Fuck. Fuck," he murmurs incoherently while I take him deeper and deeper.

A smile curves my lips, proud to have him at my mercy. He breathes hard against my soaked pussy and moans loudly when I let his cock slip from my lips with a loud pop.

"You are not allowed to stop back there," I tease him.

He chuckles. "Sorry. I didn't mean to, but you're sucking my brain out of my cock. If I had to think to breathe, I'd be dead by now."

It's my turn to chuckle, and when he reprises his assault on my wet and engorged clit, I let out a moan while I sink his cock deep into my mouth. I suck and lick and bounce my head up and down while Michele drives a couple of fingers into my dripping pussy and pumps as he sucks my clit.

God bless his mouth. I'm so far up the peak of my pleasure that when he crooks his fingers inside me, hitting that perfect spot, an orgasm shatters me. Wave after wave of immense pleasure that Michele drags out, sucking relentlessly on the bundle of nerves that is becoming more sensitive with every surge of my pleasure.

I let Michele's cock out of my mouth and take deep breaths. I've never come this hard.

"You should sell the imprint of your mouth to a sex toy factory. Women would pay tons of money to have it between their legs," I blurt out in the dizziness of my pleasure.

Michele barks out an amused laugh while he guides

me to lie down on the bed and peppers my inner thigh with kisses.

"I will consider that," he says, lapping up my wetness and making me squirm.

I look at him while he peeks a mischievous glance between my thighs and then prowls on the bed, hovering over my body and taking in every inch of my skin.

I drag my fingers in his hair and moan when he lowers his lips on my nipples, sucking and biting, in turn, each one of my sensitive peaks. He traces his way up to my mouth, licking, kissing, and nipping my skin, and when he parts my lips in a languid kiss full of desire, I taste myself on his tongue and drag him closer.

I need to feel his hot skin against mine, touch his muscles, trace every rise and dip of his body, and commit it to memory. It would be a shame having this glorious body against mine and not try to remember for eternity how it feels. He is so perfect, and this feels so right, that I'm almost frightened at how it seems like fate put him on my path.

"Fuck me, please," I whisper in his ear, and he lowers his gaze to mine with a smile on his lips.

"Well, since you ask so nicely," he says, thrusting lazily, his hips against mine.

His shaft rubs against my sensitive clit, building up a second orgasm I'm sure will shatter me.

He pushes himself up, and I watch him fumble off

the bed and hurry across the room, yanking open his bag like a man on a mission.

"Don't move," he mutters, not even glancing back at me.

I prop myself up on my elbows, breathless and grinning. "Wasn't planning on it."

He curses under his breath and then smiles when he finds the box of condoms, waving it at me with a grin. I can't stop an amused laugh from leaving my lips.

"Do you always pack like a responsible adult?" I tease as he finds what he's looking for.

I watch him rolling the condom down his length, biting my lip in anticipation of what is coming next.

"I'm Italian. We don't take chances with pasta or protection." He chuckles.

He returns to the bed, eyes smoldering, his voice a low growl. "Now, where were we?"

"Right about here," I whisper, pulling him down with me.

He kisses me like his life depends on it. Deep and languid and desperate to possess me. I caress his pecks, appreciating the tickling feeling of his hair under my fingertips. I feel each one of his abs and grip his cock firmly with my hand as I guide it to my waiting opening.

He smiles against my lips. "Are we impatient?" he teases me.

"After two months of looking at this God-blessed goodness, yes, I'm impatient," I remark, and he grins.

"As you wish," he whispers in my ear while pushing deep inside me in one slow stroke.

I open my legs wide to let him settle between them and accommodate his length and girth into my wet pussy. He fills me so good, I sigh when he starts pulling out and pushing in again. He does it slowly, peppering my neck with kisses. I lower my hand, grab his asscheecks, and push my hips against his, grinding my clit against him and matching his movements stroke by stroke.

My orgasm mounts again deep inside my core, and when Michele pushes up on his knees and grabs my ankles, pushing my legs up toward my head, the angle is so deep and good that when he starts thrusting deep and hard, I'm breathless.

"It's good. It's so fucking good," I moan as I study the grin on his face.

His broad chest and abs flex with every thrust, and when he lets go of one of my legs to rub his thumb against my clit, I arch my back and come in a whimpering mess.

"Come for me. Come all over my cock," he growls, a sound so deep I can feel it in my bones.

He pumps fast, deep, and hard into me, and when he comes, he lets out a low guttural sound, throwing his head back and making me breathless.

He is so powerful and masculine and perfect that it's like having one of those ancient perfect statutes fuck you silly, only definitely packing more.

I will never tire of discovering new parts of Michele I didn't know existed. The gentleman, the athlete, and now the rough sex god that turns me into a sweaty, moaning woman.

He lets go of my legs and lowers himself onto me, kissing and nipping my ear.

"If I'm selling my mouth imprint, I want a mold of your tits. They are so perfect, bouncing while I fuck you, I'll spend the rest of my days fondling the mold until there is nothing left." He chuckles, and I do too.

"Noted," I say, kissing his neck and wrapping my arms around him.

We lay tangled in each other, our skin still warm, hearts still racing. And in the quiet of this ancient cave, with the scent of him wrapped around me and his fingers gently tracing circles on my hip, I feel something shift. It's not just lust. Not just desire, but something more profound, persistent, something I'm afraid to name.

Something dangerously close to *falling*.

18

———

MICHELE

I wake up to the softest, warmest sensation in the world.

For a second, I think I'm dreaming. That Lena's touch is part of some perfect flashback of the night we just had, a night that rewrote everything I thought I knew about pleasure, closeness, and sex positions.

Then I blink against the low morning light streaming into the *Sassi* suite, and I realize she's very much real.

And her mouth is on me. On my hard cock.

I look down at her, and the mischievous glint in her eyes tells me she is up to no good. Or very much good, depending on the point of view.

"Good morning," she purrs after licking my shaft, balls to tip.

"This is by far the best wake-up alarm I have ever had," I croak. "Good morning to you too," I moan when she wraps her lips around my hard shaft and sinks it into her throat. I discovered yesterday that she can control her gag reflex and take me in deep all the way. Paradise. Not even in my wildest fantasies did a woman do *that*.

I put my hand on the back of her head and follow her movements up and down while she sucks and teases, and drives me crazy. I make a massive effort not to push up my hips and fuck her mouth hard and fast.

"Fuck. Do you want me dead?" I groan when she sucks hard and, in response, fondles my balls and squeezes a bit, just enough to make my breath catch in pleasure.

I look down at her, staring at me with a teasing smile that curves her lips and reaches her eyes.

"You are a little…" I can't even finish the sentence because she sucks hard, and I get lost in my pleasure.

Goose bumps rise on every inch of my body, and my heart starts thumping hard in my chest, while my breath is nowhere to be seen. My brain is MIA too.

"I don't want to come in your mouth. Come and ride me," I say breathlessly while I move my hand from her head.

By the time she straddles me, I'm wide awake, heart racing, and body sore in the best way possible. We barely slept. We didn't want to. We made love like we were trying to memorize each other's bodies, like we didn't know how long we'd have. Every kiss, every breath, every moan, it's all burned into me. I didn't think I could want her more.

I was wrong.

I reach up, bury my hands in her hair, tilt my head back with a groan while she lowers her soaked pussy on my shaft, but the sharp buzzing of my phone cuts through the moment like a slap.

I curse under my breath and grab it from the nightstand, fully ready to silence it, when I see the name on the screen.

Mom.

"Sorry," I murmur to Lena, brushing my thumb across her thigh. "I have to take this."

I wouldn't normally answer, even if it's my mother, but since the accident, I know she'll panic if I don't pick up soon. It will take some time for things to return to normal. I've already avoided her way too much these last few weeks, communicating with her only through texts.

Lena raises an eyebrow but doesn't stop what she's doing. If anything, she slows down, that little minx.

I swipe to answer. "*Ciao.*" I greet her in Italian, and Lena widens her eyes with curiosity.

I can't do much. I would speak English to include her in the conversation, but my mom doesn't speak a word of English.

"*Amore mio*! Finally! You don't answer your phone for *days,* and now the gossip magazines say you've disappeared with a *mystery woman*."

I close my eyes, trying to focus as Lena kisses along my chest, her breath warm and maddening. I force my voice to stay even, but it's a titanic effort on my part.

"I'm fine. I just needed some time away from everything." I avoid explaining the "mystery woman" part. I don't even know where to start with that.

I'm not usually prone to these rash decisions without at least a heads-up to my family, but I honestly can't explain why I did it without worrying them about my recovery. They will immediately jump to the worst conclusions, and I don't know how to explain something I don't know yet myself.

"Oh, sure. But the press says you're traveling with a woman. Is it true? Do you have a girlfriend?"

I glance up at Lena. She's watching me like she's trying to decipher my words, her brow slightly furrowed, her lips curved in a teasing smirk. And she is still riding me, deep and slowly. I want to reach out and fondle her perfect tits, but I won't be able to continue my conversation with my mom, that's for sure.

"Not a girlfriend," I say slowly. "Just…a woman I'm traveling with. She's…a friend," I say, locking eyes with Lena.

Her smile widens. She doesn't understand the words,

but she understands the tone. I suppose she understands we're talking about her, or maybe she has something else in mind to drive me crazy, and right now, I have too much going on to focus on understanding her intentions.

"A friend? Michele! That's the same tone you used when you first brought home your motorbike. You loved that thing."

I chuckle, barely suppressing a groan as Lena grinds her hips in slow circles. "Well, she's less dangerous." Barely.

"Don't joke! Your leg, how is it, *tesoro*? Are you in pain?"

I close my eyes, trying to focus on my mother's worry through the haze of pleasure clouding my mind. It's hard. I'm almost tempted to call her back later.

"No. *Sto bene*. I'm really okay. I'm resting, I swear. She makes sure of that." I glance pointedly at Lena, who bites her lip like she knows exactly how *not* restful this trip has been, especially after last night.

Damn it! Focus Michele. You can't go there, not with your mother on the phone.

"I hope you bring her home. I don't care what the magazines say, I want to meet the woman who stole my son away for the summer."

"Hmm…"

"If you don't bring her to visit soon, I'll come find you myself. Wherever you are." She cuts me off with her scolding tone, the one that put all of us kids in line when we were young. It will never cease to make my ears perk up even now that I'm an adult.

I laugh out loud. Lena pauses, startled, and I can see her itching to ask.

"She's *not* my girlfriend. And I can't guarantee anything. It's not like I can bring random girls to meet my parents." I try to make her reason, but I'm not sure I will succeed.

"But she's *there*. With *you*. That's already something." Her tone is hopeful. She has been worried for years that I will never have a family and will end up alone and miserable. It's difficult to explain to her that with this kind of job, it's challenging to figure out if someone is after me as a person, my money, or the fame that comes with it.

I sigh softly, warmed by her voice and the familiar affection in it. "*Ti voglio bene.*"

"I love you too, *amore*. Be careful. And tell her I say hello." I can hear the smile in her voice. She has already decided she is my girlfriend. Nothing will change her mind.

I hang up with a smile still tugging at my lips.

Lena tilts her head. "Okay, who was *that* important?"

I grin. "My mom."

She freezes.

"*Your mother?!*" Her eyes go wide. "I was literally riding you while you were talking to your *mom?*"

"She called *three* times yesterday while we were doing other *things*," I say, trying not to laugh. "You left me no choice."

"Oh my God," she groans, burying her face in my chest. "I can't believe I just did that."

"You didn't know," I tease, dragging my fingers along her spine. "And if it makes you feel any better, it was the best phone call of my life."

She lifts her head just enough to glare at me. "You're the worst."

"But you're still on top of me," I murmur, my voice dropping.

"Only so I can *kill you* slowly."

"Death by orgasm?" I arch an eyebrow. "There are worse ways to go."

She laughs in spite of herself, and I love that sound, bright and reckless, like she's forgetting to protect herself from me.

We're still joined. Still moving, even as we laugh. It's the most absurdly intimate moment I've ever had.

She straightens her spine and rests her hands on my pecks. "Are you ready to pay for this?" She winks at me.

"Absolutely!" I grin.

And, as she promised, she rides me slowly to the

brink of pleasure countless times before letting me come with a deep, long groan.

When she lowers herself on my chest, spent and satisfied, I wrap my arms around her, burying my face in her neck, breathing in the scent of her skin.

She's still catching her breath when I say, almost too softly, "My mom wants to meet you."

She jerks her head up to look at me, wide-eyed, almost *terrified,* and I laugh.

I shouldn't have said that, not now, not like this, but I can't help it because suddenly, the idea of bringing her home doesn't scare me. It makes something settle deep in my chest. And maybe I don't want to fight that.

19

LENA

I didn't think olive trees could be romantic, but now, as we cruise down a narrow dirt road flanked by endless, twisted trunks stretching toward the pale blue sky, I'm suddenly convinced they are. The silver-green leaves catch the sunlight just right, glinting like they're part of some long-forgotten fairy tale. And maybe it feels that way because Michele is next to me, one hand on the steering wheel, the other resting casually on the gearshift, his jaw is shadowed with stubble, his sunglasses reflecting the road ahead.

I sneak a glance at him. I've been doing that all morning.

I said yes. I said yes to meeting his family because he promised they think I'm a friend, not a girlfriend. Because he assured me their expectations were already settled. Because he swore they were down-to-earth and warm and kind.

But mostly, I said yes because when he talks about them, his whole face softens. His voice changes. I've seen the way his eyes light up when he mentions his mom's cooking, his father's terrible jokes, or how his sister used to drag him into her dance routines as a kid.

There's so much love there, so much pride, and it reminds me of my own family—loud and affectionate and a little too involved in each other's lives. I get it. I love it. I miss it.

Still, my stomach won't stop flipping.

"You're quiet," Michele says, not taking his eyes off the road. The car dips slightly as we hit a bump, and I grip the door handle tighter than I mean to.

"I'm just…" I inhale slowly. "Thinking."

His mouth quirks. "Thinking looks a lot like panicking."

"I'm not panicking." I pause. "I'm *pre-panicking.* There's a difference."

He lets out a low laugh, like he's been expecting this. "We're twenty minutes from the house. You had all morning to freak out. Why now?"

"Because *now* it's real. There's a literal house at the end of this dusty road, and people in it who raised *you.* It feels like walking into a test I didn't study for."

He glances at me, really looks, then makes a split-second decision. He pulls the car off to the side of the road, tires crunching over dry gravel, and shifts into park. I squeak in surprise.

"Lena."

I blink at him. "Are we…breaking up, or whatever you do in our *situationship*, in an olive grove?"

He smiles and reaches across the center console to take my hand. His grip is warm and steady. "You don't need to be nervous."

"Oh, no? Let me list all the reasons why I *do*." I tick them off on my fingers. "One: I'm not Italian."

He raises an eyebrow. "You speak it better than half my cousins."

"Two: I'm not your girlfriend."

"That's a relief. Less pressure."

"Three: I've seen you naked and making very unholy sounds in a holy cave-town."

That makes him laugh, full-bodied and so loud it bounces around the car like music.

"Okay, I'll give you that one," he says, still grinning. "But let me counter."

I narrow my eyes. "This should be good."

"One: My mom already loves you because she heard the joy in my voice when I talked to her."

I open my mouth, then close it. How do you counter a sentence that makes your heart do a backflip in your chest?

"Two: You make me laugh even when you're stripping me of my last shred of sanity."

"Romantic," I mutter.

"Three: My parents don't want perfection. They want *me* to be happy. And I am." He squeezes my hand. "Because of you."

I stare at him.

It's ridiculous how much those words melt me. How they slip under my skin and curl around my heart like they've always belonged there. We've never said out loud what we are, whether friends or something more, but it's clear that our feelings for each other run deeper than mere acquaintances. I don't sleep with someone just for fun; I was never the one-night-stand kind of woman, and this trip shows it.

We've driven for weeks down the entire length of Italy, being together twenty-four-seven, sharing exhausting hours in the car, and laughing our heads off at the stupidest things. We became friends, and then we took it a step forward. We have had all the time in the world to make that decision, and it's not just about sex. I *know* I feel something deeper, and at this point, I know Michele enough to be sure he feels it too.

"You really think it's gonna go that smoothly?" I ask, trying to keep my voice light.

"I think my mom's gonna try to feed you until you explode, my dad's gonna pretend he doesn't cry but absolutely will when he sees me, and my sister is gonna corner you and ask if I still snore when I sleep. I don't know about my brothers because they're idiots, and just say whatever crosses their mind in the moment."

"Do you snore? I haven't had the chance to *sleep* a lot when you're around." I raise my eyebrow.

"No comment."

I laugh in spite of myself. He leans across the seat, tugs me toward him, and kisses me senseless. His mouth moves over mine with purpose, reassurance, and something deeper I don't want to name yet, but feel all the same.

When we part, I'm breathless, and no longer nervous.

"Let's go, then," I murmur.

He smiles like the sun. "*Bene.*"

He shifts the car back into gear, and we roll forward, deeper into the grove. The house appears in the distance, white stone and flat roof nestled among the trees like a postcard. A breeze lifts dry leaves as we approach.

I watch it get closer—this home he gave his parents with the initial money he earned playing the game he loved—the house he donated with gratitude. And I realize I'm not just about to meet his family.

I'm about to meet the people who made *him.*

As we drive closer to the house, I realize it's not just *a* house. It's massive.

Not in a flashy, Beverly Hills kind of way, but sprawling and warm, with white stone walls that seem to glow under the sun and dark wooden beams that peek out from the arched doors and windows. Olive trees frame it like a painting, and prickly pear cacti cluster along the stone paths that curve between the buildings.

"Michele," I say slowly, staring out the window. "You told me your parents had a house. You didn't mention a *compound*."

He chuckles, eyes on the long gravel drive. "Technically, it's a *masseria*."

"A what?"

"A fortified farmhouse, from the 1700s. We renovated it years ago when I bought it for them. There are a lot of these in Puglia. Most are hotels now."

I blink. "You told me your parents had a house. Not that they live in a historical landmark." I gape at the building coming closer and closer.

"They needed the space," he says with a shrug, like that explains everything. "With all the siblings and grandkids, it gets chaotic, especially on weekends." He is way too nonchalant not to suspect he is hiding something important.

"Today is Wednesday," I state, already hearing the note of suspicion creeping into my voice. I hope he'll say something, but he doesn't speak, raising all the alarms in my head.

He doesn't even look at me. Instead, he pulls the car into a turn that leads toward the courtyard in front of the main house.

And that's when I see the kids.

There must be five or six of them, running around barefoot on the terracotta tiles, shrieking and chasing each other like mini whirlwinds. One of them spots our car and lets out a high-pitched squeal, waving wildly.

"Zio Michele! Zio Michele è arrivato!"

The others echo the call and take off like a stampede toward the house. A moment later, more figures begin pouring out—adults, teens, toddlers. A whole wave of people filters through the arched stone entrance like they've been waiting their whole lives for this exact moment.

I count quickly, then stop because I lose track of the numbers. At least thirty people are now standing in front of the car. Smiling, chatting, waving, clapping, even.

I whip my head toward Michele.

"You *liar!* You said your parents might be home. Maybe some grandparents. *This is a wedding reception.*"

He grimaces but doesn't look even a little bit sorry. "It's Wednesday. My siblings should be at work."

"Then why are there *thirty people* waiting to mob us?"

He shrugs. "They probably heard I was coming and came for lunch."

"Oh my God," I whisper under my breath while my gaze rolls over the people still pouring out of the door.

Before I can say anything else, he kills the engine, and then we are surrounded. The moment the doors open, it's a *full assault.*

I barely have time to plant one foot on the ground before a petite woman with thick curls and sparkling eyes rushes toward Michele and crushes him into a hug, murmuring in rapid-fire Italian. A second later, she pulls back, eyes shining, and throws her arms around me.

I freeze.

She kisses one cheek, then the other, then cups my face in her warm hands and smiles like she's been waiting to meet me since I was born. Before I can even recover, someone else—an older man with wild salt-and-pepper hair—grabs me in a bear hug and lifts me clean off the ground. Another woman presses a kiss to my temple and mutters something in Italian too fast for me to even try to understand. A teenager with braces hugs me like we're old friends. A tiny child clings to my leg like a koala.

I look over at Michele, who's trapped in his own cyclone of greetings, shaking hands, and getting his hair ruffled like he's still twelve.

"Michele," I hiss through my smile as another set of lips lands on my cheek. *"Do something."*

He glances over at me and bursts out laughing.

I scowl at him, but it's hard to keep it up. There's just…*so much love* here. Unfiltered, uninhibited affection. The kind of joy you can't fake. And I get it. I really do. I'm used to family affection. I grew up in a house full of noise and hugs and people who couldn't care less about personal space.

But I'm still American. And this is a whole other level.

I'm being kissed and hugged and introduced to sisters and brothers and kids whose names I'll never remember. I'm being dragged from one pair of arms to another like I'm a prize on parade, my feet barely touching the ground.

And I'm laughing. I'm laughing because it's too much and too loud and *so very Italian,* and when I catch Michele's eyes across the crowd and shoot him a desperate, pleading look, he just grins wider.

I think I might murder him.

Later. After lunch.

If I survive this welcoming committee.

20

MICHELE

The scent of roasted tomatoes, fresh basil, and something sweet I can't quite place fills the air, thick and familiar, as I lean against the worn stone wall just outside the kitchen. The midday sun pours through the open windows, casting long beams of light over the chaos inside.

There, right in the center of it all, is Lena. She's standing at the massive wooden table, sleeves pushed up, listening intently to *Zia* Carmela as she gestures wildly, trying to explain how to slice the mozzarella *just right*. Lena nods thoughtfully, brows furrowed, with a knife in hand, and I watch her bite her bottom lip to hide a smile when she very clearly doesn't understand a single word coming out of my aunt's mouth.

Francesco, my thirteen-year-old nephew, is at her

elbow, translating in a mixture of broken English and exaggerated hand signs, his chest puffed out like he's just been given a military assignment. Annalaura, his younger sister, pipes up now and then with corrections, bossing him around in both languages. I could go and play the knight in shining armor, rescuing her, but she doesn't need to be rescued. She is perfectly capable of handling my crazy family, and somehow, she enjoys it.

Lena laughs, nods, and tries again.

Something soft breaks open inside me. It's only been a few hours since we got here, and already, she's managed to slip into the rhythm of my family like she's always belonged. She's not just smiling through the chaos, she's *living* it, leaning into the noise and warmth the way someone does when they know exactly how precious it is.

I drag a hand through my hair, feeling something shift deep inside me, slow and relentless, like tectonic plates realigning. It's shaking me to my core like an earthquake I can't escape.

One night. We had one night together. One night of reckless, incredible sex that still buzzes in my blood when I let my mind wander. And yet it feels like I've known her forever. Like every chaotic, joyful part of my life has been leading up to this moment, where I stand in my parents' home and watch a woman I barely knew a few months ago fit herself right into the center of it.

"*Sei innamorato, fratellone?*"

The teasing voice makes me turn. Mariasole, my youngest sister, grins up at me, a dish towel slung over her shoulder, flour dusting her jeans. Her dark eyes sparkle with mischief, the same way they did when she used to steal my cleats before a game just to mess with me. I don't miss the hope in her voice when she asks me if I'm in love. She's always had a soft spot for my love life and tried to set me up with every woman she deemed worthy of her big brother.

"*Ciao, Sorellina,*" I say, ruffling her hair even though she's almost thirty now and will probably murder me for it.

She swats me away, laughing, then nods toward Lena. "So. Spill. How did you meet her? And don't you dare say 'it's complicated.'"

I chuckle under my breath, shoving my hands into my pockets. "It's not complicated. We met in Milan. She's a friend."

"Just a friend, huh?" Mariasole arches a brow, unconvinced.

I shrug, even though my heart is still tight from watching Lena laugh with Francesco. "We are friends. We…traveled together." Well, at least that is true. The other part is…well, complicated.

She smirks. "And now you bring her home. To *this.*" She gestures around us, at the noise, the heat, the dozens of relatives already fighting over who gets to sit next to Lena at lunch. "Pretty serious for a friend, no?"

I shake my head, but I'm smiling too. "Don't start planning a wedding, Mariasole."

"Too late. *Mamma* already whispered something about grandchildren."

I groan, tipping my head back against the wall. "*Dio, aiutami.*" And I really need God's help if this is the way it's going to be after just a few hours.

Mariasole laughs and bumps her shoulder into mine. "You're happy. I can see it."

I look at her, really look, and realize she's not teasing anymore. She's just happy for me.

I glance back toward the kitchen where Lena is throwing her hands up in victory after finally mastering the mozzarella technique; Francesco and Annalaura clap, as if she just won a medal.

I don't say anything. I don't have to, because, yeah. I am happy.

And for the first time in a long, long while, I don't feel like something is missing. I don't feel like I'm still running after something I can't quite catch. I think I've already found it. And she's laughing in my mother's kitchen, completely unaware she's making me fall for her a little more every second.

THE SMELL OF GRILLED LAMB, FRESH FOCACCIA, AND simmering tomatoes wraps around me like a blanket as I carry a heavy tray out to the long wooden tables set up under the shade of the olive trees. Plates clatter, glasses clink, and laughter bounces off the stone walls of the masseria.

It's beautiful chaos.

Kids race between the tables, chasing each other with half-eaten pieces of bread. My aunts shout at them to sit down, using that particular tone that sounds more like a song than a scolding. Uncles debate loudly about soccer teams and politics, waving their forks like weapons. Wine is poured into glasses without ever asking if you want more—*of course* you want more.

Lena is right there, wedged between *Zio* Pietro and my cousin Martina, laughing as she tries to navigate the *antipasti* laid out in front of her. Olives, cured meats, roasted vegetables, and little fried balls of bread. She's trying everything, encouraged by enthusiastic nods and hand gestures. Annalaura sits in front of her, diligently translating bits and pieces, but Lena's smile never wavers, even when she's not entirely sure what she's eating.

I lean back in my chair, letting the noise wash over me, feeling full not just from the food, but from being *home.* From seeing the people I love surround the woman who's somehow slipped into my life like she's always been meant to be there.

"*Finalmente sei tornato.*"

I turn to see Antonio, my big brother, slide into the seat next to mine, balancing a plate piled so high it looks like a small hill. His beard is a little grayer than the last time I saw him, but his eyes are the same: sharp, attentive, and too damn perceptive for his own good. Yes, I'm finally back home and I love the feeling.

"It was time," I say simply, reaching for a piece of bread.

He glances toward Lena, who is gamely trying to explain the concept of "peanut butter" to an utterly baffled Zio Pietro. A small smile pulls at the corner of Antonio's mouth.

"She's special," he says quietly, so low only I can hear it under the din of the lunch chatter.

I tear a piece of bread in half, my heart thudding harder than it should. "Yeah."

"You serious about her?"

The question doesn't feel like an interrogation. Antonio's not like that. It's more of a brother checking in. Wanting to understand. He's never made a fuss about my companions, even when it was clear to everyone but me that they were with me more for my fame than me as a person.

I drag a hand over my face, then glance at Lena

again, her golden hair catching the sunlight, her laugh filling the air as naturally as breathing.

"I don't know," I admit. "It's new. Fast."

"But?" Antonio prompts, raising an eyebrow.

"But it feels…" I trail off, swallowing. "*Right,*" I say finally, feeling the truth of it settle heavy and sure in my chest.

Antonio nods, like he expected that. He chews thoughtfully, then asks, "What happens after the summer? When she goes back to Los Angeles. When you go back to the fields."

A band of panic wraps around my ribcage, cutting off my breath. I wish I had an answer. I wish I could say something confident and easy, like, *We'll figure it out. It'll be fine.*

But the truth is, I don't even know if I *can* go back to the fields. My leg, though better than I ever dared hope, still carries the memory of pain like a shadow. I'm not the same player. Not yet. Maybe not ever.

I look down at my plate, pushing a roasted pepper around with my fork.

Antonio seems to read all of that in my silence. He puts a big, warm hand on my shoulder and squeezes once with a reassuring grip. A brother's way of saying *I see you. I'm with you.*

"I believe in you," he says simply, before turning his

attention back to his mountain of food like the conversation never happened.

I sit there for a moment, letting the weight of his words settle over me. He believes I'll go back, as if it's a given. But I'm not so sure.

Yet for the first time in a long time, the uncertainty doesn't hollow me out. It doesn't feel like failure looming over me. It just feels open, like anything could happen.

I glance back at Lena, who's just been handed a plate of *orecchiette con cime di rapa* and is making a face like she's just found heaven. She beams at me across the table, her whole face lighting up with pure, infectious joy.

Yeah.

Anything could happen, and that's not so terrifying after all.

THE KITCHEN SMELLS LIKE FRESH COFFEE AND BAKED sugar, and the last of the *crostata* is cooling on the counter. I lean against the heavy wooden table, watching Lena fumble adorably with the ancient *moka pot*, her tongue peeking out at the corner of her mouth in concentration.

"You're going to break it if you twist any harder," I tease, reaching around her to loosen the top.

She bumps her shoulder against mine, smiling. "*You* said to twist it tight."

"I said *firmly,* not like you're trying to strangle it."

She snorts a laugh just as the door creaks open and my parents walk in, still wiping their hands on kitchen towels, cheeks pink from the sun and the heat of cooking.

My mother's gaze drops immediately to my leg. She crosses the room in three quick strides and fusses with the hem of my shorts like she's looking for new wounds that aren't there.

"*Amore di mamma,*" she mutters under her breath, her forehead wrinkling with worry. "*Come va davvero? Non farmi preoccupare.*"

Lena watches, puzzled, clearly catching the concern in my mom's voice even without understanding the words.

"She wants to know how my leg is. How I'm really doing," I tell her softly, covering my mom's hand with mine to still her.

"And?" Lena asks, her voice just as soft, just as worried.

"I told her it's getting stronger," I say, even if it's not entirely true, then turn to my mom and reassure her in Italian. She doesn't look convinced.

Then my mother rounds on Lena with a fierce look in her eye, wagging her finger for emphasis. *"Diglielo tu!"* she insists. *"Digli che lasci stare le moto, o si ammazza."*

I smirk, even as my ears burn. I never thought I would be in my mother's kitchen being scolded like a child in front of a woman I just brought home.

"She says you have to tell me to leave motorcycles alone because I'll kill myself on one," I translate.

Lena's eyebrows shoot up. "Wait, *motorcycles*? As in more than one? I knew only about one."

I don't want it to become a big deal and drag Lena into the never-ending back-and-forth I have with my parents since I brought home my first bike.

Before I can brush it off, my father, silent until now, points a firm finger toward the courtyard. *"Garage."* One word. Full of meaning.

I groan. "They want us to see the bike."

"Now?" Lena blinks.

"Now," I say grimly.

I take her hand and lead her out through the stone archways, the late afternoon sun slanting low and soft through the olive trees. We cross the courtyard to a heavy wooden door. I pull it open, and the smell of oil and metal wraps around us immediately. My parents don't follow us. The sight of the motorcycle is still too much for them to handle.

Inside, the motorcycle sits in the corner like a wounded beast. Or what's left of it.

The front is twisted beyond recognition, the frame crumpled like paper. One handlebar is completely sheared off. The paint is scratched and torn, with patches of the car's red color blooming over the battered metal.

Lena freezes, her fingers tightening around mine.

"Oh my God," she breathes. She steps closer, almost reverent and scared at the same time, like she's looking at something sacred and terrible all at once. "*How* did you survive that?"

I swallow hard. "A miracle," I say simply, my voice rougher than I mean it to be.

For a long moment, neither of us speaks. The weight of it hangs between us. The crash, the recovery, the fear that maybe I hadn't told her the whole truth about how close I came to not walking away.

She turns to me then, her eyes shining with emotion that she doesn't bother hiding. Her fingers trace the scar on my thigh, featherlight, as if making sure I'm really here, solid and breathing.

"You scared them," she whispers.

I cup her face in my hands, brushing my thumbs over her cheeks, feeling her tremble slightly under my touch.

"I scared myself," I admit.

Her eyes search mine, wide and vulnerable and *real.*

I bend down and kiss her, soft and slow, pouring into her everything I can't say aloud. Gratitude. Hope. Something bigger than either of us expected. My tongue grazes against hers in a slow dance that has nothing sexual in it, but pure, undiluted affection that I can't hide anymore.

When I pull back, I rest my forehead against hers.

"I promise," I whisper, "no more motorcycles. Ever."

Her breath catches, and for the first time, I realize the weight of the promise I just made. It's not about the bike. It's about *her*. About the life I still want to build, the one I'm starting to see more clearly with her in it.

And I don't feel trapped by that realization.

I feel free.

21

LENA

The night air caresses our skin with warmth, and the scent of jasmine curls through the flickering candles on the table. We're still sitting at the long table under the pergola, plates pushed aside, the remains of dinner scattered across the cloth like a battlefield of crumbs and empty wine glasses.

I'm tucked between Martina, Michele's quick-witted cousin, and his grandmother, who, despite her small size and white crown of hair, has enough energy to fuel an entire city. Martina has appointed herself my official translator, flitting between Italian and English like it's nothing, while the women of the family close in around me with bright eyes and curious smiles, like I'm some rare creature they've been dying to examine up close.

"So," Martina says, grinning as she leans closer,

"*Nonna* wants to know if you can cook." Her tone is full of mirth, and her eyes sparkle with a laugh that threatens to bubble up her throat.

I blink, laughing nervously. "Um, not really. I mean, I can follow a recipe. Sometimes."

Martina bursts out laughing and rattles off my answer in Italian. Instantly, the whole group—Michele's mother, grandmother, aunts, even some cousins—erupts into good-natured teasing. Hands wave, someone pats my arm, and someone else says something that sounds suspiciously like *we'll teach her.* I don't know what I'm getting myself into, but I'm pretty sure it will be a life-changing experience.

Another question fires off, and Martina wiggles her brows mischievously. "Okay, serious question now. *Mamma* wants to know if you want children."

I nearly choke on my sip of wine. That's something Americans typically don't ask after just a few hours of meeting someone, but I assume it's not the case with Michele's family. They took me in as if they had known me forever, and they make me feel like I'm part of the family. I suppose these questions come with that privilege.

My gaze flickers to Michele a few seats down, where he's laughing with his brothers, his head thrown back, his whole body alive with energy. I consider how he plays with his nephews and nieces, and I can easily imagine him with a couple of kids running around the house. The question is, will they be *my* kids too? Just the thought makes my stomach flip in a sensation I can't quite place.

"I…think one day, maybe," I say carefully, my cheeks burning a bit from the alcohol, and even more from the intimacy of the question.

Martina translates, and there's a collective, approving hum around the table. I swear someone whispers *brava*.

Before I can recover, Martina leans in again. "Favorite color?"

"Blue," I answer quickly.

"Favorite season?"

"Spring."

Those questions come from her, trying to lighten an otherwise heavy conversation that sounds a lot like an interrogation, one nobody warned me I'd be participating in.

"Do you get homesick?"

This question comes from Michele's mother, and when I study her eyes, I see a motherly concern in her gaze. My heart swells with gratitude for her concern. It's rare to find someone who genuinely cares for you, even if they don't know you, especially in the shadows of the Hollywood hills.

"Sometimes. But here feels…easy." I pause, realizing how true that feels, and how quickly I've slipped into this feeling.

Since coming to Italy, I have never once felt the urge to return to my family and hide in the comfort of my childhood home. I don't know if it's Michele's company or the fact that Italy has something to marvel at around every corner, but I feel more in control of my emotions, more balanced, more grounded here.

They nod thoughtfully, as if this answer means more than it seems. Then Michele's grandmother tugs at my wrist gently and asks something with so much tenderness that Martina pauses before translating. She looks taken aback by her grandmother's question, and something that resembles tears veils her eyes.

"She wants to know," Martina says softly, "what makes you cry."

The question hits me right in the chest. I open my mouth, then close it. I'm not even sure my ex, the person who claimed to love me, ever asked me that. The depth of this question makes me feel naked and vulnerable, but when I look around the table, I find only honest faces, and I'm sure that my answer will be treated with all the affection and care that it needs. There is not a single ill-meaning person surrounding me at this table, and amid all these smiling, curious women, it's startlingly easy to answer.

"Injustice," I whisper. "Saying goodbye. And happy endings. Always."

Martina translates, her voice dropping into the hush

that has fallen over the table. When she finishes, Michele's mother reaches out and squeezes my hand warmly, and the *nonna* nods like I've passed some invisible test.

Another flurry of questions comes: whether I like animals (yes, especially dogs), if I can handle chaos (better than most), if I believe love should be easy or fought for (both, I think). It's overwhelming and comforting all at once, a river of affection and interest that sweeps me off my feet. I realize these women want to know the deeper part of me, the one that will bring Michele happiness, and I feel strangely relieved that there are so many people looking out for him.

They don't ask about Hollywood, about acting, about the career that usually defines me before anyone even learns my middle name. Here, it's like none of that matters. Here, I'm just Lena. And somehow, that feels more precious than any applause I've ever received.

As the night deepens and the candles burn lower, the older women begin to gather their shawls and kiss cheeks goodnight. There's laughter and slow steps as they disappear into the big stone house, the sound of the heavy wooden door thudding softly behind them.

The table empties slowly, leaving only a few lingering conversations spoken in quieter tones.

I stand, needing to stretch and breathe. The terracotta tiles are warm under my bare feet as I walk toward the courtyard, letting the peacefulness soak into my bones. My fingers trail along the low stone wall, and I tilt my head back to catch a glimpse of the stars.

Somewhere near the table, Michele's laugh rumbles low, and a warmth spreads through my chest. The earlier whirlwind of questions clings to me like a second skin, not heavy, but comforting. Like I've been wrapped in something I didn't realize I was starving for. Family. Belonging. A future that doesn't feel so impossible.

The night feels like it's holding its breath, waiting. Even the crickets don't make a sound. And even though a part of me still wonders if I'm dreaming, another part, the part that has stolen glances at Michele all night long, already knows the truth. I don't want to wake up.

I'm tracing the rough line of the stone wall with my fingertips when I hear his footsteps. Even before I turn, I know it's him. Something about the way my body wakes up, like a current surging through my veins, tells me he is coming closer.

Michele steps into the glow of the courtyard lights, hands tucked into the pockets of his jeans, his dark hair ruffled by the soft summer breeze. He doesn't say anything at first, just watches me with that half-smile that makes my heart squeeze painfully tight.

"You disappeared," he says quietly, his voice a little hoarse from laughing all night.

"I needed some air," I whisper, trying to steady my breathing. "Your family is amazing. Intense. Wonderful." I laugh under my breath. "I just needed a second to process."

He chuckles, low and warm. "They like you."

The way he says it makes something shift inside me, like a stone dropping into a pond, rippling out further than I'm ready to admit. I was craving this confirmation from him.

"I like them too," I murmur, and it's the truth. It's easy to love them, their chaos, their *love*.

We fall into a soft silence. There's something about the night—the scent of the prickly pears carried by the breeze, the low hum of cicadas, the way the old stone walls cradle the heat of the day and release it slowly— that makes everything feel sweeter, familiar.

Michele moves closer, and when he's near enough that I can feel the warmth of him against my skin, I have to force myself not to lean in, not to reach out and touch him. It feels almost forbidden to do it here, a few steps from the people who love him uncondi-tionally.

His eyes search mine, like he's looking for an answer to a question neither of us has asked aloud yet.

"You fit in here," he says finally, almost like he's

thinking out loud. "Like you've always been part of this."

The words hit harder than they should. My throat closes up. Because this awareness clashes with the reality of our lives and the ocean that separates them.

"I know," I say, my voice barely above a whisper. "And I want to."

I don't even know if I mean this house, this family, this country, or *him*. Maybe all of it. I've never felt like I belonged to something so new and yet so familiar. And the feeling is not at all unwelcome.

The air between us grows thick, heavy with words that neither of us speaks. I tilt my head back to look at him properly. He's close enough now that I can see the faint line of stubble along his jaw, the tiny scar near his temple, the flecks of gold in his dark eyes.

God, he's beautiful.

And not just in the way people are beautiful. In the way mountains are beautiful. Solid. Immovable. Eternal. Michele is all this. He is a beautiful soul wrapped in a beautiful man.

He lifts a hand slowly, like he's giving me time to stop him, and when I do not, when I *couldn't* even if I wanted, he brushes a lock of hair behind my ear, his fingers grazing my cheek.

It's such a simple touch, but it unravels something deep inside me. I sway toward him, caught in the pull of gravity that only exists between two people who are about to change everything.

When he kisses me, it's nothing like the fiery, frantic kiss of that first night. It's slow. Deep. Reverent. Like he's making a promise. Like he's *asking* for something. And I give it, whatever it is, without hesitation. My hands find his chest, his heart hammering under my palms, and I press closer, needing the anchor of him. His arms wrap around me, strong and sure, like he could hold me here forever.

I don't even realize I'm trembling until he pulls back just enough to whisper against my lips, "Hey. It's okay. I've got you."

God. If only he knew how much I want that. How much I crave someone I can trust blindly and count on. Someone I can see in my future, when we're old, and we smile at the memory of a life spent together.

An olive branch creaks somewhere behind us, and we break apart, reluctantly, turning toward the sound.

It's Mariasole, Michele's younger sister, stepping into the courtyard, barefoot and grinning mischievously. She folds her arms and says something rapid-fire in Italian that makes Michele groan softly.

He turns to me, his mouth twitching.

"She says she set up two bedrooms for us," he translates, his voice teasing but a little rough around the edges. "Because, you know, as open-minded as my parents are, they're not *that* open-minded."

I blink, feeling my cheeks heat. The implication hangs heavy between us. *Two bedrooms. Because we're not official.* Because even though we've kissed, even though we've shared a bed once, even though tonight feels bigger and deeper than anything I've ever known, we haven't *talked* about what we are.

But his family has already decided. They see us as a couple, something real, something serious. And somehow, I realize that the idea doesn't terrify me. It fills my heart with a quiet, yet dangerous kind of hope.

Michele looks at me, one eyebrow raised, giving me the chance to say something, to joke, to deflect, to change the subject.

I don't.

I just smile, small and a little shy, and say, "Lead the way." And as we walk inside together, the night warm and heavy around us, I know that whatever happens next, we've already crossed a line we can't uncross.

22

LENA

There's a soft thump in the corner of the room, like someone's gently nudging the old stone walls. I blink awake, the moonlight casting silver shapes across the terracotta floor. My window is half-open, letting in the scent of warm earth and jasmine, and the distant sound of crickets buzzing in the olive groves.

I squint toward the doorway, heart picking up pace, until a familiar, tall shadow steps fully into view.

"Michele?" I whisper.

"Shh." He presses a finger to his lips, eyes sparkling as he closes the door behind him with exaggerated care. He's barefoot, in a white T-shirt and sleep-rumpled shorts, hair wild like he's been tossing and turning in bed. "I didn't mean to wake you. I stepped on something outside your door. Think it might've been a Lego."

"A Lego? In a centuries-old fortified farmhouse?"

"We're a modern family."

I choke down a laugh. "You scared me."

He crosses the room in just a few steps and crouches by the edge of the bed, elbows on the mattress. "Sorry, I couldn't sleep."

"Did you try counting sheep?"

"Yeah, but they all looked like my cousins and started asking me when I'm getting married."

That gets a giggle out of me, and I swat at him lightly. The room feels smaller now, filled with his presence. The citrusy clean scent of his skin, the warmth rolling off his body, the low husk of his voice in the quiet of the masseria tickles all my senses in the best way.

The walls are thick here, whitewashed stone that holds the day's heat outside, guarding our sleep while the earth outside releases the intense temperature of the scorching sun. My room is spare but cozy, with high ceilings and exposed beams. The bed is soft and creaky, the kind that hugs your weight and promises heavy dreams. There's a lace curtain swaying at the window and a painted ceramic bowl on the nightstand with dried lavender tucked inside. The whole place smells like summer and old stories.

"You're sneaking into my room like a teenager," I tease, shifting onto my side to face him. My voice is soft, sleepy.

"I feel like one. Except back then, I didn't have legs full of screws."

I touch his wrist gently. "How's your leg?"

"It's fine," he says quickly. "Doesn't hurt unless I overdo it."

I narrow my eyes. "So you overdid it."

"Maybe." His smile is sheepish, and for a beat, we just look at each other. The silence stretches, but it's not awkward, it's warm, like a familiar quilt pulled over our shoulders.

I pull the blanket back in invitation, and he doesn't hesitate, climbing in beside me like he's done it a hundred times. He lies on top of the sheet, his bare legs brushing mine, and it feels dangerous and easy all at once.

"How do you feel?" he asks, brushing a strand of hair from my cheek.

"About what?"

"Today. My family. This whole…mess."

I laugh, but quietly. "Your family isn't a mess. They're a force of nature."

"True."

"I feel weirdly peaceful." I stare at the ceiling, where

the moonlight dances across the beams. "I forgot about LA today. Forgot the scandal. The headlines. Even forgot that I'm Lena Sinclair for a few hours."

His fingers find mine under the sheet. "You're still *you* here."

"But not *that* version of me. Here, I'm just a woman sitting at a too-long table, trying to explain what kale is to your grandmother."

"She said it sounds like cow food."

"Exactly." We both laugh again, muffling the sound into the pillow.

He shifts, propping his head up on his arm to look down at me. "You were amazing tonight. They all love you."

"I was grilled like a swordfish."

"You passed the test."

"I didn't even study."

His grin is lazy and a little crooked, and a sharp feeling settles in my chest, both wonderful and terrifying. "I mean it. No one's ever fit in like this before."

"Like what?"

He shrugs one shoulder. "With them. With me."

There's something thick in the air between us, like a string pulled taut. I want to grab it and wrap it around my fist, hold onto it before it slips away. Instead, I ask, "Are you going to get in trouble?"

"For what?"

"For being in here."

He pretends to gasp. "Lena. Are you trying to seduce me?"

I roll my eyes. "You snuck into my room, Moretti."

He leans in closer, lips brushing the shell of my ear. "Maybe I missed you."

His breath is warm, and my skin breaks out in goosebumps. "We've been apart for what, an hour?"

"Exactly." He kisses my neck gently, reverently, and I shiver. I know where this is going. And I know where it won't.

Not tonight. Not here. But in between there's still something electric, something playful and dangerous and real.

"You're not going to try anything," I say, my voice way too breathy.

"Me?" he whispers. "Never."

His mouth trails kisses down the side of my throat and lower, and even though everything about the masseria feels safe and timeless, my heartbeat races like a kid sneaking into the neighbor's pool at midnight. It feels dangerous and forbidden and so exciting.

"Michele…" I start to protest, but he grins, wicked and boyish, looking up at me from under his thick lashes.

"Shh," he says again. "Bet you can't stay quiet."

He kisses me between my breasts while he grazes his

thumbs over my peaking nipples under the fabric of my tank top.

"You're terrible," I half whisper, half moan.

"I'm Italian," he murmurs, biting my breast lightly.

"What does that even mean?" I chuckle.

He raises my tank top over my stomach, nipping and licking his way down toward the waistband of my panties. I think I'm losing the battle of keeping it quiet.

"According to the stereotype, I'm a charmer and passionate in bed," he teases with a smirk on his face.

That makes me snort. "Not a valid excuse."

He ducks under the sheet like a ghost, and my laugh dies on my lips when his mouth touches the inside of my thigh and his fingers slip my panties down my legs. My breath catches in my throat when, with a series of wet kisses up my inner thigh, he reaches the apex where my clit is already begging for attention. Michele licks along my folds, sucking on the bundle of nerves.

I grab the pillow and press it over my face, biting it so as not to moan and beg for more. Knowing his parents are just around the corner makes me feel naughty, reckless, and alive at the same time. He licks and nips and sucks with such an intensity that I don't think I will last long before the orgasm pooling in my lower belly will explode like fireworks.

When he slips one finger into my wet core, I whimper

softly in pleasure. When he slips a second, I have to press the pillow over my face to not let the moan escaping my lips reach anyone's ears. When he starts pumping them in and out of my wetness, I tense and arch my back, pushing my hips against his face, giving him more space to suck on my clit and build my approaching orgasm.

It takes him a few masterful strokes, bending his fingers inside me to make me come undone under his expert tongue. Wave after wave of pleasure ripples through my body, making me want to scream my lungs out. I press the pillow firmly on my face and let out a moan I'm sure everyone can hear.

He doesn't let up. He keeps sucking and teasing, prolonging my pleasure to the point that my sensitive bud wants to beg him to stop. My teeth almost hurt from biting the pillow.

I don't win the bet. God, it's a miracle if we don't wake up everyone in this house.

When I finally breathe again, my chest is rising like I've run a marathon. He kisses my hip, the inside of my knee, then the hollow just above my belly button before slipping back out of the covers.

His hair is a mess, and he looks extremely proud of himself.

"Now, who's seducing who?" I whisper.

He smirks, kissing the corner of my mouth. "I should

go. Before my mom catches me and tells you we're too young to make babies."

I giggle against his chest. "You're afraid of your mom."

"You should be too. She makes her own sausage."

I grab his wrist when he starts to move off the bed. "Stay."

He freezes. Not in hesitation. In temptation. But then he brushes his lips against mine, gentle, grateful, full of something that scares me more than any paparazzi ever could.

"I'll be back tomorrow," he whispers. "Bright and early."

"You better bring espresso," I say, stifling a yawn.

"Only if I get a kiss first." He smiles sweetly.

I give him one. And then another. And another.

Until he finally pulls himself away, slipping out of the room like a dream you will remember in the morning.

THE DOOR SHUTS SOFTLY BEHIND HIM, AND I LIE THERE motionless, the covers tangled around my knees, the ghost of his mouth still between my thighs.

I should go back to sleep. But I don't want to. Not yet.

The fan in the corner hums softly, stirring the curtain

with each slow sweep. Outside the open window, the cicadas are still singing their endless lullaby, the kind that has underscored every Italian night since we started this journey together. I close my eyes, soaking in the scent of basil from the garden, warm limestone, and a hint of the soap Michele uses.

It feels surreal how light I am. How weightless. I haven't felt like this in…I don't know. Years?

In LA, even sleep doesn't give me peace. There's always something: an email, an alert, a phone call at three a.m. from my publicist telling me I've been tagged in a headline I didn't agree to, didn't participate in, didn't even know existed. It's like being on a merry-go-round you can't get off, spinning faster and faster until your stomach flips and your brain is a blur.

But here, in this old stone room with a creaky bed and a door that barely closes, there's silence. Not emptiness, just stillness. Safety. A slowness that makes your body relax and your mind drift to a pleasant space.

And Michele.

I press my fingers to my lips, remembering the way he kissed me before he left. Slow. Certain. Like he knew exactly what it meant. Like he wasn't scared of how deep we were falling. But I am because this was supposed to be simple. A fling. A distraction. Something golden and glittering between the cracks of what broke me back home.

Only he's no longer a distraction. He's a center of gravity. And if I'm not careful, I'll start orbiting him. Maybe I already am.

I shift in bed and roll onto my stomach, then sit up and swing my feet to the floor. The tiles are cool beneath my toes. I pad to the open window and rest my forearms on the windowsill.

The courtyard is quiet now. The candles have all gone out. The big fig tree casts long shadows under the moon, and I can just make out the curve of the vineyard rows on the far edge of the property. It's like standing inside a painting. Or maybe a dream.

How did I end up here?

The woman I was in June—the Lena Sinclair who pressed pause on her Hollywood life and disappeared from the scene—couldn't have imagined this. That woman was brittle and hollowed out, weary of pretending she was fine, tired of smiling on cue.

But here I'm not smiling because I have to. I'm smiling because I can't help it. I press my forehead to the wall beside the window and close my eyes.

I can still hear Michele's laugh echoing in my memory, loud and low and utterly unfiltered. I think that's what drew me in first. Not his body, not the way he looks at me like he's memorizing every detail, but that laugh. Like he's not afraid to be happy. Like he's not afraid to *feel* things all the way to the end.

And God, the way he touched me tonight. The way he looked up at me from under the sheets, daring me to stay quiet like it was the most fun game in the world. And the way he ran off after, scared of his mother catching him, like we were in some kind of teenage sitcom.

I grin in the dark. He's this fascinating contradiction: confident and grounded and so damned sexy, and also a little bit afraid of his *mamma.*

It's adorable. And weirdly sexy too.

My stomach twists, a slow ache curling inside me. I thought I knew what this was, just two people making the most of a sultry Italian summer. But I don't think I'm going to be able to leave this behind untouched. Unbroken.

My heart's already cracking open.

The weight of that settles over me slowly. A realization, not a revelation. I've been falling for him in tiny steps since day one. Since the way he brushed the coffee stain from his shirt, and didn't make it a big deal. Since the way he listened whenever I talked, even about the most ridiculous things. Since the way his family looked at me tonight, like I belonged, even though they barely know me.

Even his sister, Mariasole, went out of her way to be kind. To respect the weird limbo of whatever we are. *Two bedrooms,* she said with a gentle smile. *Just in case.*

Like she was saying: we love you already, but we won't push.

And now here I am, standing barefoot in an old masseria in Puglia, my heart threatening to beat straight out of my chest, wondering how the hell I'm supposed to walk away from this. From him.

The cool air brushes my skin, and I sigh, pulling the blanket from the foot of the bed and wrapping it around my shoulders. My feet take me to the doorway, then back to the bed, then to the mirror, restless, nervous energy thrumming under my skin.

There's so much I still don't know. I don't know what will happen when I go back. If Hollywood still wants me. If the headlines will cool down. If I'll get to reclaim my narrative, or if I've already lost control of it for good. But I do know this: I feel like myself here.

More than that, I feel like the *best* version of myself. No makeup. No press. No curated brand, stylists, or pretenses. Just me. Just Lena. And Michele sees her. All of her.

And maybe he's starting to fall in love with her too.

My eyes sting, and I blink hard. I'm not used to feeling this way. I'm not used to feeling *safe*. But with him, I don't feel like I have to earn love. I just get to feel it.

Even if it's not forever. Even if this ends in a week or a month, or when the summer sun finally fades. I know it's real. I know *he's* real. And that's something no head-line can ever take from me.

I climb back into bed and pull the sheet up over my chest, nestling into the pillow that still smells like lavender and faintly like him.

I let the night hold me. Let the summer wrap itself around my bones, and I fall asleep smiling, already dreaming of him sneaking in again tomorrow night.

23

MICHELE

The morning sun filters through the lace curtains, casting soft shapes across the terracotta floor. The scent of freshly brewed espresso wafts through the air, mingling with the earthy aroma of the masseria. I balance a tray with two cups, a small bowl of sugar, and a plate of almond biscotti as I tiptoe down the hallway.

Lena's door is slightly ajar, and I push it open gently. She's still nestled under the linen sheets, her hair a tousled halo around her face.

"*Buongiorno, tesoro,*" I whisper, setting the tray on the bedside table.

She stirs, blinking sleepily. "Mmm, what's that smell?"

Her voice is groggy from sleep, and I smile when she

peels an eye open to peek at me. She is adorable when she's all sleepy and confused.

"Espresso. Thought you might need a little pick-me-up. You know, after my performance last night," I tease her.

She groans and puts the blanket over her head. "You are terrible."

"You weren't complaining last night. On the contrary, you seemed very, very pleased." I smirk at her and she gives me the side-eye, but a smile tugs at her lips.

She sits up, and the sheet slips to reveal her bare shoulders. "You're spoiling me," she says, eyeing the tray on the nightstand.

I hand her a cup, our fingers brushing. "Only the best for you." I wink and she blushes, hiding a smile behind the porcelain rim.

We sip our coffee in comfortable silence, the morning light dancing across her features. Outside, the cicadas begin their daily chorus, a soundtrack that reminds me of my childhood.

After dressing, we make our way to the pergola-covered patio where my mother, father, and *nonna* are already seated, enjoying the morning breeze.

"*Buongiorno*, Lena!" my mother exclaims, rising to greet her with a kiss on both cheeks. "Did you sleep well?"

I translate for her, realizing how much work my

cousin and sister did yesterday to keep the conversation flowing and merging the two languages.

"Very well, thank you," Lena replies, smiling warmly.

My grandmother pats the seat beside her. "Come, sit. Eat. You must try the fresh focaccia," she says in Italian, and I translate for her.

We join them, plates filled with sun-dried tomatoes, olives, and slices of pecorino. It's so late for my family that they've already had breakfast and are at their mid-morning snack. If we can call it that. There is enough food on the table to feed a family for several days.

The conversation flows easily, laughter punctuating stories of family and local gossip. My mother and grandmother don't refrain from telling Lena about my embarrassing moments when I was a kid. They chuckle when she throws her head back in a sincere laugh and ask questions that my mother eagerly answers. My father, always a man of few words, looks between his wife and Lena and smiles, from time to time throwing a glance at me. I know he has something to say, but he will keep it for himself until we are alone. He is not a man who shows his feelings easily.

I watch Lena interact with my family, her laughter blending seamlessly with theirs. She fits here, in this moment, as if she's always been a part of our lives. The thought fills me with a warmth I can't quite describe.

After breakfast, I take her hand. "Come, I want to show you something."

We walk through the olive groves, the ancient trees standing sentinel over the red earth. Their gnarled trunks twist and turn, each one a testament to centuries of resilience.

"These trees are incredible," Lena says, running her fingers along the bark. "How old are they?"

"Some are over thousands of years old," I reply. "They've seen empires rise and fall."

Sha gapes at me, but I shrug. I was stunned, too, when they told me how these trees stood proud throughout invasions and wars. It's a miracle they're still here.

"No wonder the olive oil is fantastic." She smiles, and I chuckle.

Lena has discovered fresh-baked bread, or focaccia, drizzled with olive oil, and said from now on she will eat only that for the rest of her life. My mom chuckled at this, especially after she had said the same thing for another dozen plates of food my family had cooked.

"I'll make sure you'll always have some, even when you're in Los Angeles." I wink at her and she lights up in a grin that takes up her whole face.

We continue walking until we're out of sight of the masseria. The sun filters through the leaves, casting dappled shadows on the ground. I sit under an olive tree, resting my back against it. Lena sits next to me, facing me slightly. She rubs a hand over the cargo pants covering my scar.

She frowns, probably noticing the stiffness in my muscles, and turns to face me. "How's your leg?"

I sigh, looking down. "It's…not great," I admit. At this point, it is impossible to hide anything from her or my family. They both know me well enough to call me out on my bullshit.

She studies me for a long moment. "What do the doctors say? And don't give me the usual nonsense you tell everyone who asks. What do they really say?"

I smile, grabbing her hand massaging my leg and intertwining our fingers. "The doctors say I might need surgery, but there's no guarantee I'll be able to play at the same level again."

She nods thoughtfully. "Is it something that could improve your mobility?"

"Maybe. They'll have to take apart my muscle and restitch it together, hoping this time it will heal right. It's kind of massive. The recovery time is uncertain." I confess my biggest fear. "I don't know how long it will take to heal. My body didn't react as the specialists had hoped, and they're all at a loss as to what to do. If the guys from the ambulance who peeled me from the side of the car hadn't recognized me, they would have probably amputated my leg. It was *that* bad."

She places a hand on my arm. "But you don't know how much time it will take to recover either way, right? Surgery or not."

I nod slowly, considering her words. She doesn't pity me with the usual "I'm so sorry for you," I've heard a million times since it happened. She just puts something into perspective that I've already discussed with my agent, Marco, a million times.

"Right. However, there's also the problem that the procedure's not guaranteed to fix my leg. It could get worse and leave me limping for the rest of my life. We can't know. Most of the specialists I found don't want to risk their careers to try and fix something that probably can't be fixed. I'm famous, way too famous to put their names on the line for a surgery that could damage me and their career. My leg works as it is now. Badly, but it works."

"But you still feel pain and limp more often than you care to admit. Your life is already upside down because of this injury. Maybe it can't be fixed, but maybe it can, making your life better."

I nod, considering her words. She's not completely wrong. I mean, it's not like I'm going to lose my leg, at least not that I know.

"Then maybe it's worth trying," she says gently.

I look into her eyes, finding a strength in her gaze I didn't know she had. Not for me, anyway. She looks like she wants to infuse hope into my heart somehow, and the thought scares me to my bones. I can't hope. I can't afford to, because if it's crushed, I'll be dead.

We sit in silence for a long moment, the weight of the conversation settling between us. Then, without a word, she leans closer, wrapping her arms around me.

I hold her tightly, the scent of her hair mingling with the earthy aroma of the grove. Our lips meet, a tender kiss that deepens with each passing moment. The taste of hope and love lingers on her lips and fills my chest with heat.

There is no rushing this moment between us. We kiss and nip each other's skin, tasting and breathing in our scents. It's a moment of discovery for both of us. The chemistry we had in bed the last time leaves room for something else, something more profound. It's like we discovered our bodies the first time, but now we're discovering our souls.

I grab a fistful of Lena's blonde hair and tilt her head to deepen the kiss. She moans in my mouth, pulling a groan from deep in my chest. Her tongue fights with mine in a dance that leaves both of us breathless. When we separate, she locks her eyes with mine and grabs my T-shirt, leaning back and pulling me on top of her.

Her eyes are hooded, filled with lust and love I didn't expect to find there. It unlocks something in my chest I didn't even know was buried beneath the surface. I crush my lips on her again, deepening the kiss and nestling myself between her legs.

I feel my arousal build against the heat of her sweet thighs and can't stop the urge to roll my hips against hers. She moans deep in my mouth, and I enjoy every single second of it, feeling it reverberating in my chest, down to my groin.

"Are you uncomfortable?" I whisper against her lips when I realize she is stretched out on dirt and leaves.

She shakes her head. "Please, fuck me, Michele," she moans.

I chuckle. "Since you ask so nicely," I murmur, tracing a path of kisses along her neck.

She grabs the hair at the base of my neck and pulls slightly, eliciting a groan from my chest. I kiss my way down her collarbone, reaching the swell of her breasts, slipping a hand under the yellow sundress that's been driving me crazy since seeing her this morning, and caress my fingers over her soaked panties.

"Fuck," I murmur when I feel how ready she is for me. For us.

She squirms under my touch when I pull her panties aside and slip a couple of fingers over her wet folds.

"More, please," she whines while she grips my hair firmly, closing her eyes and throwing her head back. She is so beautiful when she lets herself go that it almost hurts to look at her.

I push inside her with one finger, and I enjoy the moan escaping her lips. I add a second one and smile when she parts her legs wider to give me full access. I stroke her with slow, lazy movement, watching her lips part and her eyes flutter shut. I push deeper into her and she bites her lip, encouraging me to draw my fingers almost out and push them inside even deeper, then rewarding me with a deep groan.

"Please, Michele, fuck me," she pleads, locking her eyes on mine.

I chuckle, but it soon dies on my lips when I realize what that entails.

"Fuck," I groan lowering my head on her chest.

She tilts her head up and frowns at me. "What?"

I look at her with a sheepish smile. "I don't have a condom," I confess.

She smiles. "Wasn't your plan all along to seduce me in the olive grove?"

I give her a don't-mess-with-me look, but a grin pulls at my lips.

"Actually, this wasn't planned, but you're so irresistible I can't keep my hands to myself."

She rolls her eyes playfully. "Are you Italians always so flirty?"

I pretend to be offended. "We're always flirty, it's in our DNA."

She chuckles, but her smile sweetens. "We can go without it, if you want. I'm on the pill and clean."

Her proposal takes me by surprise. It's a big deal going without a condom, but she looks at peace with it, no trace of doubt on her face.

"Are you sure? I mean, I'm clean, too, but it's not like we have to do it." Even if my cock throbbing between her thighs begs otherwise.

She nods. "I'm sure," she says, kissing my head.

The knot in my stomach flips and then dissolves into a warm feeling that spreads all through me.

She helps remove my cargo pants and boxer briefs while I take off her panties. I nestle between her legs again and put my elbows on either side of her, looking her straight in the eyes, while aligning my shaft to her entrance and slowly pushing inside her.

"Fuck…" A growl escapes my mouth. This feels so intimate my body trembles against hers. She lets out a soft moan and wraps her arms around my neck, her legs over my butt. I cradle her body against mine, and I thrust into her, slow and deep. I take my time savoring the feeling of our sensitive skin against each other.

She raises her hips, matching my thrust with hers. I feel her hip bones against mine in a dance that alters the space and time around us. I'm so lost in the sensation of her heat around my cock, that when she puts her hands on my buttcheeks and pushes me against her, I completely lose the battle of restraining myself and thrust deep and fast inside the most delicious being I've ever made love with.

Because this isn't casual sex, not anymore. Not for me, and from the way she's looking at me, not for her either. Our bodies dance in sync, the sound of skin against skin drawing out the sound of the cicadas and crickets around us. Or maybe they're just silent and blushing in view of this spectacle of love and lust and everything in between.

"Come inside me, Michele. Please," Lena whispers against my ear, and it's the only permission I need to worship her body even harder and faster.

She clenches around my cock with a moan muffled by her mouth biting my shoulder and I come undone, pushing deep inside her and releasing my pleasure, trembling and breathing hard, leaning my forehead into the crook of her neck and almost whispering those words that press against my lips. *I love you, Lena.* And I've never been more sure about something in my entire life.

I roll to the ground next to her, breathing hard and tightening my grip around her body, dragging her against my chest. The ancient olive tree above us stands witness as we come down from a high that drained our bodies but filled our souls, because I feel deep in my gut that everything changed today.

In this moment, everything else fades away—the

uncertainty, the pain, the fear. All that remains is us, here, now.

As we lie together beneath the canopy of leaves, I realize that this isn't just a summer fling. It's something deeper, more profound.

And I don't want it to end.

24

LENA

The smell of grilled zucchini, lemony sea bass, and something fried mingles with the warm summer air as I sit beneath the pergola outside Michele's parents' masseria. The air is thick with the scent of jasmine and rosemary, and the sun has only just dipped below the horizon, painting the sky in dusky pink and amber. Now that the stars are peeking out, the string lights above our heads glow like fireflies caught in a dance.

It's beautiful. Too beautiful. One of those nights you know you'll remember for the rest of your life.

A vintage radio plays somewhere behind us. A soft, sentimental Italian song croons through static. It adds the perfect touch, like a movie scene you didn't know you'd been waiting your whole life to live.

I've got a glass of white wine in my hand, a plate full of grilled vegetables in front of me, and the kind of joy in my chest that feels both light and dangerously full.

Michele sits beside me, looking more relaxed than I've ever seen him, his hand brushing mine every time he reaches for his glass. He doesn't even notice. Or maybe he does. Either way, I don't pull away.

To my left, Gianna—his childhood friend, now married with a toddler and a knack for storytelling—is leaning forward, her elbow on the table as she eyes me with a grin. "So," she says, "has he told you about the treehouse?"

I raise an eyebrow and glance at Michele, who suddenly looks very interested in his wine.

"No," I say slowly. "But I'm already intrigued."

Andrea, a tall, slender guy with hair that could only be described as 'perpetually windblown,' snorts into his glass. "He was twelve. Decided he'd build his own treehouse. Got halfway finished with the ladder before realizing he had no idea what he was doing."

"I had a plan," Michele mutters beside me.

"Yeah," Alessandro chimes in from across the table. "A plan that involved climbing up with three planks of wood and a single nail in your pocket."

Gianna's already laughing. "He got stuck halfway up the olive tree and yelled for his mom like it was a life-or-death emergency."

Lucia, from a few seats away, waves a hand through the air. "I had to put back the ladder he'd let fall and drag him down myself while he clung to a branch and swore he saw a snake."

"It moved," Michele insists, clearly reliving the trauma.

Everyone laughs, and he scowls at no one in particular.

I lean into him, whispering, "You were twelve, building a treehouse with one nail. What exactly did you think was going to happen?"

I can't hide a chuckle escaping my lips.

"I didn't expect to be ambushed years later by my own dinner guests," he retorts, eliciting a new round of laughs around the table.

I bounce my shoulder playfully against his and he glares at me, but a smile is tugging at his lips. He's embarrassed about the stories his friends are sharing, but I'm convinced he enjoys spending time with them. I see it in his eyes, from the way he looks at them, full of love and a hint of melancholy.

"You invited them," I point out with a grin.

"That was a mistake," he rebukes, but I know he doesn't mean it. The grin trying to escape from his lips says otherwise.

Laughter ripples around the table, warm and contagious, and I find myself laughing too, really laughing, the kind that hurts your ribs and cramps your cheeks but makes your heart settle in an easy rhythm.

"Wait, wait," Gianna says, wiping tears from her eyes. "What about the pool incident?"

Michele's groan is immediate. "No. Absolutely not."

He rubs a hand over his face when it's clear that his friend has no intention of holding back on this story, and I have to admit I'm curious to hear it. They're telling me so much, I'm pretty sure he's lived ten lives. I haven't done even a fraction of what he did when he was young. He was reckless and completely out of control. I can see how starting his career so young helped him straighten out his head.

"Oh, yes," Andrea says, already grinning. "He was fifteen, trying to impress Serena. Remember her? Long legs, no patience?"

Lucia raises a brow. "Still no patience, that one. We were at the public pool, right? School had just let out a week prior."

She doesn't seem that fond of the girl Michele was crushing on, and I can't hide a smile spilling from my lips.

"He climbs up onto the roof of the pool storage shed," Andrea continues, "says he's going to dive in like a pro."

A groan escapes Michele's chest, and I grip my hand around his. I see a few glances from his friends who notice the gesture but say nothing. I would normally be conscious of public displays of affection, but right now I feel so at ease with the people surrounding us that I don't mind showing this side of myself, even if I did just meet them a few hours ago. Michele doesn't seem to mind either, and a flutter starts in my chest when he absently caresses my hand with his thumb.

Alessandro shakes his head. "And he would've, if he hadn't miscalculated the distance he needed to reach the deeper side of the pool."

"You distracted me with your chatter and jokes," Michele mutters, but Alessandro shushes him with a wave of his hand.

"Landed where the water was a bit too low. It was memorable."

Everyone laughs, and a cheer goes around the table, as if celebrating that he didn't die during that stunt.

"I limped for a week!" he points out, but everyone shakes their heads in unison.

It's Gianna who voices their thoughts. "You limped for attention because Serena was all over you when you got out of that pool."

Alessandro raises his eyebrow in agreement, and I feel my cheeks heat up when I realize a part of me is jealous of a teenage girl, now an adult, who is not even here right now.

I can't breathe from laughing. "Please," I gasp.

"Keep going. I need more stories to torment him with later."

Michele looks at me like I've just committed the ultimate betrayal. "Et tu, Brute?"

"Absolutely," I grin. "I'm just trying to understand the man I'm…" I pause. Dating? Seeing? Sleeping with? Falling for?

He arches a brow, waiting for me to finish. This is a discussion we've both avoided after the latest developments, and right now, my brain is scrambling to find the right word without appearing like a complete idiot in front of his friends. They didn't ask us if we were together, or at least they didn't express this thought to me, but I saw the curious gazes between us when they joined us tonight.

"…having dinner with," I conclude, taking another sip of wine but never letting my gaze leave his eyes.

A small smirk appears on his lips while he studies me intently. I can't tell if he's happy with my definition of our relationship, or lack thereof, but I decide not to bring it up here, and neither does he. But this is something we have to discuss at some point, because we are clearly not just friends anymore.

Laughter erupts around the table again, bringing us back to reality, and his hand slides beneath the table to rest against my thigh. It's innocent. Almost. Because when he reaches the hem of my dress, he caresses my inner thigh way too intimately for a dinner with friends. Thank God, Italians use a tablecloth for every meal. Otherwise, his mother would be horrified.

The rest of the night is a blur of food, wine, and stories. Lucia makes her rounds like a queen holding court, pressing more focaccia into my hand every time I so much as glance toward my empty plate. Michele's younger cousins dart to and from the table with the energy only teenagers on summer break can have. Someone starts pouring limoncello from a bottle that appears to be older than most of the guests.

Eventually, the stories give way to quieter conversations. Candles flicker low. The cicadas sing in the trees.

I lean back, sipping my drink, and let the moment settle into my bones. I've never felt this kind of belonging before. Not on a movie set. Not even at one of those exclusive Hollywood parties with champagne and string quartets and gowns that cost more than my car.

This is real.

Michele's mother walks by and sets a warm hand on my shoulder. "You're part of the family now, *tesoro*. Whether you like it or not." Her smile is so soft that, as her son translates it to me, my heart almost explodes in my chest.

I blink hard against the tears that threaten to rise. "I think I'm okay with that."

Michele looks at me, and something passes between us, unspoken words that warm my chest. He reaches for my hand again and threads his fingers through mine.

I squeeze.

I want to remember everything. The glow of the lights, the sting of the limoncello on my tongue, the scent of summer in the air, and the way Michele smiles at me like I'm the most precious thing he's ever had the nerve to want.

In this moment, surrounded by laughter, flickering candlelight, and the low hum of an Italian summer night, I think I might love him. I might really, truly love him, and that might be the most terrifying, wonderful thing I've ever felt.

THE WINE HAS GONE TO EVERYONE'S HEADS IN THE BEST possible way. Some of his friends are still telling stories about their childhood, while others are walking between the olive trees, trying to digest the Italian dinner we just had. Some others pour another glass of limoncello, with flushed cheeks and watery eyes.

Michele's hand slides over my knee under the table, squeezing lightly. I turn my head, and he's already looking at me with a lopsided grin.

"I'm getting you out of here before Andrea tells the watermelon story," he murmurs.

"What watermelon story?" My eyes light up with curiosity while my cheeks beg me to take a rest from laughing.

"Exactly," he says, already pulling me to my feet.

"Michele!" I half laugh, half scold as he tugs me away from the table, down a stone path a few meters from the pergola, near a cluster of fig trees and an old radio propped on a barrel. The music is low, a slow and romantic tune, the kind that makes the cicadas seem quieter in comparison.

He stops and turns, slipping his arms around my waist. "Dance with me."

My heart does its usual backflip, like every other time Michele looks at me with those intense eyes. He makes me feel seen, loved, and a part of something. He sees the real me, and I'm not afraid to show him the most intimate part of myself. I don't even remember the last time I wore makeup this summer, maybe a few days into our journey.

"You're saving yourself from public humiliation, aren't you?" I raise an eyebrow, challenging him.

He smirks. "Absolutely. But also, I just wanted you

in my arms again," he whispers in my ear while he pulls me against his chest as we sway to the slow song.

God. How is it that he says things like that with zero hesitation? Like it's inevitable. Doesn't he know that my legs go weak when he says things like that? Even my words fail to give him a reply.

I loop my arms around his neck, and we dance slowly, our bodies pressed close and following the rhythm. The night air is warm and honey-sweet, and the candlelight from the table flickers across the stone wall of the masseria. His hand is splayed across my lower back, and his fingers sift through the fabric of my sundress.

"So," I say, tilting my head to look up at him, "you really played the same song every night for a whole summer?"

He groans. "You said we were done with this."

I grin.

"I lied. Was it a ballad?" I tease him.

"Lena." He growls my name in a way that I don't know if it's a warning or lusty desire. Heat pools in my lower belly.

"Did you do the whole kneeling-down thing? Maybe some tortured eye contact?" I press teasingly, wanting to know how the young Michele was. Was he as confident as he is with me now, or was he shy around the girls? I find it sweet that he played the same song for the entire summer because the girl he had a crush on loved it. It somehow fits the Michele I know now, thoughtful and romantic.

His eyes narrow playfully. "You're walking a very dangerous line."

And I'm not even done yet.

"Did you make a video clip for her with that song? Did you have backup dancers? A costume? I feel like there was glitter involved." Now it's hard to hold back a laugh.

That's when he retaliates with a swift tickle to my waist that makes me yelp and jerk in his arms. His deft fingers are playing my body way too well.

"No! Stop! Michele!" I gasp, laughing so hard my ribs ache.

He grins like a boy caught sneaking cookies, looking smug and stupidly beautiful, the shadows from the fig trees softening the angles of his face.

"You deserved that," he says in a low voice. More serious.

My fingers skim the back of his neck, toying with the edge of his dark hair. "It's nice, you know. Hearing all those stories. It means they really love you."

"They tolerate me. Barely." He playfully rolls his eyes.

"They love you," I say again, more firmly. "And they

included me. Like I've always been here," I add more to myself than to him.

In their eyes, we are a couple, something serious and definitive, as if we have already figured out the rest of our lives, unaware that we are far from that outcome.

He's quiet for a beat, watching me like he's trying to solve a puzzle with no rush to the answer. I can't read his thoughts, but there is a bit of longing in his gaze, covered by a layer of uncertainty.

"I think they've already decided you're staying," he says, his voice soft. "Even before we figure it out."

My heart kicks against my ribs. The conversation is too close, too tender, and mirrors my thoughts exactly. It's too important and delicate to talk about here, when anyone could interrupt us, leaving us more confused than we are now. So I cover this seriousness with a grin.

"I mean, after you serenade a girl with her favorite song and fall off a roof, what else is left but marriage?" I wink at him, and a smile spreads across his face, lightening the tension between us.

He laughs, and I kiss the corner of his mouth—just a tease—but when I pull back, he doesn't let go.

He shifts one hand to cup my cheek, fingers tracing my jaw like I'm something rare. The kiss he gives me isn't rushed or playful. It's slow, thorough, and deeply aware of where we are, of the laughter still echoing in the background, of the fact that anyone could see. And someone does.

A whistle cuts through the air, followed by clapping.

"Finally!" Gianna shouts from the table.

Andrea raises his glass. "About time!"

My cheeks flame, but Michele just presses his forehead to mine and chuckles.

"Well," he murmurs, "I guess that makes it official."

"Looks like it," I whisper, not moving from his arms. Because if I move, I'm not sure I can stand on my own. My legs are weak, and my stomach trembles, succumbing to the flutters that are wreaking havoc in my chest.

Five minutes ago, I didn't know how to define our relationship, but now it seems we've chosen a path to follow in the most public way possible. And strangely, it doesn't feel too fast or too exposed. It feels right. Like we've landed in the middle of something we didn't even know we were heading toward, and everyone else already knew.

Under the stars, with summer wrapping us in her warm, fig-scented arms, I kiss him again because I want to, because I can, and let it be known that I'm all in.

Even if I'm terrified of how hard I'm falling.

25

LENA

The scent of wild herbs floats through the open windows of the masseria, mixing with the distant hum of bees and the faint clinking of plates from the kitchen. It's late morning, and the light plays with countless shapes against the whitewashed walls and clay-tiled floors. I'm curled up on the couch in the sitting room, with a book in my lap, and I haven't turned a page of it in fifteen minutes, distracted by the sound of Michele's voice echoing down the hallway as he talks to his father.

Everything feels easy lately. Effortless. Lazy kisses in the garden, naps under the olive trees, meals that last hours. I've never known time to stretch like this. But even in all this calm, there's a pressure building, something we both keep not talking about.

That something comes crashing into our sanctuary less than an hour later. The door slams open, and Marco's voice cuts through the house like a blade.

"I've been calling you for weeks, Michele. Fucking weeks."

I hear footsteps, a low thump of wood on tile, probably Michele's chair pushed back, and I'm already up on my feet, my heart thudding in my chest. I move closer to the doorway, hidden but listening. I shouldn't be eavesdropping, but I justify my action by telling myself I can't understand a word of what they are saying in Italian. But I can guess the vibe of the conversation just hearing the tension in Marco's voice.

"I know," Michele answers, his tone flat.

"You know," Marco repeats, incredulous. "And yet here I am, flying all the way down to the middle of nowhere because you're ignoring every single attempt to reach you. What the hell, Michele? What is this charade with the hot American?"

My stomach drops because I may not know what they are saying, but the Italian word for American is pretty similar for me to recognize in his harsh tone. I guess I'm part of this conversation, but I already knew it because my life is so intertwined with Michele's right now that it's impossible to talk about him without saying my name and vice versa.

I step into the room just in time to see Michele's jaw clench. "Don't talk about her like that."

Marco glances at me, then back at Michele, raising his hands with a guilty expression. "Alright. Sorry. But come on, man. What's going on? You disappear, blow off therapy, and ghost me. We've got press hounding us, sponsors asking questions, and people starting to wonder what's going to happen with your career. You think this is a vacation?"

His tone is frustrated, and his disheveled appearance, a crumpled shirt that has seen better days and creased linen trousers, tells me he is having a rough time. I suspect our impromptu trip is the topic of this argument.

"It's not a vacation," Michele growls.

"Could've fooled me." Marco gestures broadly, his voice rising. "Beautiful estate, wine, romantic countryside… And no physical therapy. No rehab plan. No communication. What am I supposed to tell people?"

Michele moves toward him, chest rising with each breath. "Tell them the truth. That I'm fucked," he says in English, dragging me into the conversation in the worst way possible.

The words drop like a bomb. My breath catches. Marco blinks, caught off guard. There is a long silence where time seems to stand still. Even the cicadas shut up.

"I tore my leg apart six months ago," Michele continues.

"I've done everything. Therapy, trainers, even acupuncture. You name it. And it still hurts when I do anything more than walk. Still buckles when I push too hard. What am I supposed to do, pretend everything's fine? Go back on the field and make it worse?" His tone is so somber, and his words so discouraging, that my heart aches for him.

I know the situation is grim, to say the least, but hearing Michele say it like this to his agent feels so final that my heart bleeds for him.

"You could at least talk to me about it," Marco says, softer now, the conversation switched to English for my sake. "We've been through too much for you to shut me out like this."

Michele shakes his head. "You're not hearing me. I'm not just worried about missing a few matches. I'm worried I've already played my last one."

The room is silent. Even the light breeze outside seems to pause. I press my back against the archway, guilt blooming inside me like a bruise. I'm the one who dragged him through this madness, making him forget what he's worked for all his life. I'm the one who can resume her job anytime, while he's missing an essential part of his rehabilitation as we pretend to be lovers all over Italy.

Marco exhales, then crosses his arms. "Look. If you need time to figure this out, take it. But you can't disappear, Michele. I can't do my job if you cut me out. Either you decide what the hell you want your future to look like…or I walk."

His tone is soft but firm, and I can understand his point. He's doing his job, making Michele look at a reality that he doesn't want to face. But he can't run from it for the rest of his life. At some point, it will catch up with him and make him pay with a vengeance.

Michele doesn't flinch. "So walk."

My breath hitches. My brain is struggling to comprehend the weight of this sentence.

Marco stares at him. "You don't mean that."

But Michele just folds his arms across his chest, jaw tight, emotion flickering behind his eyes. "Maybe I do."

There is no hesitation in his voice. Not a single hint indicating he's saying this purely out of rage, or even spite.

A beat passes. Then Marco turns on his heel and walks out without another word. The front door clicks shut behind him, and it echoes through my bones.

Michele stands still, unmoving. His hands twitch like he doesn't know what to do with them, like his body is physically reacting to a decision that will alter the course of his existence.

I take a step forward. "Michele."

He looks at me then, and the hurt I see guts me. Not just the pain in his leg, or the frustration with his career. It's the helplessness. The fear of losing everything he's worked for and maybe losing himself along with it.

"I'm sorry," I say quietly. "This…all of this. I didn't mean to pull you away from your life."

A knot of guilt forms beneath my ribs.

"You didn't pull me," he says, voice rough. "I walked away from it."

"But if I hadn't…" The words struggle to get past the lump in my throat.

"Lena." He closes the distance between us, cupping the side of my face. "You didn't ruin anything. You're the only part of my life that's made sense lately."

His words hit me like sunlight, blinding and warm. But the guilt doesn't leave because I know there is still a future for him. A future where he can do what he loves and thrive doing it. But he can't see the hope, the light at the end of the dark, cold tunnel he is in right now.

I search his face. "You love playing. I know that. I've seen it in your eyes when you talk about it. I don't want to be the reason you stop."

"You're not," he replies, almost resigned to his new life. "My body is the reason. Not you."

Still, the pressure is building. The scandal I ran from, the paparazzi, the weight of his career teetering on the edge—how can we survive this bubble when the outside world starts pushing back?

I blink fast, pushing back the tears. "I think I got used to pretending none of it matters out here."

He sighs and rests his forehead against mine. "Then let's keep pretending a little longer. It's not that bad living in this fantasy, right?"

I let out a soft laugh, though it sounds like a sob. "God, you're so bad at finding a solution."

He smiles and shrugs. "I usually just kick a ball and score goals. That is what I'm good at, not problem solving."

And this is what terrifies me, because football is his life, and while he's upset now, with his agent's ambush slamming reality in his face, he'll regret his decision not to try and let his fears take the helm of his future.

"You're decent at kissing," I murmur, deciding not to voice my worries.

His arms tighten around me. "Decent?"

I manage a small grin. "Slightly above average."

He kisses me before I can tease him more, slow and full of something I can't name. And in that moment, I feel it again, that deep, gnawing truth: I'm not walking away from this summer whole. I'm already too far in. And falling harder every day. And I think maybe he is too.

THE NIGHT HAS SETTLED OVER THE MASSERIA LIKE A soft blanket, thick with the scent of jasmine and the gentle chirp of crickets. I step out onto the patio, where the stone holds the sun's warmth from earlier. Above me, the sky is black velvet stitched with stars, and through the kitchen window, I catch a glimpse of Michele's mother preparing the sourdough for tomorrow's baking, while his father pours himself a glass of grappa.

They were quieter than usual during dinner. Kind, polite, but subdued. And Michele was practically silent. He spoke in low, clipped tones to his parents all afternoon in the living room, too fast for me to follow. But I didn't need to know Italian to read the tight set of his jaw, the weight in his shoulders, the worried glance his mother cast his way when she thought he wasn't looking.

I've waited all day to talk to him, letting him have space. But now, I need him to let me in. I find him by the olive trees, where the moonlight turns the leaves silver. He's sitting on the low stone wall, elbows on his knees, a beer dangling from one hand.

"You disappeared after dinner," I say softly, walking toward him.

"I needed air," he replies without looking at me.

I sit beside him, close but not touching. We listen to the wind rustling through the branches for a few seconds before I speak again.

"So…are you going to tell me what's gnawing at

you?" I already know the answer, but I need him to acknowledge it too.

He leans back, tipping his face toward the sky. "You saw it. Marco showed up, acted like a dick, and I kicked him out. That pissed me off and put me in a foul mood."

"That's not what I meant." My voice is soft but firm. I don't want him to avoid the conversation again.

His jaw ticks. "Then what do you want me to say, Lena? That I've been lying to myself for months? That my body betrayed me? That the career I built from the time I was a kid might just be gone?"

The words are sharp, but not cruel. More like they're cutting him open as he says them. And they are cutting me, too, deep and sharp and painful. My heart bleeds with him for what he has almost lost.

I don't flinch. I reach out and place my hand over his. "Do you still want to play?"

He looks at me then, really looks. The fire in his eyes is dimmer than it used to be, flickering but not gone.

"Yes." His voice cracks. "God, yes. It's all I've ever wanted. It's all I know how to do."

"Then why does it feel like you've already given up?"

That hits him. He blinks and pulls his hand away, dragging it down his face. There is so much pain and exhaustion in his eyes that I know it's not physical, that his soul is what's carrying the weight of his accident.

"Because maybe I have." His voice is raw now. "Do you know what it's like to go from being at the top, having people chant your name in stadiums, watch you like you're a god, to suddenly wondering if you'll ever run without pain again? I didn't plan for this. I never even thought I'd need to. I thought I had more time." He lets out a bitter laugh. "But time doesn't give a shit. Neither does a mangled leg."

I shift, turning to face him fully. "You don't have to be on top to still love what you do."

He shakes his head. "That's easy for you to say."

"No," I say firmly. "It's not. My whole life blew up back in LA, remember? I lost everything, my image, my credibility, my trust in people, and maybe my career. But I'm still here. Still breathing. Still trying. You don't get to quit just because it got hard."

His eyes lock on mine, and for a moment, I see the storm behind them begin to settle.

"You have money. You have a name. You have people who love you," I continue, softer now. "If you never played another match, you'd still be okay."

He swallows hard, and for the first time since Marco stormed in, I see something real break through his armor. Not pride. Not anger. Just fear.

"I don't know who I am without it," he admits, voice barely above a whisper. "Football is the only version of me I've ever trusted."

I slide my hand back into his. "Then maybe it's time you get to know the rest of yourself while you try to go back. But you should play because it's what you *love* to do, not because you don't want to discover who you really are."

He doesn't respond at first. His gaze drops to our hands, his thumb brushing over my knuckles.

"I think you should get the surgery," I say gently. "If it gives you a shot, even a small one, then you owe it to yourself to try."

He doesn't argue. He just listens.

"It might take time. A lot of time. You might have to fight your way back from the bottom. But if you still love it, really love it, you'll find a way. Not for the fans. Not for Marco. For you. Think back to when you started playing. Was it for the money? For the fame? Or was it just because you loved it?"

A silence stretches between us. The night hums in the background. The stars blink down like they're holding their breath, waiting.

Finally, he turns his face toward me. "How do you do that?"

"Do what?" A small smile curves my lips.

"Cut right through the noise and say exactly what I need to hear," he whispers.

I smile faintly. "It's a gift."

He laughs under his breath and presses his forehead

to mine. "You're not the reason I'm lost, Lena. You might be the reason I find my way again."

My throat tightens. I lean into him, breathing him in, the faint scent of beer and soap and summer skin. His hand comes up to cradle my cheek, and his thumb sweeps across my skin like he's memorizing me.

In the quiet of this grove, with the weight of all we are and everything still unknown, I whisper, "The way to find who you are is in here." I put a hand on his chest. "*The road to you* is through your heart."

He kisses me then. Slow and deep, like an anchor, like a vow. For the first time all day, I feel him begin to come back to himself.

26

LENA

The fan whirs in the corner of the room in lazy, rhythmic circles, stirring the warm summer air just enough to make the sheets flutter over my legs. I lie awake in what has become my bedroom in the last week, staring at the textured plaster overhead, and lulled by the soft creak of the old house around me.

Michele is asleep in the next room. We didn't speak much after our talk beneath the olive trees. We walked back inside holding hands, and his mother offered us a plate of almond cookies without asking questions. He kissed my temple, said he was tired, and disappeared down the hall. I let him go.

Now I lie in a bed that smells faintly of laundry soap and lemon, a lace curtain fluttering at the window, and I wonder if it's possible to live a whole other life in the span of a summer. Because I think I have, and the worst part is, I don't want it to end. But reality doesn't wait just because the stars are beautiful and someone makes you feel seen for the first time in years.

I shift onto my side, pressing a hand to my chest like it'll help hold everything in place. It doesn't, but it's worth a try. The ache is sharp and familiar, that creeping sense that something good is slipping through my fingers, and I can't stop it.

I've been hiding. Not laying low, not healing my broken heart, hiding. The scandal, the press, the endless opinions about me, about my relationship, about what's left of my life, it was too much. So I ran. I told myself I needed time to follow my publicist's advice, and everything would resolve itself. But the truth is, I've been afraid. Afraid to be back in a world where people don't care who I really am, just what they can take from me.

Yet I miss acting. God help me, I do. I miss the rhythm of a set, the smell of coffee and cables, the way everything goes still when someone yells "Action." I miss becoming someone else for a while and finding pieces of myself in the process.

I reach for my phone on the nightstand. It's 2:08 a.m., too late, or early depending on the point of view, to do the math and figure out what time it is in Los Angeles, but I'm pretty sure it's safe to call. I scroll to the contact I haven't called in weeks. *Vivian Blake,* my manager. The only person besides my publicist who kept me in the loop about what Hollywood was thinking of my crumbling love life.

I press call.

It rings once. Twice.

She picks up on the third. "Lena?" Her voice is breathless, but she calms down quickly. "Is everything okay?" I hear ruffling sounds and the thump of someone running on a treadmill. She is at the gym, but then I hear a soft click, followed by silence, and figure she went somewhere quiet to talk.

I sit up, pressing the phone tightly to my ear. "I think I'm ready."

There's a pause. "Ready?" There is surprise in her voice, and maybe a bit of expectation.

"To come back," I say, even if it's not necessary, because she knows me so well, sometimes I don't even need to speak for her to know what I want to do. But this time is different, this entire situation is out of character for me.

I told Michele that he needs to discover himself to understand how vital soccer is for him, and I have to do the same. Throughout my life, I've known what I wanted to do, and I achieved it. But I never stopped to think if I loved acting as much as the romantic idea I have of it. This forced break, this summer, living my life instead of thinking about my next project, has put everything in perspective. I love acting, my life, what I've built, and the path I've paved for myself.

This summer was a magical adventure I will never forget, but it's not my reality, it's not who I am, and I can't live this dream longer without losing myself in the process. My heart aches because it means that I have to leave something behind, something that changed me forever. I have to leave a piece of my soul with the only person who has made me feel seen, alive, and loved. Michele.

Vivian is quiet for a breath, then exhales like she's been holding it for months. "Oh, honey. Are you sure?"

"No." I laugh softly, rubbing my temple. "But I know I can't stay here pretending the rest of my life doesn't exist. It's time."

Another pause, then she lets out another excited breath. "Well, it's good timing. There's something I didn't tell you before."

I blink. "What?"

"There's a director, Alain Faure. He's been asking about you."

The words take some time to register in my brain, but when it happens, my heart stutters. "What? *The* Alain Faure?"

I cover my mouth because my squeal is so loud that everyone can hear me in the silence of the night.

"Yes. He's working on a new project. Big-budget.

Bilingual. People will leave the theater emotionally wrecked. It's dramatic as hell. Your name was the first one out of his mouth. But you were off the radar, so I told him you were taking a break. He respected that. Didn't push. But he's in Rome with his family this week. Vacation. He said he'd be open to a casual meeting if you're nearby."

The underlying excitement in her voice is something I've never heard from her. She's the epitome of calm and professionalism, but this news is so massive that she can't hide her enthusiasm. And neither can I. This is the chance I've been waiting for—the big movie that could launch my career to a whole new level.

And he's in Rome. Five hours away. If that's not fate, I don't know what is.

"I can set it up," she continues, her tone gentle now, like she knows this means slicing something open in me. "You don't have to commit. Just meet him. Talk. See how it feels."

My fingers tighten around the phone. I stare out the window, where the moon hangs low over the fields. The same moon that Michele is sleeping under. I think about the way he kissed me last night, like he meant it, as if it were a beginning and not just a beautiful ending.

"I'll go," I whisper.

Vivian doesn't say *I told you so.* She just says, "I'll

send the details this evening, or morning for you. And Lena?"

"Yeah?" I whisper.

"I'm proud of you." Her voice is so soft that it makes my heart break even further.

After I hang up, I sit there in the quiet, the decision echoing through my bones. My chest feels full and empty at the same time, like I'm gaining something and losing something all at once. Because how do you say goodbye to a summer that felt like freedom? To a man who looked at you like you were more than your broken pieces?

You don't. Not yet. But I know in my heart this is my path to follow.

THE SUN IS STARTING TO SET BEHIND THE OLIVE TREES, casting a golden glow across the gravel paths of the masseria. The sky is a watercolor of apricot and lavender, and the air smells like rosemary, with a hint of a storm that never came.

Michele is in the courtyard, sitting on the low stone wall with a bottle of Peroni in his hand. He hasn't seen me yet. His gaze is far away, like he's watching the wind move through the leaves but not really seeing any of it. I hesitate in the doorway for a beat, heart thudding too loud in my chest. Then I step outside and walk toward him, each step heavier than it should be.

He looks up when he hears me, offering me a soft smile that doesn't quite reach his eyes. "You okay?"

I nod and take the seat beside him, leaving just enough space for the words we haven't said yet to settle between us. "I called Vivian last night."

His brows lift slightly, but he doesn't speak. He just waits, because he knows me now, he knows I'll get there in my own time.

I press my palms against the rough edge of the wall, grounding myself. "There's a director. A big one. He wants to meet me. He's in Rome this week."

There is a beat of silence, one that stretches our hearts. Michele's gaze is focused on me, but I'm not brave enough to look at him. Not yet.

Then he asks, gently, "Are you going?"

There is no annoyance in his voice, not a hint of anger, just a subtle hurt he is trying hard to hide. He won't make a scene, he won't make me feel guilty for it, but it doesn't mean I don't feel it just the same, deep in my gut.

I nod. "It's just a meeting. No commitment. But I need to go." I finally look him in the eyes, and my heart breaks a little bit more.

He looks down at the bottle in his hands. His fingers tighten around the neck like he's holding back something he doesn't want me to see. Hurt. Not because he doesn't want to appear vulnerable, but to make the choice easier for me. At this point, I know enough about Michele that I'm certain he is doing it for me, not for him.

"That's good, Lena. I'm glad."

But his voice cracks a little on *glad*.

I swallow the lump in my throat. "I didn't plan for this. I wasn't running from work when I came here, I just I needed to take a break for a while. And then I found you. Or maybe you found me." I laugh softly, but it's tight, frayed at the edges. "And now I don't know how to leave."

He turns to me, his eyes so full of everything he can't say. "You're not leaving, Lena. You're going after something that matters to you."

His voice is soft and desperate at the same time. In this moment, I know he loves me as much as I love him, and this awareness makes my breath catch in my throat. This is the Michele I've come to know. Loving, selfless, and always doing the right thing when it comes to the people he loves. The same man who bought this house to repay his family for the sacrifices they made for him, the man who picked up a broken heart in Milan and healed it one smile at a time. A man who will live forever in my heart.

"And you?"

His jaw clenches. "What about me?"

"You matter to me." The confession slips out of my mouth, and I don't regret it because I need his help to find the strength to go to Rome and not fall apart.

He closes his eyes for a moment, like he's bracing himself against something invisible and overwhelming. When he opens them again, they're shining. "You matter to me too."

There's a silence that stretches, long and full and aching. Then he says, "You should go to Rome. Meet this director. Take the job if it feels right for you. The world hasn't seen the best of you yet."

His words hit me hard in the chest.

"I'm afraid," I whisper.

"Of what?"

"That this, what we have, will just fade when I leave. That it'll turn into some dreamy memory of a summer that never had a chance."

He exhales hard, then reaches for my hand, threading his fingers through mine. "It won't fade for me."

My chest aches. "I wish I could stay."

He leans in, pressing his forehead to mine. "And I wish I could ask you to."

I close my eyes. "But we both know we can't."

His thumb brushes against my wrist, slow and tender. "I knew this would end. I just didn't know it would hurt like this."

I nod. "I didn't think I'd fall in love with you."

His breath catches. He pulls back just far enough to look me in the eyes. "You did?"

He seems genuinely surprised, and I can't stop a small smile from escaping my lips.

"Of course I did," I say softly. "How could I not?"

His lips part, like he's about to speak, but then he just wraps his arms around me and pulls me in tight, burying his face in my neck. I hold him just as hard, feeling the tremble in his body, the quiet heartbreak we're both pretending we can survive.

When he finally pulls away, his voice is barely audible. "I love you, Lena."

Tears blur my vision. "I love you, too, Michele."

We sit there in the last golden light of the day, clinging to something we can't name, something bigger than either of us. Something we didn't plan, but that happened in the sweetest way, and that changed us both. And even though I'm leaving, even though Rome, and everything after, is waiting, a small part of me hopes that love is enough to find its way back.

27

MICHELE

The air is still cool when I slip out from under the sheets, careful not to wake Lena. She's curled on her side, one hand under her cheek, the other stretched toward the space I just left. For a moment, I just stand there watching her softly breathing, tangled hair, the early morning sun painting gold along her bare shoulder.

We didn't have the strength to sleep in separate rooms last night, not after the confession that broke our hearts into a thousand pieces. If my parents complain about it, I'll explain, but I think my mother already knows what happened. Her eyes never left Lena and me during dinner, her mother's intuition ramped up to a higher level, if that's even possible.

I step outside, basking in the scent of coffee and freshly-baked bread. Under the pergola, the world is silent except for the soft rustling of olive branches and the distant coo of doves waking with the sun. I sit on the stone bench and rest my elbows on my knees, pressing my palms together. My leg gives its usual throb, a quiet, cruel reminder of what might never be again.

Marco's words echo in my head like a bell I can't un-ring. *"Make a decision or I walk."* He's not wrong. I've been floating. Avoiding the mirror. The rehab. The calls. Hell, my own thoughts. But my talk with Lena last night brought everything back in full force, slamming against me, pushing me down, suffocating the breath in my lungs, and squeezing my heart in my chest.

She made the decision for both of us, and even though I wasn't ready, I'm glad she did. The bubble we've been living in was always meant to pop at some point, and I knew it would hurt. Just not this much.

"You're up early," Mamma says from behind me. I turn as she pads over in her house slippers, her cardigan pulled tight around her body even though it's already warm.

"Couldn't sleep," I murmur.

She sits beside me without another word. I don't speak either. We just sit there for a long moment, the kind of moment only mothers and sons know how to share.

Then she asks softly, "What's bothering you, *tesoro mio*?"

I let the breath out slowly. "Marco gave me an ultimatum. He says he'll drop me if I don't make up my mind about how to fix my leg. About playing again."

"And what do you want to do?" Her voice is soft, like every time she guides her kids through a difficult decision.

She has always been like that, always listening, always the light of reason in our confused minds.

"That's the problem." I rub a hand over my face. "I don't know. I keep waiting to wake up with clarity, to just know. But instead, I keep waking up like this: tired, confused, angry."

She hums, watching the olive trees sway. "Why do you think it's so hard for you to decide?"

I stare at the ground, at the tiny cracks in the stones between my feet. "Because what if I say yes, and I fail? What if I try everything and still can't play like I used to?" My voice tightens. "What if I've already reached the top and I'm just falling now?"

The only thing I know for sure is that I love to play, I don't want to do anything else in my life, but it may not be possible for me anymore, and I have to decide on the next chapter of my life.

She's quiet, but when she speaks, her voice is gentle. "And would that be such a terrible thing?"

I blink at her, surprised by her words. I expected some pep talk on how to conquer my fears, but not this.

"You've played football since you were six. You gave up birthday parties, school trips, and summers with your friends. You missed weddings. You trained in the rain, the snow, injured or not. You gave everything to the game, Michele." She puts her hand over mine. "You gave your youth."

I swallow hard, unable to look her in the eyes.

"You lived the dream of millions of boys," she continues. "You won trophies. Wore the national team jersey. You were loved, still are. Maybe now it's time to collect the rewards from all of that." There is a hint of something she is not telling me, but I have an idea about what it is.

Lena. She saw me happier than she's ever seen me. Hell, I was never that happy in my life, not even when I won everything it's possible to win with my team. Because Lena makes me feel happy in a more complete, grounded way.

I shake my head, but my chest starts to constrict, not like heartache. It's tighter, sharper. Like the room is shrinking around me, except I'm outside in the open.

I grip the edge of the bench, breathing through my nose. But my throat is thick. My fingers tremble.

"Michele?"

"I don't want to stop," I choke. "I don't want it to end

like this. I want it to end on my own terms. When I'm ready to let it go."

And the truth of it, the clarity I've been waiting for, punches through me so hard I think I might fall over. My lungs burn, but I gasp through it, sucking air like I'm surfacing after drowning.

"I don't want to give up," I say again, steadier this time. "Even if it's hard. Even if it takes months, even if I never make it back to the top, I need to try. I need to know I didn't walk away when I still had something left." Even if it means losing Lena for good.

Mamma exhales, and it sounds like relief.

"Well," she says, squeezing my hand, "then there's your answer."

I nod, my throat still tight.

She tilts her head toward me. "And if tomorrow you change your mind, and you decide you'd rather move to Hollywood and become an actor with Lena, I'll support you all the same." There is a hint of amusement in her voice that she can't hide.

I huff a laugh, wiping the corner of my eye, realizing a tear escaped. "I don't think I'd be very good in front of a camera."

"No," she agrees with a smile, "but you'd look good doing it."

I laugh again, the panic in my chest fading, replaced

with something steadier. It's still uncertain, still painful, but grounded now in purpose.

"Do what makes you happy, Michele," she says, standing. "That's all I've ever wanted for you. You don't owe anyone anything. Not the fans. Not Marco. Not even me. Just your heart."

She kisses the top of my head, the way she did when I was a boy, then disappears into the house, leaving me there with the olive trees and the sky and the thrum of my pulse finally settling into something I can carry.

I lean back, close my eyes, and let it all settle. I'm not done yet. Not with football. Not with her. Not with this life.

THE SKY IS FULLY AWAKE NOW, STREAKED WITH PURPLE and pink, and the scent of jasmine floats on the breeze. Lena is still asleep, and the house is quiet except for the distant clinking of breakfast plates and the occasional coo of a dove.

I sit with the phone in my hand for a full minute before I make the call. My thumb hovers over Marco's name, heart thudding against my ribs like a warning or a promise, I'm not sure which.

Then I press the screen. He picks up on the second ring.

"Well," he says, voice dry but tight at the edges. "The prodigal finally returns."

"*Ciao*, Marco," I say, trying to keep my tone even. "Got a minute?"

"For you? After you ghosted me for weeks? Ignored texts, calls, my actual physical presence?" He lets out a sound, somewhere between a sigh and a bark of laughter. "Sure, I've got a minute."

I close my eyes for a second, half smiling at his words, half feeling guilty. "I needed time."

"You could've told me you were still breathing. Just a text. Even an emoji," he points out bluntly, as usual. This is why I chose him all those years ago. He doesn't sugarcoat anything, but he's always been fair and loyal.

"I know. I'm sorry."

There's a pause. And then, softer, "Are you okay?"

"No," I say honestly. "But I'm getting there."

Another beat of silence. "So why the call?"

I know he's wondering if I want to go back or give up entirely. His ultimatum was real, not something he said out of anger or spite. It was his way of waking me up and making me realize I had to make a decision.

"I want back in," I say more firmly than I expected my voice to sound.

He exhales like he's been holding that breath for days, since he left my parents' house in a fury. "Finally. Thank God."

"I'm serious," I say, sitting up straighter. "I've thought about it. I'm not done. I can't walk away from soccer without giving it everything I've got first, even if it's hard, even if it's slow. I want to play again."

"Okay," Marco says, his tone shifting into business immediately. "I'll see what I can… Well, no. I'll tell you the truth."

"Go ahead." I already know it will be a hard truth to swallow.

"I never stopped looking, even when you were MIA. But the interest right now is from minor teams. Nothing from *Serie A* or abroad. Everyone's watching your leg like it's a ticking time bomb. No one wants to commit without knowing if you'll fully recover, or when. The uncertainty is a red flag."

I let out a slow breath, lowering my head into my palm. I grit my teeth, but I expected this. "I get it. No one bets on a broken horse."

"Michele…" he starts softly.

"I'm not mad," I cut in. "I just need you to keep the door open. Please let them know that I'm working on getting answers. I'll meet with the surgeon again, get a better idea of the timeline, and start the recovery for real this time. PT, the scans, everything. I'll send you updates so you've got something concrete to pitch. But for now, if a lower league team wants me, I'll listen."

"You serious?" he sounds surprised.

And when I search for words to answer his question, I realize it's the truth. I just want to play. "Yeah. I need the practice. I need the ball at my feet again. Even if it's not a stadium full of screaming fans."

Marco lets out a breath. "This is the first real conversation we've had in months. It's good to have you back."

"It's good to be back," I say, and I mean it.

"Okay," he says. "Give me a week. I'll start putting feelers out again. And let me know the second you get confirmation from the surgeon. If we can give them a timeline, even a vague one, that changes everything."

"I will."

There is a pause, a long one pregnant with meaning.

"And Michele?"

"Yeah?"

"I'm proud of you. For calling. For not giving up."

I stare out at the olive grove, the breeze stirring the branches. It's the first time I've heard something like this coming from his lips. He's never been one to hand out compliments; advice, yes, but not praise. It's almost overwhelming.

"Thanks," I say. "But I'm not doing this for pride."

"Then what?"

I smile. "For myself. For the game. To discover what I'm capable of doing when I'm not effortlessly at the top. For the girl still asleep in my bed."

Marco chuckles. "You're a romantic under all that charm, huh?"

"Always have been," I mutter, ending the call with a smirk.

I set the phone down beside me and let the stillness wrap around me again. This is the beginning of the climb, and this time, I'm not afraid of the fall.

28

LENA

The car is packed, the sun is barely over the horizon, and everyone is in the courtyard like we're leaving for a six-month expedition across the globe instead of a five-hour drive to Rome.

Michele's mother hugs me for what feels like the hundredth time, whispering, "*Mangia bene, dormi bene, e ricordati che qui hai sempre una casa.*" Eat well, sleep well, and remember, you always have a home here.

My throat tightens.

She tucks something else into my arms, another bag. "*Focaccia,* the one you like. And some *taralli.* And this olive oil is from our own trees. Don't let airport security take it, eh?"

I laugh, but my eyes are stinging. "*Grazie,* really. I don't even know how to say thank you for everything."

"Say it by coming back," she says, cupping my face and caressing it like I'm her daughter.

She has no idea what this means to me. It feels like I'm not only leaving Puglia and Italy soon, but I'm leaving behind Michele and a new family that accepted me as their own. I've never felt so emotionally unstable in my entire life, and I barely manage to keep my tears at bay. When I came to Italy a few months ago, I thought I would eat well, relax a bit, and take my life slowly. But I found more, so much more.

She squeezes my hands tightly before letting go, and I glance around the courtyard. It smells like olive trees and morning dew. It's warm, like a memory you don't want to let go of. Michele's father hugs me with a firm but affectionate pat on the back. Even Mariasole, Michele's sister, has come down to say goodbye.

It's surreal how loved I feel here. It's as if I've slipped into someone else's life and found it fits better than my own. Michele's cousin, Martina, tears up as she waves a dishtowel like a flag. "Don't forget us when you're in Hollywood again!"

She makes me smile, and I blow her a kiss. "Only if you forget I was the one who beat you at *burraco* four times in a row."

They all laugh. There are more hugs, more cheek kisses, more well wishes in fast, melodic Italian. I don't catch every word, but I catch the meaning.

Love. Fondness. Belonging.

Way too soon, we're walking toward the car, the trunk already full of bags and wrapped-up care packages. My arms are overflowing with food, my heart overflowing with something I don't have the words for.

I glance at Michele. He's quiet, too quiet.

He is not the playful, talkative, teasing version of himself that comes out around his family. His shoulders are tense as he loads the last bag, like he's bracing for something heavy. I understand his feelings, because they're the same ones that weigh in my chest.

Once we're in the car, and the gravel crunches beneath the tires, I turn toward him. The road winds ahead, but I watch his profile instead.

"You're quiet," I say.

He hums in response, eyes on the road. I understand being sad because you're leaving your family, but he's not disappearing from the world; he's just accompanying me to Rome. He seems almost angry, and I don't understand this reaction from him.

"You've never been this quiet with your family around. Did I do something? Are you mad I'm dragging you away from them?"

His grip on the steering wheel tightens for half a second before he releases it. He forces a smile, but it's the kind that barely touches his eyes. "Everything's fine, Lena."

I know it's not. I also know that this journey is coming to an end, and my heart is torn, but I'm not getting angry. I'm just trying to figure out what to do to survive.

"Michele," I say gently, "you're a terrible liar."

He exhales, slow and heavy, but doesn't answer immediately.

"I just don't want to talk about it, Lena," he finally says in a whisper, letting me see the Michele I've come to know. The caring, sweet one.

I can do that. I can give him the time he needs to process everything that's happened in the last few days.

I let the silence hang between us like a question neither of us wants to answer. Outside the window, the landscape shifts from rows of olive trees to busier streets, from the peace of the masseria to the sound of other cars. I already miss the courtyard, the clink of plates, his mother's singing in the kitchen, the warmth of that house, which felt like it had roots, history, and love in its walls.

But the silence inside the car is louder than anything outside, and it tells me something else: this summer, whatever it was, whatever it became, is ending, and what waits ahead in Rome feels different.

More like reality. Definitely like goodbye. I don't know yet if I'm ready for either.

THE COUNTRYSIDE ROLLS BY IN SHADES OF GOLD AND green, but I hardly see it.

The road trip to Rome is silent. Not the kind of comfortable silence we've shared before, when words weren't necessary and his hand rested on my thigh and we laughed when a song we both loved came on the radio.

This silence is suffocating.

Michele keeps his eyes on the road, one hand on the wheel, the other fidgeting on his knee. I keep thinking he'll say something. A joke, a sigh, a comment about the sheep crossing the road an hour ago. But nothing comes. I don't know what to say either. What do you say to a man who said I love you, and you said it back, and that you are leaving for good? There are no words that can fill the silence between us, as there are no words to fill the emptiness carved in my chest.

The hum of the tires on the asphalt fills the space between us, louder than it should be. Every kilometer we drive feels like peeling away from something I'm not ready to leave. It's strange how something can feel so much like the beginning and the end at the same time.

I glance at him, hoping to catch his eyes, but he doesn't look at me. He's somewhere else entirely. And that, more than anything, makes the ache spread through my whole body. Michele is not in this car with me. He is in a place I can't reach, somewhere else entirely, that doesn't include me.

I know what this is. It's the unraveling. It's the slow slipping of something beautiful through my fingers, like sand I can't hold onto no matter how hard I try. It's a feeling I'm finally experiencing in its full force, and it's washing over me like a wave I can't contain.

I always knew this summer had an expiration date. We left Milan without a plan. We built a bubble out of sunrises and wine and midnight swims and mornings tangled in each other. But real life was always waiting. Watching. Tapping its foot. We pretended it wasn't there. We gave it our backs and laughed, ignored its calling. But that doesn't mean it didn't exist. We knew that at some point it would outrun us, but we thought we were faster, smarter, immune to its pull.

We were wrong.

I just didn't expect it to hurt like this. I didn't expect that I'd want to stay so badly. I didn't expect *him* to mean so much to me.

Michele shifts in his seat, adjusting the hem of his T-shirt that is rising up, and I watch the way his jaw tightens. The way he doesn't reach for my hand. The way he closes himself off.

Michele is slipping away from me, and I don't know how to stop it. I don't even know if I *should* stop it. Even if I could, what's the cost? Maybe we prolong the ache a bit longer, hoping it will be better when our lives take two different paths? It won't get better, it will get ugly, because our frustration and resentment will get mixed in with the beautiful thing we have. I want to treasure this summer in my heart as the best journey of my life. I don't want it to become something we fight over.

I turn to the window and press my forehead to the glass, hoping the coolness will calm the heat in my chest. But it doesn't. The pressure there is sharp. Real. Like heartbreak already half-formed, waiting for the final blow.

I thought I was strong enough for this. I thought I could say goodbye when the time came, but I'm not ready. Not even a little. And I think, maybe for the first time, that I don't want this summer to be the end of our story.

29

LENA

The lobby of the Hotel de Russie is the epitome of quiet elegance with its soft-spoken guests, clinking porcelain, and the faint rustle of designer shoes against marble floors. Everything about this place screams luxurious Italian vacation, and I'm not surprised that Alain Faure chose it to spend time with his family. If he needed a space to relax far from the Hollywood chaos, this is *the* choice.

Lush gardens surround this place, and luxurious small alcoves dot the hotel and the surrounding area, providing guests with space to spend time in privacy while enjoying the amenities, such as the bars serving colorful delicacies for dessert.

I spot him instantly. The director, the visionary, the one whose films have won awards I used to dream about from the back seat of my mom's car. Alain Faure is the most sought-after director for every actor who wants a legitimate chance at winning an Oscar. He doesn't do blockbusters or mainstream movies, but he's gained the kind of recognition that assures you every movie he makes is an Oscar nominee contender.

He doesn't even make movies very often, releasing one every three to five years, and that's why it's such a big deal that he asked for me.

He's sitting in the corner, tucked into a velvet armchair near the windows that let in the kind of Roman light that makes everything look like a movie. His signature round glasses are perched on his nose as he frowns over a bunch of papers he is reading. He's known for not using technology; he prefers old-school scripts printed on paper.

The closer I get to him, the tighter the grip on my stomach. I've had hundreds of auditions, screen tests, and talks with various directors and colleagues throughout my career, but he still manages to intimidate me. When he sees me, he stands with a warm smile, his expression familiar and curious.

"Lena," he says, like we've known each other forever.

We shake hands and sit. There's already a cappuccino waiting for me, a small gesture that makes my heart flutter. He didn't need to find out I'm addicted to coffee, but he obviously did his research. He studies me like he's trying to read my soul. His gaze isn't creepy, just intense. Intentional. Like he's flipping through invisible pages of me in his mind. And I squirm under his scrutiny.

"I've watched everything you've done," he says, voice low and rich with his French accent. "Even the films you pretend don't exist."

I started my career as a child actress, but when it came to working with prominent actors, I had to begin at the bottom, gaining respect through less polished movies, if you can call them that. I don't regret those movies. They were part of my training to become better at my work, but that doesn't mean I'm not embarrassed when people bring them up in conversation.

I laugh, blushing. "That's bold of you to admit."

"It's part of my job. I don't just want an actress. I want a woman who can haunt the screen. And you—" He gestures toward me, eyes lighting up like a man seeing the solution to a riddle. "You *are* her."

Hearing something like that come out of Alain's mouth is like a storm hitting your face. You don't understand what's happening, you're disoriented, but you know deep in your gut that this is something massive that could change your life.

"Her?" I ask, wrapping my hands around the warm cup, trying to ground myself with the warmth radiating from the ceramic.

He leans forward slightly. "The protagonist. The center of the storm. The woman who has to confront the darkest corners of her mind after a brutal trauma. It's a psychological thriller that delves deeply into the complexities of the human brain. Huge budget. Complex script. No open casting for her. I wrote this character with you in mind."

I stop mid-sip and almost choke on my cappuccino. Vivian told me he wanted me specifically, but she didn't mention that he wrote the script *for* me. What god did I please to be noticed by him?

I blink. "Seriously?"

He nods, and his eyes sparkle with excitement, leaving me breathless.

"I've seen what you can do," he says, with absolute certainty. "And no one else can give her the edge and the fragility she needs. No one else makes me believe she's real."

My heart thunders in my chest, and my breath catches. I haven't felt like this in so long. Wanted. Seen. Not in my job, at least. Because Michele makes me feel all those things together and even more. My heart makes a flip thinking about him, but I focus my attention on the man in front of me.

I'm not just a gossip headline in his eyes, but an artist. A woman with something to say, something to give. This is the most empowering compliment someone could give me, and I smile timidly, not sure if I can live up to his expectations.

"Send the script to my manager," I say, a little breathless. "I'll read it as soon as I get the chance."

He nods, satisfied. "Take your time. But not too much," he adds with a grin. "We want to shoot this fall."

I nod, and I feel the knot in my stomach relax a bit.

We chat a bit longer about the production, the cast he's assembling, and the composer he's trying to lure in. Every word stokes the fire in my gut that I thought had gone out after everything that happened this year. When you're focused on saving your reputation, everything else gets dragged through the mud that the magazines stir up. Michele and this journey across Italy did a good job of taking my mind off of my problems, but it also made me forget what I'm meant to be. An actress. An artist.

Something else slips into my chest, warming me from the inside out. Maybe everything that's happened to me lately was meant to guide me in this place. Maybe it was fate guiding me through Italy with a man who made me discover myself, only to end up a mere five hours away from this hotel, from this life-changing moment.

Fate was just waiting for something like this to happen.

When we finally stand to say goodbye, Alain takes my hand and squeezes it lightly. "It's good to see your eyes sparkling with excitement, Lena. That's how I know I've found my lead."

My legs buckle slightly, but I work to stand tall and smile. I thank him, not sure how I manage to walk out of the hotel without floating straight into the Roman sky.

Outside, the sun hits me full in the face. It's warm and blinding and unapologetically bright. And I smile like an idiot, like a child, like someone who just remembered who she is.

I'm back, and whatever happens next, I'm ready.

MICHELE

The room smells like antiseptic and polished metal. It's too clean, too cold, too quiet.

I sit on the edge of the examination table in a pair of gym shorts, my knee bouncing with nerves I can't hide. Across from me, the specialist, the man everyone swears is the best in the country, clicks through images on a screen mounted to the wall. X-rays, scans, my history in shades of black and bone.

Marco and the orthopedist who followed my recovery helped me find this doctor and secure an appointment in just one day. They performed a miracle, considering it's a two-year-long waiting list. I don't know what they promised him, but at this point, I don't care. I would do anything to fix this crippled leg. And the bonus is that he has a private office in Rome.

Being here helps me not think about the fact that Lena, right now, is meeting with the director, and she is probably changing our future completely. I don't blame her for accepting this meeting. It's her career, and I totally support this decision, but that doesn't mean it doesn't hurt.

We've reached the end of the line, and we both know it. We've always known that after the summer, we would return to our normal lives. Just now, I'm realizing how much I'm not ready for this to happen.

The doctor doesn't speak at first, just makes a low sound in the back of his throat as he studies the mess inside my leg.

"It looks almost clean from the outside," he says eventually, turning toward me. "But inside, it's a different story."

I nod. I've known that for months. What I didn't know was *how* bad it really was. Now that he's high-lighted the different shapes in my muscles with red marks on the screen, I start to understand how many scars are hidden underneath my skin. Not the visible ones on the surface that are slowly fading. There's a constellation of more subtle ones running up and down my muscles like small, creepy worms.

He gestures for me to stand, and I do. My leg tightens the moment I straighten it, like it's trying to protect itself. I'm constantly guarding it, always bracing for the pain to shoot up my leg and spine. He runs me through a series of strength tests, including balance drills, resistance band exercises, and uneven step challenges. By the end, sweat clings to my shirt, and my thigh feels like it's going to give out.

"You okay?" he asks.

His tone is even, but there is a concern behind his stern composure that unnerves me.

I shrug. "It hurts."

His gaze softens a fraction.

"Of course it hurts," he says, tapping his pen against my file. "And it's going to keep hurting. That's the point."

He sits, wheels himself closer, and points to one of the scans. "Your injury—" he makes a big circle with his fingers around the black shades of the scan, "—it didn't just tear the muscle. It mangled it. It tried to regenerate, but the healing process went wrong. Scar tissue formed in all the wrong places. That's why it can't stretch or respond like it should. You're compensating with other muscle groups just to walk."

I clench my jaw. I already knew something wasn't right. I've felt it every single morning. Every time I try to run. Every time I imagine myself on the field again, my body screams *no* before I even move. Those small strikes across the muscle are the reason for that.

"So…what's the solution?"

He shifts slightly, and his voice is steady. "Surgery. A very specific one. We'd need to remove the scarred tissue and reconstruct the muscle. In your case, I recommend a muscle flap transfer. We take healthy muscle from another part of your body, typically the other thigh or the back, and use it to reinforce and rebuild the damaged one. Along with tendon work."

That sounds ominous. No way would I let him touch my healthy leg, but even my back is a bit concerning. I can't play with a messed-up back.

I stare at him, the words landing slowly. "So I'd have…two injuries? Temporarily?"

"Yes. You'd need rehab on both the donor site and your leg. But—" he holds up a hand, "—this procedure has a decent success rate in athletes like you. I'm confident that we can help you regain your full strength. Not just walking. Not just jogging. Playing."

Decent success rate is not very encouraging. "So why did no one want to do the surgery before if it's that easy?"

The doctor inhales deeply and takes his time to answer. I like that.

"Probably because the risks are significant. The part of the muscle that we have to replace is bigger than usual, and considering how your recovery went the first time, they probably don't want the risk"

I open my mouth to object, but he raises a hand to stop me.

"But I wasn't with you right after the accident. I wasn't in the OR, and I don't know what doctors were dealing with, but I've seen enough injuries in my career to *know* that they were trying to save your life and your leg. They had to repair major arteries, stop the bleeding, and try to put together the bones without amputating the leg. They did a great job with the bones. We wouldn't be here talking about another surgery if that weren't the case. Additionally, as an athlete, all the muscles in your body work together to support the injured leg, and you can't underestimate this. It's a risky surgery, yes, but it's worth the risk."

I appreciate his honesty, but I want to understand all my possibilities here.

A breath escapes me, half relief, half terror. "And if I don't do the surgery?"

His voice softens. "Then you'll keep losing strength. You might still walk fine. Live a normal life. But playing professionally at your level? You'll never get there without intervention. The leg simply can't function the way it needs to."

Silence falls in the room, and I can hear my heart beating so fast I'm afraid it's going to explode out of my chest. I stare at the scans again, my own failure mapped in shades of gray. The fear hits me like a low wave, rolling heavy in my chest. What if I go through with the surgery and still don't make it? What if I lose both sets of muscles and I'm worse off than before?

"I don't just want to play," I say, more to myself than to him. "I want to feel like me again."

"And you can," he says, meeting my eyes. "But not if you keep avoiding the hard part."

I nod slowly, breathing in through my nose.

"Let me know when you're ready to schedule," he says, standing.

I look at my leg. Then back at the screen. He's so sure I can do it that it makes me nervous. I consider everything I've built, everything I've lost. The dream I've held in my hands since I was a kid.

And then I think of Lena, her voice when she said, *"You don't have to play for them. Play because you love it."* I still love it. I haven't stopped, and that's enough to face the fear.

"Okay," I say, finally. "Let's do it."

31

LENA

I haven't moved from this spot in over two hours.

My legs are curled beneath me on the hotel bed, the duvet slightly twisted, and my laptop is warm on my thighs. A cappuccino has long gone cold on the nightstand, untouched since the first ten pages.

I can't tear my eyes away from the screen. The words, the scenes, the dialogue, they hit me like electricity. This script is *alive*. It wraps itself around me, the way all good stories do when you forget you're just reading lines and start *living* them. The character is raw, wounded, complicated. She is someone who has everything on the outside but nothing holding her up inside. She's spiraling. She's haunting. She's unforgettable.

By page thirty, I already know how I'd play her.

By page fifty, I can *feel* her in my blood.

This isn't just a movie. This is *the one*.

I close the script and lean back on the pillows, breathless. My heart is pounding like I just sprinted for miles. I stare at the ceiling, smiling like a lunatic, clutching the laptop as if I can absorb the script and make it mine.

This could change everything. Not just a comeback, but a *breakthrough*. The kind of role they write about in *Variety*. The kind that gets whispered about during awards season. The kind that earns you respect in a town that forgets women like me by the time they turn thirty.

Alain Faure directing it changes everything for a completely different reason. I won't be Preston Livestone's girlfriend anymore. I will be Lena Sinclair, the actress who played the lead role for one of the best directors of our time. Yes, Preston is a great director; he gave me the chance to shine in so many roles, and I will give him that. But they were always talked about like couples' projects, with our names intertwined. I couldn't fully shine on my own. With this movie, I have the chance to prove myself again and leave my past behind, including the part that ties me to Preston.

I blink fast while a slow breath melts the tightness. This could make them remember me even when I'm old, like the great names in Hollywood history, legends who stay in people's memories for a long, long time.

I grab my phone without thinking. My fingers move faster than my thoughts, dialing Vivian's number.

She answers before the first ring is over. "Tell me everything."

"I *love* it," I blurt, still half laughing. "Vivian, I *love* it so much I want to call the director right now and tell him yes before I even see the damn contract."

She exhales with a pleased tone in her voice. "I had a feeling. He's serious, Lena. He's not shopping this around. He wants *you*."

"I can't believe this is happening," I say, standing now, pacing the soft carpet of the hotel room. "It's everything I didn't know I was waiting for. The story, the tension, the way it sits in your chest. God, I've missed this. I've missed feeling like this."

And it's true. While I loved playing the roles in my previous movies, I always felt like something was missing. They were good movies. I'm not complaining about them or even regretting them, but they weren't special. At least, not anything that makes my heart pound in anticipation.

Vivian doesn't speak right away. I hear her typing, and she is probably already sending follow-up emails. "Then let's do it. I'll tell him you're interested and get the studio on a timeline. I'll make sure the contract reflects the kind of performance this will demand. We'll negotiate hard, Lena, but this is yours if you want it."

"I want it," I whisper, stopping by the window.

As soon as those words leave my lips, I can feel the rush of adrenaline pumping in my veins. I shiver, feeling the excitement grow inside my chest, making my heart beat erratically.

Rome sprawls outside in front of me, drenched in sun and marble and afternoon light. I press my hand to the glass, feeling the city alive even from behind it. I've never believed in fate, at least not like something that guides your life without you having a say in it, but this feels a lot like fate. It's the butterfly effect where all the pieces fall perfectly into place. Even the heartbreak of Preston cheating is a long-ago memory that doesn't feel real anymore.

"I want it so bad I can taste it," I confess.

I hear Vivian chuckle slightly on the phone. I can imagine her leaning forward in her office chair, smiling, and typing away on her laptop, as if she already knew I would accept it. And maybe she did. She has been with me for so many years, she knows exactly what I like and what I don't, and this is the movie we've patiently waited for.

"All right, then," Vivian says. "Let me go move mountains."

The call ends, and I let the phone drop to the bed. I rest my forehead against the window, the smile still spreading across my face. For a second, I let it all sink in.

I bask in the silence, the possibility, the *certainty* that this encounter brought into my life.

Then I step back, walk to the small balcony, and push open the doors. The sun hits me like applause—warm, full, and vast as the sky. I close my eyes and laugh softly, the kind of laugh that comes from your chest when you *know* something is about to change.

I feel like I'm right where I'm meant to be.

32

LENA

When the door clicks behind him, I'm still in my robe, standing on the balcony with the city buzzing below. I turn, my heart lifting automatically at the sight of him, until I see his face. Michele strolls into the room at a slow pace, almost dragging his feet.

Something's off.

His eyes are tired and a little dull, like the light inside him has been dimmed. His jaw is tight, his shoulders tense. I realize with a jolt that I don't even know where he went. We didn't talk about it. Didn't plan it. He just left this morning, and I was too distracted by my own excitement to ask.

I feel bad about it now. Michele does not do things without a reason, and I'm sure he didn't just go for a stroll the entire afternoon. He kept it from me for some reason I can't understand, or maybe because he wanted to give me space to get my thoughts together about the script and the encounter with Alain. But I don't accept being cut off from his life, not now that we're close enough to trust each other. Not now that it's all coming to an end.

"Hey," I say softly. "Where were you?"

He doesn't smile, doesn't come close, like my presence is somehow making him uncomfortable. It hurts, but I don't point it out.

He waves a hand, brushing it off. "Nowhere important."

His tone is clipped, like he is trying hard not to be harsh in my face, but I can see the tension in the set of his jaw and how his eyes scan the room without meeting mine.

I blink. "Seriously?"

My tone is pissed enough that he finally looks at me. His eyes are full of a turmoil I've never seen before in him, and my heart squeezes in my chest. Michele is never one to be so upset he can't speak. Yes, he didn't immediately tell me some things about his life, but we didn't know each other at that time. The thing I love the most about him is the emotional maturity so rare in most men. I don't recognize him now.

"It's nothing, Lena."

He heads toward the small couch and sinks into it, rubbing his hand down his face, clearly exhausted. But something about the way he says it, *it's nothing*, makes my stomach twist.

"No," I say, stepping inside and letting the balcony door click shut. "Not this time."

He glances up at me. His brows furrow, puzzled, and I notice the tension in his injured leg. Worries creep up my spine, tingling with a silent alarm.

"I'm not asking to pry," I add quickly, "but you can't just shut me out. Not when we're…this close to the edge of everything."

He watches me for a second. His eyes flicker, and then, finally, something lets loose inside him, and the real Michele resurfaces like a person who was drowning and finally takes a breath.

He exhales a long breath and leans forward, elbows on his knees, voice low. "I went to see a specialist. About my leg."

I didn't expect that, and I'm a bit scared because he didn't tell me anything about it. Hurt punches my chest, but I keep quiet.

I walk slowly toward him, sitting across from him on the bed. "And?"

"He wants to operate," he says. "The muscle's not healing right. It can't stretch the way it needs to. That's why the pain's not going away. He showed me everything. Tests. Scans. He thinks he can fix it…use another muscle to replace what's not working. Said I could recover almost completely."

This is a significant step, considering how little hope there was even a few hours ago, but his eyes tell me he's troubled, and I don't know if I want to peel away that layer because I have a feeling I know where this is going.

I reach for his hand. "Michele…that's amazing."

He gives a tired smile. "Yeah. It is."

"But?" I can't hold back.

His jaw tightens again. There is a storm behind his eyes—one that is difficult to ignore and somehow out of reach. I want to reach out and hug him, but I worry that if I do, the conversation will wither out, and we need to have it. No matter how much I'm dreading this moment, we have to talk about it.

"When all of this returns to normal," he says, "when I'm in rehab or back in Milan or wherever I end up, and you're filming some major movie in LA…" His voice cracks slightly. "I don't know what happens to *us*."

My throat closes. "Oh."

My answer is stupid, I know, but the truth is it's difficult to put into words what is going on inside my chest right now. I knew this was coming. There is no going around it; no amount of pretending will change the fact that we have two completely different lives. With our jobs, having a relationship is difficult even when you live in the same country, but on two different continents? It's a disaster in the making.

He looks up at me. "I feel like I'm drowning, Lena. I finally figured out what I want, for my career, for my body, but I have no idea what to do with my heart."

I can feel the knot tightening in my throat, making it hard to breathe. No matter how many times I told myself this thing between us was temporary, my heart didn't get the memo. It fell hard for the man sitting in front of me, making this moment even more bittersweet. I want my career, but I also want Michele, and even if we dream of having a long-distance relationship, reality tells us that we would both be miserable. It's unfair to put us through this.

My fingers squeeze his. "I… I accepted the part," I say quietly. "Told Vivian to move forward. Filming starts in a few weeks. Maybe less than a month."

He can't conceal the hurt in his eyes, but he tries to tug his lips into a small smile. "I'm happy for you. You deserve that part," he whispers softly.

The knot in my throat makes it hard to breath, let alone speak, so I just nod, knowing it's not enough to thank him, but it's all I can manage right now.

His eyes close for a moment. The silence that fills the room is thick, heavy, like grief before a goodbye. Neither of us says it out loud, but we both hear it.

Time's up.

Whatever this summer gave us—the escape, the intimacy, the magic—it's unraveling, thread by thread. The real world is already pulling at our sleeves.

I want to say something. Anything. That we'll figure it out, that we'll try, that love should be enough. But I don't know if it is.

So I just sit still, my fingers laced with his, and hold onto him like I can stop the world from turning if I just grip hard enough. And still, it turns.

33

LENA

I don't sleep the night before I book the flight.

The script I printed out sits open on my hotel desk. Its pages are dog-eared and full of my scribbles, as if my handwriting could anchor me to this moment, to this city, to this version of my life, to Michele. Now that reality is sinking in, my chest is becoming increasingly tighter, and I don't know how to stop it from imploding. I'm certain, at some point, I won't be able to breathe anymore.

Yet the world is spinning again, fast and loud, and I can't press pause. It doesn't wait for me, for us, for this life we created inside this summer bubble. It forces us to spin with it. It doesn't care if we are keeping up or stumbling to jump into the reality that is threatening to squash us.

The next morning, I book my return flight to Los Angeles. My heart is heavy during every step of the process.

When I tell Michele, we're sitting at the little café near the hotel, the one with the chipped tables and terrible coffee that somehow became *ours*. I didn't want to do it in such a public place, but the heaviness between us is almost unbearable, and I can't drag this moment out any further.

His eyes narrow, and for a moment, I wonder if he heard me right.

"I leave Friday," I say again, softer this time.

He sets down his cup too hard. The ceramic clinks against the saucer. "Then I'm coming with you."

The words are so instantaneous, so impulsive, they knock the air out of me.

"Michele…" I start, but he's already shaking his head.

"I'll figure things out from there. I can have the surgery in the States, it doesn't matter. I don't want to be apart."

God, a part of me wants to say yes. Wants to scream it, but the part of me that has always survived, always protected the dream when everything else fell apart, finds her voice first.

"No," I whisper. "You can't."

My voice comes out strained, mirroring the vise that

is constricting my chest. I see how much he is grasping at this dream, not wanting to let go. He doesn't want this to end, *us* to end, but I can't see a way out of it. It would be unfair for both of us to drag this out until it tears us apart, transforming something perfect into something ugly.

He looks like I just slapped him. "Why not?"

I lock my eyes on his hurting ones, and my heart screams to listen to him, almost drowning the reasonable voice in my head.

"Because you need to have that surgery. You need to *heal*," I say firmly

"I can heal in LA," he says in a rush, but I can hear the doubt in his voice. We both know that if he wants to have a chance to climb up to the top teams, he has to be where the top teams are, be visible, remind them how much he is worth, how his healing is progressing. And that place is not Los Angeles. It's here, in Italy, where everyone lives and breathes soccer.

I shake my head. "That's not the point."

He's quiet now, watching me. He knows what the reason is, but he doesn't want to admit it. Part of me would like to say "fuck it, we'll figure it out," but it's not a solution, it's only delaying the inevitable.

"I can't be the regret of your life, Michele," I say, voice trembling. "I won't be the reason you didn't fight for your career."

His brows knit together. "You wouldn't be."

His voice is more certain now, and I know that he really believes it. He is sure he won't regret this choice, but I've thought a lot about what I would do if I decided to stay instead of flying back, and I felt a part of me die.

"You say that now. But what about two years from now? Five? When you're watching a game and your chest aches because you *could* have been out there. When you wonder if you gave it up for someone who was never supposed to stay."

He winces. "That's not fair."

"No, it's just the truth. Do you think I haven't considered the idea of staying in this country with you?" A sad smile graces my lips when I see the surprise on his face.

"Yes, I thought about it, and I realize that's not fair to me either. I could stay, try to learn Italian, and try to rebuild my career in the Italian movie industry, but it means throwing away what I worked for my entire life. Because I can't just waltz in here and assume I'll find someone to give me a chance to prove I'm good at acting in Italian. It doesn't work like that. And I can't keep working from here with LA-based directors either, because like you, I need to be there to be seen."

I reach across the table and place my hand over his. He is warm, familiar, and my heart cracks. He doesn't say a word, and I suspect he is trying to keep himself together, not let his emotions overwhelm him.

"I love you," I whisper. "God, I love you so much it hurts. But we knew it would end. We said it, remember? That summer has to end at some point."

He doesn't speak. Just stares at our hands like he's memorizing the way they fit.

"We're living two different lives," I say. "And we can't pretend that love is going to erase the distance between them."

He pulls his hand away, slowly. Pain flickers in his eyes, but then he nods.

Once.

And somehow, that hurts worse than anything else.

We don't talk much after that. Back at the hotel, the silence settles between us like a blanket too heavy to breathe under, but when his fingers find mine in the dark, I turn to him.

My lips meet his, tentatively at first, but when he wraps his arms around my waist, I melt into his embrace and tighten my arms around him. I need it, I need this contact, this tightness between us, where no space is left between our bodies.

There's no rush, no firestorm. Just a slow, aching kind of tenderness. His hand runs up my back like he's memorizing the shape of me, every curve, every dip, every place he's touched before, but now treats like something he'll never touch again. My skin tingles beneath his fingers, not from desire alone, but from the weight of what this is.

The last time.

The realization lands somewhere deep in my chest and cracks open a pain I didn't think I was ready for.

I press my forehead to his, our breath mingling. His eyes are open, searching mine, and I see the grief, the want, the helplessness. He doesn't say a word, but he doesn't have to. I feel it in every kiss, every lingering touch, every soft stroke of his thumb across my cheek. It's all there, his love, his goodbye.

When we undress each other, it's quiet. No teasing, no banter, no playful looks. Just reverence. He peels away each layer of clothing like it's sacred, like beneath them is something fragile and precious. And maybe it is. Maybe we are fragile in this moment.

He lies beside me and pulls me to him, our legs tangling, our bodies pressing together in a way that feels less like lust and more like a plea, a promise, a memory in the making.

The room is dim, the city outside muffled by thick glass and the hour of night. But in here, it's a different world. In here, nothing exists except the warmth of his body and the rhythm of our hearts pounding against each other like they're trying to find the same beat.

We make love slowly, deliberately. There's nothing frantic or urgent. Just a shared desperation not to let go too soon. I clutch him like I can anchor time, but it keeps slipping away so fast it takes my breath away.

He kisses the curve of my shoulder, the edge of my jaw, the space just above my heart. I kiss him back everywhere I can reach, afraid I'll forget the taste of his skin, the way he sighs when I whisper his name. There's something mournful in the way we move, like we're both already grieving what we haven't lost yet, but know we will.

I close my eyes and let it all wash over me: the love, the loss, the *everything*. He moves like he's trying to keep a piece of me inside him. Like he already knows he's losing me, and I hold him like I can stitch us together with my bare hands.

When it ends, we stay like that, wrapped in each other, breathing the same breath. I want to speak, to say something meaningful, something that might make it hurt less. But the words are tangled somewhere between my ribs, and I can't get them out. I think if I do, I'll cry. And if I start crying, I might never stop.

So I press my lips to his bare chest and just hold him tighter. This is goodbye, and neither of us says it, because saying it would make it real. And I'm not ready, maybe I never will be.

Somewhere between the quiet breaths and tangled sheets, I realize that loving him might be the most beautiful heartbreak I'll ever have.

THE CAR RIDE TO THE AIRPORT IS A GRAVEYARD OF unsaid words.

The windows are cracked open, letting the warm Italian air sweep through, but it doesn't clear the heaviness from the car. Michele's hand is on the gear shift, his jaw clenched, eyes locked on the road. I sit beside him, spine straight, hands fidgeting in my lap like they're searching for something to hold on to, but there's nothing left to grab, no moment to stretch, no miracle to delay the inevitable.

I'm leaving, and he's not coming with me.

The highway signs flash past us like countdowns. Rome Fiumicino. Departures. Terminal.

I want to scream. I want to beg time to stop, to stretch this ride out forever. To never reach the place where I have to let go, but instead, I stay quiet. We both do.

Inside the airport, the fluorescent lights loom above us, too bright, too sterile. The scent of roasted espresso and cold metal fills my lungs, and still, I can't breathe right.

Michele walks with me through the check-in process, silent as a shadow. When I lift my suitcase onto the scale, his fingers brush mine. I pretend it doesn't shatter something in me.

We say nothing, but we move like we've done this before, as if we know how to survive a goodbye. But we don't. Not like this.

When we reach the TSA line, it feels like standing at the edge of a cliff. One more step and I'll be falling. I turn to him, and for a moment, we just *look*. His eyes are dark and wet, his face tight with the effort of staying composed.

He steps closer, and then his hands are on my cheeks, warm and trembling slightly, like he's cradling something delicate. Like he's holding a memory he never wants to lose. His lips brush against mine in a soft, slow, reverent kiss.

It's not a kiss goodbye. It's one full of *if onlys*. If only we had met at a different time. If only love were enough. If only summer never had to end.

I don't pull away. I let myself live in this moment. Let the tears slip down my cheeks as he kisses them away without saying a word.

When we reluctantly part, I can't speak. My throat is sand, and my heart is glass. I step into the TSA line, handing over my passport with numb fingers. I glance back once and twice because I *have to*, because leaving him behind feels like tearing out part of myself.

He's still standing there, his arms hanging uselessly by his sides, his eyes locked on mine. Neither of us waves. We just *look* like we're burning the image of each other into our skin.

Then the line moves, and I walk forward. Each step hurts more than the last. When I reach the metal detector and turn one last time, he's still there, but the moment I step through, he's gone.

Out of sight. Out of reach. I don't make it five feet before the tears come again. I don't try to stop them. My vision blurs, and my heart aches so painfully that I clutch my carry-on to stay upright. The ache is too big for my body.

I left him behind, and the sound of my heart breaking is the only thing I hear as I walk toward my gate.

34

LENA

The paparazzi lost interest weeks before I even landed back in LA. The cheating scandal, the gossip, the screaming headlines, it all burned hot and fast and then vanished like a spark in dry grass. That's how it works here. Frenzy one day, forgotten the next. By the time I stepped off the plane, I was yesterday's story.

Still, I was glad I stayed longer in Italy. I'm glad I stretched out those final days like silk slipping through my fingers, even if now, four months later, I wake up every morning with an ache in my chest that just won't go away. Even now, as I sit in the makeup trailer with a script full of scribbled notes and a heart that feels like it's still bruising.

The mirror lights buzz softly above me, casting a

golden glow over the counter cluttered with powders, brushes, water bottles, and the script open to today's scene. It's an emotionally brutal one, the kind of performance actors dream of, and all I feel is hollow.

I'm trying to focus, but my brain's been foggy all morning. Too much weight pressing down on me. I pick up my phone to distract myself, scroll aimlessly, and then I do the thing I shouldn't.

I stop on a photo.

It's Michele, laughing in that unguarded way he has, surrounded by his friends in his parents' backyard in Puglia. There's a bottle of wine on the table, and his cousin is mid-gesture, clearly telling a story with too much passion and too little accuracy. But Michele is the center of it all. Head tilted back, eyes crinkled, a grin that could light up a city.

My thumb hovers over the screen, and the ache comes fast and sharp. A knot closes up my throat. God, it still hurts. Like he's been carved into my bones and I can't shake him loose.

"You okay, sweetheart?" Julia's voice breaks gently into my spiral.

I glance up in the mirror. Julia's been with me every day on set. Her hands are steady, her eyes warm, and she's one of those women who knows when to talk and when to just quietly hand you a tissue.

I nod, but it's weak. A shrug, more than anything.

"Yeah. I'm just..." My voice cracks. I don't even bother finishing the sentence.

She steps closer, peering at the photo over my shoulder, and makes a soft sound in the back of her throat. "He's handsome. And that smile? That's a man in love."

I place the phone face down on the counter. "Yeah. He was."

Julia doesn't press. She dabs a bit of concealer under my eye with a featherlight touch, but I can feel her curiosity building.

"Why didn't you try long distance?" she asks softly after a beat. "I mean...forgive me for prying, but it's kind of obvious. You're still in love with him."

I inhale slowly. The air feels thick in my lungs. I hate how easily my eyes sting. "Because fairy tales don't exist," I whisper.

She pauses, sponge in hand. "That's...bleak," she says, not unkindly. "Especially coming from someone who makes a living pretending they do."

I laugh, but it's small, humorless. "Yeah, well... pretending is easy. Living it?" I shake my head. "We live on different continents, Julia—different time zones. I'm here, working twelve-hour days on a set that's chewing me up, and he's over there, trying to put himself back together. What were we supposed to do? Text good morning and hope it doesn't fall apart?"

She studies my face in the mirror. "But you don't know that it would've fallen apart. You didn't even try."

"That's the thing." My voice is steadier now, but there's something brittle underneath. "I didn't want to try. Not because I didn't love him, but because I did. Because I still do. I didn't want to stretch something beautiful until it broke. I didn't want to ruin it."

Julia is quiet again. The room is filled with just the gentle tap of a brush against powder. She's letting me speak, letting me spill.

"I want to remember him like that," I continue. "Like in that photo: laughing, happy, full of life. Not through a screen at two a.m., fighting about missed calls and timing and not being able to touch him. I didn't want to become his regret."

I feel the tremble in my hands and press them into my thighs. "I didn't want him to wake up someday and hate me for being the reason he gave up everything he worked for."

Julia finally sets the brush down and turns me slightly in the chair to face her. "Maybe he wouldn't have. Maybe he'd have chosen you anyway."

I look at her, blinking away the tears threatening to spill. "And maybe we'd have resented each other. Or maybe we would've lasted three months and ended it over a bad phone connection and missed flights. I didn't want 'what ifs.' I wanted to leave it while it was still good. While I could still close my eyes and remember what it felt like to fall in love under the Italian sun."

Julia tilts her head. "Do you still talk?"

I shake my head. "Not once. Not since the airport."

"Do you think he moved on?"

That question slices deeper than I expect. "Maybe," I whisper. "I hope he's happy. I want that for him. But God, some nights I wish he'd call. Just once. Just to say he misses me too."

Julia places a gentle hand on my shoulder. "You know, fairy tales…they're not perfect. But sometimes, they find their way back around."

I meet her eyes. "You really believe that?"

She gives me a small, knowing smile. "I work in a trailer where people play make-believe all day. But the realest love stories I've seen are the ones that don't go according to script."

I look down at my script, the one waiting for me to channel heartbreak I don't have to fake.

Because I already feel it. Every day.

35

MICHELE

The cold December air burns my lungs with each inhale. It's the kind of sharp, biting chill that cuts through sweat and settles into bone, but I welcome it. I *need* it. It keeps me awake and focused.

My foot presses gently against the ball, guiding it forward along the turf. Not a sprint. Not even a jog. Just controlled movement, what my therapist calls "progressive reintroduction to strain." It's not flashy, not even close to what I'm used to do, but it's something. For a long time, I wasn't sure I'd ever get even this far.

One step, then another. Controlled. Measured. When I plant and gently tap the ball back to myself, the movement is fluid. Not perfect, but mine again.

Marco stands a few meters away, bundled in a puffy

coat and scarf like he's filming in the Arctic, his phone steady in one hand. "Give me a smile," he says, grinning like an idiot. "Make it look like you're having the time of your life, come on."

I force one. It's thin. Hollow. Fake. But it's all I have.

I go through another set of drills—slow ball control. Light passing against a wall. Nothing dynamic yet. No jumping, no fast pivots. Just slow, careful reminders of what I used to do effortlessly. Each motion makes my grafted muscle tug, like a foreign thread stitched inside me. The pain is there, deep, dull, but it's pain with purpose. And that, at least, is something I can live with.

Marco stops filming as I limp over to the bench and sit down slowly, wiping the sweat from my neck with a towel. "You're ahead of schedule," he says, passing me a water bottle. "Dr. Conti said he's never seen a muscle flap recover this fast in someone your age. You're killing it, man."

"Feels…functional," I say between breaths. "Still tight. Still weak. But yeah. It's coming back."

"It is," he agrees. "And teams are starting to sniff around again. Cautiously, but they're watching. I've got a few emails flagged for you. One coach wants a video update next week."

I nod. I should be elated. I'm not.

"You're frowning," Marco says, sitting down beside me. "And don't tell me it's the cold."

I roll the water bottle between my palms, letting the silence hang for a beat too long. Then I say it.

"I'm in love with a woman I can't be with."

The hurt in my chest is almost as unbearable as the first days after surgery, when I thought my leg was on fire. I clenched my teeth then and pushed through, and the leg is getting better. My heart is not even close.

Marco exhales, long and slow, like he's been waiting for me to admit it. "Still?"

"Always," I say, gripping the water bottle tightly in my hand, and staring down at my white knuckles.

He studies me, eyes narrowing. "You've been walking around like a ghost since she flew back to LA. You're grinding through rehab like it's penance, not recovery. You think I don't notice?"

I don't respond. What should I say? That I feel like my life doesn't make sense anymore? I went through this massive surgery to play again. I knew the recovery would take around eighteen months to two years. I did everything right to get back even sooner because I wanted to play and go back to the field, but I still feel empty, even after recovering faster than expected.

"What happened, Michele? You two looked like you were building something real. I thought you were gonna fight for it."

Soon after my decision to do the surgery, I told Marco I wanted to get back on the field, and that he needed to start planning my return to the scene. I was sure by now I'd feel better, motivated, ready to work my ass off to get somewhere. But I'm not. Yes, physically I feel better, I see daily progress, I can feel that I'm going in the right direction, but my chest is empty.

I shake my head, throat tightening. "She told me not to come with her. Told me I had to finish what I started here. That I had to chase the dream I've fought for since I was a kid. She didn't want to become my regret. And she was right. I *do* want that."

"But?" Marco's tone is serious, but not angry. He wants to understand because, as my agent, he needs to know what I think to pursue the right path in my career and push me in that direction.

"But I also want her." As soon as the words come out of my lips, my chest feels lighter. Not healed, but at least I can breathe easier.

Marco leans back against the bench, his breath visible in the air between us. "You think that has to be a choice? Soccer or her?"

"I don't know," I say quietly. "I really don't. She's on set all day, every day. I'm here, in rehab, trying to convince my leg to behave like it's mine again. It's not just distance. It's timing. Life. Everything."

This situation is such a mess that I can't even get my thoughts straight. Some days I think I can do it, go back to my old life, and other days I feel like I did everything wrong, and the latter are more frequent than the former.

"She's still the background pic on your phone," he says dryly.

Marco is not the kind of man who beats around the bush. He's willing to do anything to make his clients' dreams come true, but he also wants the path to be clear. No change of plans, afterthoughts, or anything that derails his work left and right. And I chose him because of this determination. I need him to be my reason, especially now that I feel lost.

I glance down and look at my phone, which I left on top of my gym bag. He's right. It's a photo from Puglia. She's barefoot on the beach, wearing one of my shirts and laughing at something I said, her face lit up like I hung the moon.

"I miss her," I murmur. "I miss how she smelled like lemon and sunblock. How she always managed to burn toast but still insisted on making breakfast. I miss the way she'd ask me a million history questions just to hear me rant. I miss…God, I miss everything." I've never told anyone this, but I don't feel embarrassed to pour out my deepest secrets because I know Marco won't judge.

He watches me quietly for a moment. Then he says, "Your graft's healing better than anyone expected. You're young, marketable, and you've still got it. You're gonna be ready for the second half of next season."

I nod, but it feels mechanical. A nod that belongs to another version of me, the one who still believed that soccer was enough. Until I met her. She taught me that I love soccer, yes, but I love her too, and now I feel torn between two choices that don't feel like choices at all. They feel like punishments.

He nudges me. "But it's not gonna mean shit if you keep walking around like your soul's been ripped out."

A faint laugh escapes me, bitter and hoarse. "It has."

He doesn't say anything after that. Just lets it hang in the air between us, like the echo of something we both know but can't fix.

I sip my water. My leg aches. My chest aches worse. I'm clawing my way back on the field and in my body, but without her, it all feels like a half-finished game. Like I'm winning something I can't share with the only person who ever made it feel worth it. And maybe that's the real reason I can't smile.

Because this time, the goal isn't enough.

36

MICHELE

The waiter brings a bowl of olives and a bottle of sparkling water, but I don't touch either. My leg bounces under the table. The nervous energy is coiled so tight I feel like I'll snap. My stomach is so constricted I can't eat anything.

Marco told me this morning he had "news." That's all. No hint. No clue. Just enough to mess with my head for the entire damn day. God, I hate him sometimes. I know he likes to talk in person about important things, but at least telling me if it's good or bad news would be nice.

I glance at my phone for the tenth time, checking the clock even though I know it by heart.

7:28 p.m.

Two minutes early. He'd better show.

I look toward the door and, like he read my mind, he strides into the restaurant, that cocky grin lighting up his face like he just won the lottery. The maître d' leads him to our table, and Marco claps me on the shoulder before sitting down. That happiness means good news, right? I'm so riled up after his call I can't think straight.

I'm working my ass off to get back on the field and, while it won't be an immediate return, my recovery is ahead of schedule, and the last check-up with the surgeon was promising in terms of getting back into my previous shape.

"Your face looks like someone stole your puppy," he says, laughing.

He likes to taunt me, keeping me on my toes just to mess with me. I usually wouldn't be pissed and laugh about it, but lately I feel so down I can't even take a joke.

"Just tell me," I shoot back. "I haven't been able to think straight all day. Is it a contract?"

God, I hope it is. I can't take this uncertainty anymore. I've played professionally since I was sixteen, and I'm not used to this long period of inactivity, being off the field, not having a team at my side.

He grins wider, opening the menu like we're here to debate wine pairings. "Let's order first. I'm starving."

I'm going to strangle him. I swear, if he doesn't tell me something, anything, right now, I will rip his head off with my bare hands. Prison seems a better alternative than the game he's playing.

"Marco," I warn, leaning forward. "Take me out of my misery before I lose my damn mind."

He chuckles and closes the menu. "Okay, okay. You ready for this?"

I nod once, my heart pounding in my chest. No, I'm not ready, but I will never be. I'm coming from a year of bad news, and it's difficult for me to focus on a positive mindset.

He leans back, arms stretched across the chair like he owns the place. "You got an offer. A big one. From a team in Los Angeles."

The restaurant sounds are drowned out by the blood rushing through my ears and making me dizzy. Surely, I didn't hear that right. I've always focused on Italian or European teams. I never even considered the other side of the world. When I think about Los Angeles, my mind immediately goes to Hollywood, movies, and the jet set. But I always forget that they also have a soccer team.

I blink. "What?"

He beams. This asshole is so smug I want to slap him and then kiss him.

"LA Galaxy," he clarifies, eyes gleaming. "They want you now. They're willing to work with the surgeon and your physical therapist to bring you to a full recovery in their facility in Los Angeles and have you on the field whenever you're ready. They offered enough zeroes to make your past contracts jealous."

I blink again. "Los Angeles? As in…California?"

I know it's a stupid question, but I can't believe this is happening. I know soccer isn't as popular in the US, but the teams tend to buy famous players from Europe who can boost their popularity with their fans. Usually, they go for someone at the end of their career who has already peaked but still has a few years ahead of them on the field. While their interest should be a punch in the gut because they consider me done with my career, I can only feel happiness bubbling up in my chest.

"Unless there's a secret Los Angeles in Sicily I don't know about, yes," he says, pouring himself some water. "They've been watching your recovery. Your numbers are solid, the video we shot was a hit, and they want you."

I sit back in my chair, stunned. My mind is spinning, trying to process the words. I want to play. I realize that I don't care which team I choose because I just want to go back to what I love doing. Like Lena said, I want to do it for myself and no one else.

I thought he was negotiating with *Serie A* clubs. I thought I'd be stuck in Italy for at least the next year. I was ready to forget my summer and look toward my future.

"But…why didn't you tell me you were looking

overseas?" I'm genuinely curious about this. He's never kept me out of the loop about something so massive as actively looking elsewhere than what we agreed.

He shrugs, a little too casually. "Because I'm tired of watching you mope around like a lost puppy. You've been miserable since Lena left. And you know it."

My throat tightens at her name. I glance down at the table. Yes, he's right. I tried very hard to convince my heart that the separation is the best thing for both of us, but it didn't listen. It didn't lose hope, not once. It broke down time and time again, but never gave up.

"I'm not saying this is about her," Marco adds. "But let's not pretend it doesn't help. You want a fresh start? There it is. You want a second chance? Go take it."

A beat passes, and then another. Los Angeles, her city. My heart thuds hard against my ribs. This is really happening. But doubt starts to creep into my chest, slow and icy cold.

"What if she's moved on?" I ask, quietly. "What if she realized that she doesn't want to spend her life pining over a summer fling?" Maybe it was not exactly a fling, but we both knew it was going to end.

Marco looks at me, all humor gone. "Then you'll know. But at least you'll stop wondering. And you'll still get to play again, under the lights, in a city that watches you rise from the ashes."

I take a deep breath and push down that uneasiness

growing in my chest. If she's moved on, I'll figure out what to do. But if she hasn't, I can't pass up the opportunity to go after what my heart is beating for.

The waiter appears, and we order. I barely remember what I ask for, my head is still spinning. It's everything I wanted, and everything I feared. A future and a risk.

Her.

For the first time in months, I feel like I can breathe again.

37

LENA

I'm curled up on the couch, legs tucked under a soft blanket and a steaming mug of tea nestled in my hands. For once, the house is quiet, with no call times, no frantic script changes, and no makeup smeared across my cheekbone from a shoot. Just the crackling of the fireplace and the soft rustle of pages as I flip through the last few chapters of a book I've fallen hopelessly into.

It's the first time in weeks I feel like myself. We are almost done with the movie. We have a few scenes left to reshoot after the Christmas festivities, but the majority of it is done. Thankfully, because this time, I felt drained of my last drop of strength. It was the most beautiful role I've ever played, but also the most challenging one. I had to shed all the layers protecting my heart to get into the main character's head, and at some point, I didn't know if I could get out of it again. It was scary how my thoughts didn't feel mine at all out of set.

My parents and my sister Maddie are flying in for the holidays in two days. I've already planned the menu, cleaned the guest rooms, and bought more fairy lights than strictly necessary. The house smells like cinnamon and pine—it smells like home. I can't wait to hug them and let my mind be distracted from the smiling brown eyes haunting my dreams since this summer.

God, I miss him. I miss his smile, his hugs, his chatter, and even his history rants. I miss Michele so much it almost hurts, no matter how many months I spend trying to focus on my job and anything else. There is always this hole in my chest with the shape of him that I can't fill. I wonder when I'll be able to bring up the memory of him without feeling my chest imploding.

I'm just about to finish a chapter when the doorbell rings. My brow furrows. I wasn't expecting anyone. Setting my mug down, I get up and pad barefoot across the hardwood floor, making a list of who it could be. All my contacts here in LA are either with their families or on some exotic vacation. When I reach the small screen that shows the front gate camera, I press the button and freeze.

No. It's not possible. I blink and lean in closer, sure that my eyes are playing some weird trick. But it's him. It's really him.

Michele.

Standing at my front gate in jeans, a jacket, and that expression I know too well, nervous, determined, and hopeful. His hair's a little longer, and he looks like he hasn't slept much, but it's him. I slam the gate release button and run, forgetting I'm barefoot.

Out the front door, down the porch steps, bare feet hitting the cold pavement of the path that leads to the gate. My heart is galloping in my chest, wild and unsure, but my legs don't stop. My blood is rushing, and my heart is flying. I reach the edge of the drive just as he opens the gate and steps inside.

He closes the gate behind him and looks up at me, and time fractures into before and after. We both freeze. My breath is caught in my chest in a battle to get out.

I drink him in like I'm starving—because I am. I missed him with an ache that never faded, a hollow space that no role, no city, no spotlight could ever fill. And right now, all that ache is rushing out of my chest, leaving me breathless, and letting hope take its place.

His smile is tentative, like he's afraid to hope. "Hi."

A breath escapes me. "Hi."

Neither of us knows what to say, and for a bit, the silence is almost deafening.

"I, uh…" he rubs the back of his neck. "I just came from the Galaxy training center. I signed the contract this morning."

His words come out in a rush, as if they'll lose their truth if he keeps them inside any longer. My brain struggles to keep up, and when it registers its meaning, warmth fills my chest in waves. I never dared to hope something like that would happen because the heartbreak of discovering it was just a dream would kill me.

My heart skips. "You're playing in LA?" My voice comes out small and trembling.

It's difficult to process this news without considering the implications, and I don't dare hope.

He nods, his voice steady but soft. "Yeah. I'm here now. For good."

Is this really happening? If I wake up right now and discover it's just a dream, I will scream.

I take a step forward. He watches me, eyes bright, glistening just a little. "Why?" I ask, even though I already know.

Something gets loose inside my chest, and a wave of expectation hits me in the gut. I've never believed in miracles, but this looks a lot like one.

He swallows. "Because I couldn't spend one more day wondering what would've happened if I had the courage to try. I don't know if long distance would've worked. I don't know if anything will. But I know I'm in love with you, and I had to come and ask if you'd give me a real chance to make this work."

My heart cracks wide open. Tears threaten to spill, but I keep them at bay. I don't hesitate. I don't think. I just run the last few steps and lock my arms around his neck and inhale deeply.

He grabs my waist firmly and encircles me with a laugh before pulling me against him even more tightly, like he never plans to let go again. I bury my face in his shoulder, breathing him in. He smells like sunshine, cologne, and home—my home.

"I love you too," I whisper. "I've missed you so much."

He pulls back just enough to kiss me, and when our lips meet, it's not just a kiss. It's a homecoming.

It's the unraveling of every lonely night, every aching morning, every what-if. It's slow and reverent, like he's trying to memorize the shape of my mouth, and I kiss him like I'm afraid he'll disappear again. My hands cradle his face. His thumb brushes a tear from my cheek. His lips whisper things mine have been starving for.

We kiss like time stops for us. And maybe, for once, it does.

When we finally break apart, I press my forehead to his, breathless, overwhelmed, and completely whole for the first time in four months.

"You came back," I murmur.

His smile is pure sunshine. "I never really left."

The world clicks back into place, and on this random December Wednesday, I know this is our second chance, and this time, we won't let it slip away.

38

LENA

I t's a late July morning, the kind that already smells like sunshine and jasmine, and our back-yard is drenched in warm light. The sliding glass door is wide open, letting in the scent of basil from the potted plant Michele insists on keeping alive like it's a child, and somewhere in the distance, a neighbor's sprinkler ticks in rhythm with the breeze.

My Los Angeles house somehow turned into *our* house—emphasis on the *our*, because within weeks, it started sprouting basil and rosemary like it had been waiting its whole life for an Italian man to move in and reclaim the kitchen. Now it smells permanently like garlic and ambition. And when I say *we* use the herbs from the garden, I mean I pluck them proudly like a forager in yoga pants while Michele does all the actual cooking. I provide the moral support and enthusiastic taste-testing. It's teamwork. Sort of.

Inside, I'm perched on the kitchen counter, legs swinging lazily while Michele bustles around in front of the stove, shirtless, wearing only cotton shorts and that smirk he saves for when he knows he's showing off.

"You're watching me like I'm a cooking show," he teases, tossing a handful of cherry tomatoes into the pan like he's on *Top Chef.*

I let my gaze linger, shamelessly drinking him in— every line of his chiseled chest, every flex of muscle in his thighs as he moves around the kitchen like it's just another workout. Two years post-surgery, and he's not just healed, he's *thriving*, carved back into almost peak form with that effortless grace that once made headlines and now just makes me melt. But the most breathtaking part isn't the body, it's the joy. The quiet, steady happiness that lights up his face every morning when he pulls on his gear and heads to the facility. He's not playing for the glory of a European superclub, not for trophies or headlines. He's playing because he *loves* it. Because it fills him up. And every time I see that easy, satisfied smile as he laces his cleats, I know he's exactly where he's meant to be. And that's what matters most to me.

"You *are* a cooking show," I grin, lifting my coffee to my lips. "A very sexy one with a light sprinkling of olive oil."

He looks over his shoulder and winks. "Stick around, there's going to be a plot twist."

"You burning the eggs again?" I grin, loving how I can push his buttons just by reminding him of that one debacle.

"That happened once. And they were scrambled. On purpose." He narrows his eyes at me.

"Sure they were." I smile, hiding behind the rim of my cup.

He rolls his eyes, but he's laughing, and I let the sound sink into my bones. This is how our days feel now, like love and breathless laughter and skin caressing skin in the middle of the day and night.

We've both been off work for a couple of weeks. He is between games, and I am between projects. Instead of flying to some exotic island like we swore we would, we ended up vacationing at home. Turns out, we're terrible at planning and even worse at packing. But I wouldn't change a second of it.

We sleep late. Make love in the middle of the day. Take walks to the farmers' market and fight over what gelato flavor to get like it's a life-altering decision. And sometimes, when it's quiet like now, I catch myself staring at him, this man who barged into my summer in Italy and somehow stayed for all the seasons after.

I hop down from the counter and sneak up behind

him, slipping my arms around his waist and resting my cheek against his back.

He hums. "That's cheating. I'm cooking."

"I'm bored. Tell me something I don't know."

I will never get tired of him talking about what he is passionate about, it doesn't matter if it's soccer or history. The way his eyes light up makes me fall even harder for him.

He stirs the pan, the scent of garlic blooming in the air. "About?"

"History. Come on, Professor. Impress me."

Michele chuckles, but I feel the moment his brain kicks into gear. "Okay," he says after a beat. "Did you know Cleopatra wasn't Egyptian?"

I pull back just enough to look at him. "She wasn't?" Well, there is something new to learn from him.

He shakes his head, proud. "She was Greek. From the Ptolemaic dynasty. Descendant of one of Alexander the Great's generals. But she also embraced the Egyptian culture, and is basically considered Egyptian in her way of ruling."

I blink. "You're so hot when you talk nerdy to me."

And it's true. Because no matter how hot his body is, his brain is even hotter, and his personality makes him almost perfect in my eyes. He's not perfect, I know, but he's perfect for me, and I love that feeling.

He turns off the stove and faces me, spoon in hand.

"You say that now, but you mocked my Roman Empire fact three days ago."

I pretend to be offended. "I didn't mock it. I just said your obsession is a little *too* real."

He dips the spoon into the sauce and holds it out to me. "Taste it. And tell me I'm not the superior half of this relationship." He winks and grins, knowing I don't fall for his bullshit.

I chuckle and lean forward, licking the spoon with a dramatic moan. "Okay, damn. That's unfairly good."

"I know." He sets the spoon down and leans in to kiss me, his hands sliding into my hair, warm and sure. The kiss is slow, like we have nowhere else to be. Because we don't.

When we part, I whisper, "I love you."

He presses his forehead to mine. "I love you more."

"Nope," I murmur. "Not possible."

He kisses me again. And again. Until we're laughing into each other's mouths, my back pressed against the counter while he stands in front of me, shirtless, golden from the sun, and smug as hell because the sauce simmering on the stove smells like heaven and he knows it. His chest brushes mine when he leans in, his skin warm from the heat of the kitchen and the steam curling up from the pot.

I'm not cooking, I never am, but I'm exactly where I want to be: leaning against the countertop, watching him move with the kind of ease that only comes from doing something you love. Garlic and tomato fill the air, rich and comforting, and music plays low in the background, but all I hear is the sound of his laughter and the thud of my heart when he turns around and gives me *that* look.

He reaches for me again, another kiss, just because he can, and this one is softer, lingering. A promise wrapped in warmth. I cradle the side of his face, my thumb brushing the curve of his jaw, and I think: this is it. This is everything.

No fairy tales. No red carpets. No need for the world to spin any faster than this moment right here.

Just him.

Just us.

Here.

Now.

Together.

And I never want to be anywhere else.

EPILOGUE
MICHELE

The white gravel crunches under the tires as Antonio pulls into the courtyard of our parents' masseria. My Alfa Romeo is gleaming like it's just stepped off a showroom floor. He kills the engine and glances at me, one hand still resting on the steering wheel. He's all dressed up, with a tie and everything, and the smile on his face is one of happiness and maybe a bit of pride.

"You sure you're not going to faint?" he teases, and I know he's just trying to ease the tension that's been growing in my chest since yesterday evening.

I smile, but my heart's pounding so hard I can feel it in my ears. "Not unless she doesn't show up."

God, I hope not because I would... I don't even

know what I would do. I can't even contemplate this idea without having a panic attack.

He snorts. "She flew across the world for this moment. I think she's showing up," he reassures me.

I know I shouldn't be concerned, I'm pretty sure she loves me as much as I love her, but I can't shake the nervousness gripping my stomach. I'm not having doubts or anything like that. I just want this to speed up because I can't wait to see her again.

I step out of the car, the late afternoon sun wrapping its golden arms around everything, the stone walls, the rows of olive trees, the linen tablecloths fluttering in the breeze. My family and friends spill out into the backyard, all dressed in soft hues, smiling widely, clapping me on the back, and offering congratulations.

My mother kisses both my cheeks. Her eyes are misty. "You clean up well, *tesoro mio.*"

She wasn't thrilled for me to get ready at my brother's house, but after seeing the chaos spiraling into the masseria yesterday for the latest arrangements, I was glad I made this decision. My mom needed a bit of rest to get ready, too, instead of fussing after me all morning.

"You crying already?" I ask, teasing.

Her eyes are watery, and I'm sure she has already shed some tears before I got here. My father is a bit emotional today too. I know because he's fussing with his tie and the white rose on his lapel, similar to the one I have.

"I will be," she says, placing her hand over her heart, "when she walks down the aisle."

I swallow hard. I can't think of a more emotional day in my life. I've never been so nervous, not even on my *Serie A* debut. Not when I proposed and she said yes, during a pillow fight in our living room. We were laughing so hard we almost cried, and that was the moment when my lips popped the question, even before my brain processed what I was doing. But my heart was already on board with the idea for a long time. She smiled and said yes, then she smiled even brighter, and she said yes again. Then we made love and cuddled. It wasn't the most romantic proposal, but it was our proposal. Our story started with an impromptu journey when we didn't even know each other—who cares if the ring came a few days later than the question?

We walk through the courtyard and into the olive grove where we've set everything up: simple wooden chairs lined on either side of the aisle, strings of fairy lights looping between the ancient trees, petals scattered on the grass. The air smells like rosemary and earth and happiness. It smells like the joyfulness of the people here today, celebrating with us. It smells like home.

The officiant waits by the little wooden arch we built with my father. Antonio hands me a glass of water and claps my shoulder. "Deep breaths. Smile. And maybe don't cry too soon."

Easier said than done. It's too late. My chest already feels tight, my heart is already thundering in my chest like it wants to jump out and run to her.

Then I hear it, the soft sound of the gravel creaking under the tires—the buzz of a small engine, light and uneven, growing louder. Every head turns toward the driveway that curves around the house.

When the nervousness almost eats me alive, I see it, a powder-blue *Fiat Cinquecento*, older than both of us, with little white ribbons tied to its mirrors. It sputters to a stop in the shade of the olive trees, and the passenger driver's door creaks open. Lena's dad walks around the car and opens the passenger door.

And there she is, Lena.

Her dress is simple and elegant, with lace covering the white fabric that softly envelopes her curves. Her blond hair is twisted back with tiny flowers threaded through the strands. The sun catches the shimmer on her cheeks and the joy in her eyes, and I swear, for a second, the whole world holds its breath with me.

She steps around the door slowly, and the moment she turns her head and locks eyes with me, everything else disappears.

I feel it all at once: our first kiss, our laughter, the heartbreak at the airport, the quiet mornings in LA, the afternoons filled with cuddles, and the nights tangled in happiness and promises. And now this. Her. Here. Becoming my wife.

She walks toward me, each step soft and sure. When she reaches me, I take her hand in mine, grounding myself in the warmth of her skin.

"Hi," she whispers, a soft smile playing on her lips.

I can barely get the words out in a whisper too. "You're...*sei bellissima*. I don't think I've ever seen anything more beautiful."

She squeezes my hand, and I feel her thumb brush over my knuckles, steadying me when my voice cracks. We turn to the officiant together, our fingers laced tight, and I realize I'm not just marrying the love of my life. I'm marrying my best friend, my home, my future.

I let the tears fall, because for the first time in my life, I am full to the brim with love, with joy, with a quiet certainty that this is forever.

ACKNOWLEDGMENTS

Writing a book is often described as a solitary journey, but *The Road to You* would never have made it to readers' hands without the incredible people who walked alongside me every step of the way.

To **Staci**, my editor. Thank you for your insight, your precision, and your unwavering commitment to making this story shine. You catch what I miss, challenge what needs growth, and always push me toward my best work. I'm endlessly grateful for your partnership and your care.

To **Annalisa**, my Italian editor. *Grazie di cuore*. Your guidance and passion for language bring my stories to life in a way that honors every nuance. Your support means the world to me, and I'm so thankful for your sharp eye and generous heart.

To my husband, **Dario**, and to all of my family. Thank you for grounding me when I feel lost in words, for cheering me on through deadlines and doubts, and for being my home no matter where the story takes me.

And most of all, to **you**, my readers. Thank you for every message, every review, and every word of encouragement. You are the reason I get to do what I love. Whether you've been with me from the beginning or this is your first time stepping into my world, your support is the fuel behind every book I write. I am here because of you, and I don't take a second of it for granted.

With all my love and gratitude,
	Erika

ABOUT THE AUTHOR

Erika Vanzin is the Italian Amazon bestselling author of the rock star romance Roadies Series.

After traveling around the world with her husband, she settled down in Seattle, enjoying the marvelous Pacific Northwest. She brought from Italy a couple of suitcases, fifteen boxes full of books, and her most successful novels translated into English.

While she is not writing, she enjoys reading books, watching the Kraken hockey games, and working on DIY projects.

Keep in touch with Erika via the web:

facebook.com/erikavanzinauthor

instagram.com/clumsyeki

tiktok.com/@authorerikavanzin

pinterest.com/ErikaVanzin

amazon.com/author/erikavanzin

bookbub.com/authors/erika-vanzin

goodreads.com/erika_vanzin

ALSO BY ERIKA VANZIN

Los Angeles Billionaires Series (Complete Billionaires Romance)

The Producer: Aaron

The Senator: Raphael

The Actor: Harrison

The Broker: Elijah (Novella)

The Mogul: Leonard

Roadies series (Complete Rock Star Romance):

Backstage

Paparazzi

Faith

Showtime

Betrayal